un

Trabzon

Kaçkar
Mountains

Kars

Sivas

sa

Erzincan

Erzurum

Armenia

rinkuyu
ri

Mt Ararat

Azer
bai
jan

Doğubayazıt

Malatya

Nemrut Dağı

Adıyaman

(f) Diyarbakir

(h) Van

Gaziantep

(d) Urfa

(g) Mardin

Iran

(e) Harran

Syria

Iraq

Georgia

Note: All present-day characters are fictional except for the media and political personalities in chapter sixteen and one character in chapter twenty-one: There really is a Metropolitan Ozmen at the Deur-ul Zaferan Monastery near the Turkish-Syrian border.

Descriptions of historical characters are factual. Suleyman Mahmudi did build Castle Hosap in southeastern Turkey in 1643.

The chess game in chapter fourteen derives from one played by Gustav Richard Neumann and Adolf Anderssen in Berlin in 1864, but then it was not a matter of life or death.

PROLOGUE

Zeliha Kuris sat in her living room in Konya, scarcely believing what she was watching on TRT1, the major government-run channel in Turkey. The second of the twin towers of New York was crumpling. She cried, thinking of the horrible way so many were dying. Then came a knock on her door.

She peered out cautiously. Ever since her last book, threats from Hezbollah terrorists had come as fast as the sewage ran after heavy rains. One fatwa against her read, "She has confused and poisoned Muslims with her Western ideas. She deserves death."

But it was only a man, Trafik Kurban, whose ailing mother she had helped. They had met in the room at the hospital where the old woman was dying of lung cancer. Trafik's hollow cheeks and chain-smoking habits made generational continuity likely, but he had seemed friendly enough as he joked about his favorite American film, *The Wizard of Oz*. Zeliha opened the door to him.

"I have a present for you in my car," he said, taking her hand in his own—it was sticky soft—and pointing to a white Mitsubishi that sat at the curb. "You showed yourself a true daughter of Turkey during my mother's duress, and I want to thank you."

Zeliha looked up and down the street but saw no danger signs. She smiled and followed him to the vehicle. Trafik reached in, pulled out a three-foot-tall scarecrow stuffed with straw, and handed it to her. She gave it a puzzled look before smiling and saying, "It's lovely."

Then Trafik stuck a needle in her arm and shoved her into the car.

Zeliha came to in a dank basement. At first all she could sense was the overpowering smell of onions. The odor hung in the air and left her struggling for breath. Her hands were bound behind her back, her legs tethered to a pillar. All was quiet, but then she heard movement and conversation on the floor above.

She strained to catch what was being said. A man with a booming voice. He sounded joyous. "Passed the initiation . . . Trafik, one of us . . . member of Hezbollah."

Hezbollah! So Trafik was not just a petty criminal. Hezbollah! Instantly she knew what would happen, though her tormentors made her wait. She lost track of the time and must have dozed because when she awoke her throat was parched and a glass of water sat just beyond her reach.

She often heard the man with the loud, harsh voice talking and then laughing outside the door. When the door opened, the smell of fresh bread wafted into the room. Only when her mouth was as dry as Saudi sand and her stomach cramped from hunger did the loud man enter. Even then he was patient, standing for a time just staring at her.

Finally he leaned close, smelling of garlic, his thick black mustache tickling her cheek. Spit from his mouth sprayed her face. "You wanted to be Turkey's Salman Rushdie or Taslima Nasrin, eh? They deserve to die, and you will."

On the first day he beat her. On the second day he dripped burning nylon on her, all the time complaining that he had to use primitive torture devices because her Western allies kept him from getting modern electroshock devices. He demanded information about the members of her conspiracy. She explained that there was no conspiracy, that she had only written what was true. He became furious.

Upstairs she could hear *The Wizard of Oz* playing nonstop, with the Munchkins' song turned up loud to cover up her screams. She imagined Trafik was watching the film, and her one hope was that he would come to see her so she could ask him how he felt betraying the woman who had been his dying mother's only friend. Trafik did not descend, but she heard him chortle as the Wicked Witch screamed, "I'm melting, melting."

Finally Trafik did stand in front of her, but instead of displaying remorse he held a camera. As the loud man did his work, Trafik silently recorded the ravages of torture. Summoning her remaining strength, Zeliha spat at him. "How could you do this?" But before he answered, if he answered, she lost consciousness and never returned to life.

PART ONE

INNOCENTS ABROAD

CHAPTER ONE

Providence Community Church in South Philadelphia was hosting its end-of-the-school-year rally. Five hundred members of church youth groups from the Philadelphia and Wilmington areas came to hear a rock band and enjoy a cook-out, with a skit about the danger of growing gang violence sandwiched in between.

The band was hammering at high decibels in the low-lit sanctuary. Teens stood on the pews, swaying and clapping to the music. No one noticed a young man entering through the double doors at the back. A white and blue bandanna covered his head and an obscenity-laden T-shirt hung nearly to his knees, still not far enough to reach the crotch of his baggy blue jeans.

His right arm was tattooed with spiderwebs, "laugh now, cry later" clown faces, and the name "Luis." His right hand held a .38. Before a greeter could offer a welcome, Luis sent a bullet through one guitar and another clanging into a microphone stand.

As the band members froze in confusion, teens in the audience laughed and applauded the clever opening to the skit. A third bullet tore into the bass drum and sent the band members scurrying. A lone voice yelled, "He's shooting at us! Duck down!"

The skinny youth pastor, looking not much older than the kids who packed the dark sanctuary, stood up and waved his arms wildly. "This is not the gang skit. This is for real." His voice cracked, sending the crowd into fits of laughter. Suddenly his left arm jerked wildly and a red stain spread over the sleeve of his white shirt. "Get down in the pews!" he screamed.

Kids close to him began to yell and duck under their pews. Those on the other side still thought they were part of an interactive skit. "Paintball!" one boy yelled. "Awesome!"

Luis was outraged. "Shut up! All of you just shut up! Enough of this Jesus nonsense!"

One girl whispered, "Can he say that in church?" The boy next to her shouted, "Wash your mouth out with soap!" His friends gave him high fives.

The shooter turned and glowered at them, cursing in a combination of Spanish and English, swinging the gun from side to side as he sidled away from the doors and snarled, "Where's Carlos?" He snapped off two shots, hitting a girl. She screamed, moved her hand to her shoulder, looked at her red-stained fingers, and screamed again: "He shot me!"

Her voice reflected shock and betrayal. That's when panic set in.

Across the parking lot in the church manse the old air conditioner rat-a-tatted as *Washington Post* national security correspondent Halop Bogikian finished his interview of pastor David Carrillo, known for his work with gangs. This was an unusual assignment for Hal, but reports of Al-Qaeda connections with a Hispanic gang, Mara Salvatrucha—MS-13 for short—were surfacing. His editor had thought he should learn about the gang and the possibility that it could smuggle a nuclear bomb across the border.

The journalist and the pastor sat across from each other at a round oak table in the book-lined study. Carrillo leaned back in his chair, a smile playing around his lips. Hal thought the pastor too relaxed, too comfortable in his own skin, so it was time to pounce. Leaning forward, pen poised above his reporter's notebook, thin and wiry Hal searched the pastor's face. "You're saying that hard-core gang members, even members of MS-13, get religion and turn from their wicked ways?"

"I know you don't believe it, but that's what often happens."

Hal shook his head as though dealing with an imaginative six-year-old. "Church and state issues aside, why should anyone believe that gang members will give up power—and what seems to them an efficient way to get money—for God?"

Carrillo smiled. "I'm not expecting you to take my word for it. A young man, Carlos, is waiting in the living room. He has a remarkable story to tell you if you've got the time."

Hal glanced at his watch. He wanted to get back on the road to Washington. This whole trip to Philly had been a mistake, proving once again that you couldn't trust an editor to know the elements of a decent story. He began to offer an excuse as he capped his pen, but the pastor looked like a little kid who had called him chicken. Hal removed the cap from his pen. "OK, I'll listen."

Carrillo opened the door to the living room. "Hey, Carlos, come on in." A heavy-set boy with a bad case of acne shuffled into the room, his pants dragging on the floor. His black hair was slicked back from his face, and the beginning of a wispy black goatee shaded his jaw. Though he was seventeen, his voice cracked when he spoke: "Me and my friends joined a street gang last year, La Mara Salvatrucha. Guys call it MS-13."

Hal nodded, thinking, *Here comes one more of those born-again stories.*

"A couple of weeks ago, a little after midnight, three of us were standing near a 7-11, and some chicas cruised by, shouting insults at us. Our leader, Luis, hurled a bottle at them, but they kept going. Then a few minutes later we saw this big old Chevy come by. Three guys from the South Side Locos with baseball bats. They chased us into the projects."

Hal thought, *Might as well get some more human interest.* He began writing.

"Luis said, 'Let's get our machetes and show them.' Those Locos saw us coming out and ran, man. It was funny. But one of them tripped. The others kept going, so we caught him. I kicked him a couple of times. But Luis said, 'Let's teach the Locos that they can't mess with MS-13.'"

Carlos was silent for a time. He pulled a chain out of his pocket, which he twisted and twined between his fingers. The faint roar of noise from the nearby highway continued. A car backfired.

The pastor said, "Sounds like the concert is over. I'm not hearing the bass." Hal took another look at his watch and tried not to let the kid see how impatient he was to be off.

Carlos started up again: "OK, I want to get this off my chest. Luis started to nick that guy with his machete: hands, head, all over. I tell you, Luis is more loco than the Locos. He covers his whole body with MS-13 tattoos. But when he started to cut that guy's fingers off it was bad, real bad."

Hal's pen flew over the page of his notebook. He kicked himself for not bringing a tape recorder. While he wrote, trying to capture the cadence of the boy's speech, he felt the first flutter of excitement: This could be a good column, maybe even award winning.

Across the table the boy's voice stopped. Hal looked up from his notebook and saw Carlos crying. "The guy was screaming. I was screaming. Luis kept cutting. Left only the thumb. He laughed and said the guy could hitch a ride home. That's when I decided I had to get out. My mom could tell something was wrong. She nagged me nonstop and wouldn't get off my back until I came to talk to the preacher."

Just then a young woman ran in. "Pastor, come quick." Hal took in bright hazel eyes, slender neck, soft shoulders, and a name tag reading "Sally." He had never seen anyone so lovely.

Then her words sank in: "Someone's shooting in the sanctuary. I've called 911."

Carrillo jumped up and headed out the door to the church building. Carlos's face blanched. "Luis! It's gotta be. He's gonna kill me." He looked desperately for a place to hide. Sally bit her upper lip. "Stay here. You'll be safe." She looked up at Hal as though seeing him for the first time: "You stay with him."

Hal said, "Can't. I'm a reporter." He grabbed his pad and slammed through the front door toward his car. He heard Sally's scornful voice at his back: "That figures. He wants to be first with the story." She gave Carlos a reassuring pat on the back before following the pastor.

Carrillo entered the sanctuary through a side door and surveyed the scene. Children cowered behind the pews as Luis stalked back and forth, careful to stay away from doors and windows. "I want that traitor! Where is Carlos?" he kept yelling.

Carrillo took a step into the sanctuary: "Put the gun down, son. This is a house of God."

Luis sneered and swore at him. Carrillo kept his voice even. "You haven't killed anyone," he said, hoping it was true. "The police will be here soon. It will be better for you if you put the gun down."

"Shut up! I don't want more Jesus junk like the lies you told Carlos. I should just shoot you and put you out of your misery. Want to die?"

Carrillo said evenly, "You can shoot me if you want. I'm not afraid to die. I know where I'm going."

"Don't give me any heaven stuff!" Luis screamed. "I can turn this place into hell. My boys and me are gonna nuke the city. And I'll start with you." He pulled the trigger, and Carrillo felt a piercing pain on the right side of the chest. As he crumpled to the floor, the shooter turned his gaze toward the front of the sanctuary.

Suddenly a voice from the back demanded, "Drop your weapon."

Sally stood just outside the side door through which the pastor had entered. With her foot she held the door open about six inches. She could see Carrillo on the floor. The mystery speaker was outside her line of vision. She strained to hear police sirens.

Luis ran past the side door toward the back. She could hear his heavy breathing and his heavy footfall on the tile floor. He raised his gun and fired twice. Then Sally heard an answering shot and the metallic sound of a gun being kicked across the floor. She opened the door cautiously and saw Luis on the floor, and a shadowy figure walking away.

With no time to puzzle over the identity of the second shooter, Sally pushed open the door completely and crab-walked to the pastor as he moaned and a rising chorus of cries filled the sanctuary. Carrillo's shirt was soaked with blood. Sally looked vainly for something to use to staunch the bleeding, before settling on her skirt. She unzipped it and slipped it off, then bunched it up and pressed it into the wound.

She waited for the sirens. *What's taking so long?* she thought. She hadn't prayed for a long time, but she did now, although it was more of a complaint: God, how could you let this happen? What's the point?

———•———

As the first police cars fishtailed into the church parking lot, followed by ambulances, Hal started up his Jetta, which he'd parked on the street across from the manse. The hand that had held the Colt .45 shook, and he wished that he still smoked. He didn't know if he'd killed Luis or not; he hoped not. Not knowing whether he should stay, he asked himself what the penalty was for a person with one shooting in his past using an unlicensed gun to save lives. He decided not to stay and find out.

As Hal headed onto the highway, he called his editor, gave him the outlines of the story, and said wire service reporters would be there soon. Brushing off demands that he stay and do the reporting, he used the sentence he had used many times before: "If you don't like it, fire me." Sometimes editors had complied.

He turned on the radio, scanning the stations until he found a news-talk station where some caller was blathering about delays at airport checkpoints. He was about to jab the button again when he heard a special bulletin giving brief details about the shooting. Then the soft voice of an eye-witness identified as Sally Northaway was describing the pastor's action and telling a reporter, "I've never before seen bravery like Reverend Carrillo's."

Hal scribbled "Sally" in his reporter's notebook as he tried to erase the memory of her scornful denunciation when he fled the room. He flipped to another station: "A pastor is in critical condition, and four others plus the accused gunman are wounded. It would have been much worse except for the intervention of an unidentified bystander."

Hal honked as a Mercedes cut him off. He let a Ford Focus get in front of him as they approached a tollbooth. He turned on the CD player and listened to Patty Griffin's melancholy voice:

> There's a war and a plague, smoke and disaster
> Lions in the coliseum, screams of laughter,
> Motherless children, a witness and a Bible,
> Nothing but rain ahead, no chance for survival.

Hal let himself be lost in her misery and hellish visions, preferring them to his own. Only when he reached the outskirts of D.C. and saw out of the corner of his eye an IKEA store with a sign proclaiming "Manager's special. Swedish meatballs $5.68. Comes with salad," did he think about eating. He parked in a huge lot, noting with irritation the SUVs surrounding him.

Hal entered the modern building and immediately felt himself relax. Something about the white walls, cool wood floors, and spare furniture always did that to him, though he didn't know why. Probably had to do with all the stories of human abuse and torture he'd been forced to endure at his granddad's knee: IKEA represented cool detachment.

The cafeteria was nearly empty except for a couple drinking coffee by the windows. Hal pointed at the meatballs and said, "No gravy, please. Vegetables instead of potatoes." He filled his salad bowl with lettuce and added two cherry tomatoes. The cashier rang it up: "$7.10."

Hal waited a second and said, "Taxes aren't that much, even here in Maryland. The sign said $5.68."

The cashier stared at him and replied, "That don't include the toppings on the salad."

He stalked back to the salad bar and dumped the tomatoes into their bin. He returned to the register: "How's that? $5.68?"

The cashier laughed. "Yes, sir."

Hal took a table away from the windows and as far from the register as he could get. He ate slowly, relishing the meatballs and remembering how his grandparents had told him to chew everything twice and hug every penny. Contemplating how they had nearly starved as small children during the Armenian holocaust that was a sidelight of World War I, he wiped his plate clean, then drove to his apartment in a not-yet-gentrified building east of Capitol Hill.

Outside his door, Hal took in the odor of urine that never went away. One of the neighbor kids had left a couple of Matchbox cars in front of his door. He gave them a soft kick that sent them rolling down the corridor. He unlocked his door and stepped into the living room, which was largely filled by an IKEA couch, its once-white cushions turned gray. A round pine table covered with cigarette burns, stains, and words etched into the soft surface by Hal's too enthusiastic scribbling sat in front of the room's one window.

One wall was decorated with portraits of Armenian leaders that he'd inherited from his dad. On the opposite wall an entertainment center looked forlorn, with a twelve-inch television in the space allocated for one much larger. A folder containing photos taken of Hal with important politicians was nearly buried beneath a stack of papers. He threw his rumpled blazer onto the couch and flicked on the news. The church shooting received some play, but his role merited only a brief mention at the end: "Police are trying to pin down the identity of the hero who prevented a mass killing today."

He paced the room, thinking it crazy that he had a good story but couldn't write it and even had to hope that no one would connect him with the shooting. Maybe it would be best to get out of town for a while. He could use a vacation.

Hal spent the next hour jotting down notes for a presentation he would make the next morning in response to a speech from an academic crank—not just any crank but his freshman roommate from Columbia sixteen years before. Finally, near midnight, he flopped down on his mattress, which lay on the floor next to wire baskets filled with clothes. He complimented himself on his stoicism and lack of concern for material things. But as he drifted uneasily off to sleep, he was asking himself what he did care about.

Also at midnight Washington time—seven a.m. in Antakya, Turkey, the city known in biblical times as Antioch—a man who knew what he cared about convened a meeting in a terrorist safe house to discuss his next move.

The man, Suleyman Hasan, had a Middle Eastern marquee idol's features—height, thick black mustache, and olive skin. His lieutenant, Trafik Kurban, sat to the right, sucking furiously on a cigarette and grimacing frequently, as if pressing salt on an open wound. Mustafa Cavus, his well-muscled but potbellied special agent, sat to Suleyman's left in a molded plastic chair, wiping at his nose with a gray handkerchief as he waited for the chief to speak.

Sitting in the back were Suleyman's wife, Fatima, and a friend of hers, Kazasina, along with four students: Gurcan Aktas and Zubeyir Uruk from the University of Bosphorus in Istanbul,

Sulhaddin Timur from Dokuz Eylul University in Izmir, and Fadil Bayancik from Mustafa Kemal University in Antakya.

The students all wore thick mustaches in imitation of Suleyman as well as school insignia, because their leader insisted that his new insurgents have degrees. He had told them in his loud, deep voice, "We do not want to be seen as ignorant and poor people adopting terror out of desperation. We are poets and chess players, not gunmen."

Tonight Suleyman was so bored that he was soliciting suggestions: "It would be wonderful to have a nuclear bomb, but while we are waiting, what should we do?"

Mustafa and Trafik argued for what they knew how to engineer—more bombings of synagogues and government buildings. But Suleyman shot down that suggestion: "I'd like a vacation from small-scale bombings. They're the same old same old, as my classmates at the University of Texas used to say. Interns, what do you suggest?"

Sulhaddin perked up: "How about using poisonous gas on a subway train?"

Suleyman shook his head, arguing that it was too random in its effects: "We want to show the world that terror is not anarchy, that we can be precise in dealing even with those who resist Allah."

Gurcan had been weaned on violent videos: "Let's take a hostage and film his beheading."

Suleyman stood up and began pacing: "That's a good thought. I haven't kidnapped anyone for a couple of years. But how do we rise above run-of-the-mill hostage-taking?"

The room was silent until Suleyman pulled from a bookcase a small volume with yellowed pages. "I have an idea. I have studied the work of my ancestor Abu'l-Hasan al-Mawardi, al-Ahkam as-Sultaniyyah, peace be unto him. A brilliant scholar, he died in Baghdad in 1058, but first he discoursed on how to treat captured enemies. He gave four possible actions. The first of the four is to put them to death by cutting their necks."

"Yes, neck-cutting is good," Mustafa said in his high, puffy voice. "What are the others?"

"The emir also may enslave captives," Suleyman recited, almost seeming to go into a trance. "He may show favor to them and pardon them. He may ransom them in exchange for goods or prisoners."

"That would be fun," Fadil said. "We'd see the captives squirm, competing for our favor."

Suleyman stroked his mustache and agreed: "This could be a pleasant vacation activity while our allies work on finding nuclear materials. We could show the world that we act thoughtfully, in accordance with our history."

He paused in contemplation, and the room was again silent until Suleyman clapped his hands and said, "Yes, let's do it. We may have to wait a while, but I would like to capture four Americans vacationing in our country and use all four of my ancestor's options."

"An elegant plan," Mustafa exulted.

Suleyman spelled out the details: "We will cut the neck of one captive. A second will be a woman to enslave so we can repay the Americans for the way they treat women. A third we will pardon, so that person will tell the world our story along with one important detail: that we are ready to ransom a fourth."

"Brilliant," Trafik coughed.

"Excellent," Suleyman smiled. "We will do our scouting and find the right group of four. We will all have a wonderful vacation."

CHAPTER TWO

One mile but millions of dollars away from Hal's north-east Washington apartment, Professor Malcolm Edwards climbed into a king-size bed at the Capital Hyatt. He had a big speech to give at a Brookings Institution conference the next morning and needed to get a good night's sleep.

Suddenly he let out a scream as a scimitar blade cut into his neck. He sat up in a cold sweat—only a nightmare, possibly triggered by watching Internet videos of Middle East beheadings. He checked the clock and groaned: two a.m. It would be hard to fall asleep again.

He thought about the sexual harassment claim he soon would face unless Columbia's provost could swing a deal with his accusers. It wasn't his fault that every term he taught two lecture classes totaling 500 students, 250 of them young women, 100 of them good-looking young women.

He had developed a reputation as an entertaining professor at the Columbia University Center for Ethics, one who made liberal use of music and film in teaching both International Conflict and his most popular course, The Sexual Revolution. Whether it was movies like *Last Tango in Paris* or his lectures, Malcolm didn't know and didn't care, but he still remembered how several young women during his first term had sauntered into his office, dropping hints that they'd be glad to sleep their way to an A.

Malcolm had obliged, and to guarantee similar results in subsequent terms began stressing his faith in complete sexual freedom. It had almost always gone smoothly since Malcolm kept his end of each bargain and gave not only a top grade but a sterling recommendation.

Did he have second thoughts or worry about what would happen if a problem arose? Sure, but his lectures were better when he could show his awareness of student culture by throwing in allusions picked up during pillow talk. He wasn't a commuter professor: He entered into the lives of his students.

This term, though, a student had e-mailed Malcolm some nude pictures of herself. He responded and all went pleasurably until the threatening letter showed up in his mailbox. That setup was only part of the treachery that could cost him his endowed chair.

The center's secretary, Carol, had been a bedmate until six months ago. When she criticized Malcolm's promiscuity, their sexual relations had ended, but her efficiency in filing and record keeping had soared. The provost said she had detailed logs and phone tapes of Malcolm's sexual conversations with students, along with incriminating e-mail messages.

Malcolm thought this was all unfair since all the sex they had was consensual, but maybe it was time for a vacation. Yes, it would be nice to lecture on a beach to bikinied young women looking at him with admiration. Hmmm, there was his class now, and his top student stood in front, but why was she wearing a short black dress? And why was the surf pounding so loudly, almost like a hard rapping on wood?

Malcolm woke up, looked at the clock—six a.m.—and heard someone knocking. He shuffled to the door in his boxers.

"Room service breakfast, sir," a young woman in a Hilton shirt said.

"I didn't order anything," Malcolm barked. He grabbed the paper out of her hand and read it: "That says Room 118. This is 116. What's your name? Barbara? What kind of . . .?"

But then he saw Barbara cringing and felt sorry for her. She was the age of some of his students. "Oh, never mind."

Malcolm closed the door. He sat down and examined the first page of his speech, but the image of Barbara from two minutes before occupied another part of his mind and body.

"Most cute," he mused and opened his door to look down the corridor. Perfect timing. She had just made her delivery to the next room and was walking toward him.

"Anything else I can do for you, sir?" she asked meekly.

Malcolm smiled and said, "I'm sorry about my outburst. I came down from Columbia last night to give an important speech this morning. I'm a little jumpy."

"That's all right, sir," Barbara responded. "I thought I recognized you from a book jacket. I'm a student at Georgetown." She paused and then blurted, "I've read *Pragmatic Progressivism*. My professor thinks you hung the moon. He's using the book as a text and treats everything you say as though it's exactly right." She paused to catch her breath before adding, "Has anyone ever told you that you're even better looking than your photo?"

Malcolm's smile became wider. "This could be the start of a beautiful seminar," he said. "Why don't you come into my room for a while?"

She hesitated just a minute and then shrugged: "This is my last day of work. Doesn't matter if they fire me."

———•———

Just before eleven a.m. Malcolm approached the stage of the chandeliered hotel ballroom. He frowned as he saw his cynical ex-roommate talking to a tall, white-haired woman. "My favorite nephew," Phoebe du Pont said, striding toward him in her bright, floral-print dress and giving him a hug.

Several minutes later she told the suit-jacketed audience of Brookings Institution supporters, "You know me as the widow of a financier who became our ambassador to Turkey. Today is my sixty-eighth birthday, and I am feeling old these days, so it gives me great pleasure to introduce two rising stars who are each half my age.

"Professor Edwards wrote the best-selling *Pragmatic Progressivism*, the book that is teaching us how to react to terrorism without overreacting. His students know him as a professor who involves himself deeply in their lives." Malcolm wondered how much she knew or even could know.

"Halop Bogikian is a Pulitzer Prize-winning national security reporter and columnist who has written about Islam and other religions in an equal-opportunity manner: He scorns them all." The audience laughed.

"Their backgrounds are strikingly different. Malcolm is descended from the Puritans and keeps alive their vision of America as a city on a hill, although his hill and Jerusalem are on different planets." Mild laughter.

"Hal, grandson of an immigrant who sold used mattresses, was a Massachusetts high-school chess champion. He keeps alive the immigrant vision of America as a land of opportunity, including the opportunity to shoot your neighbor." Hal grimaced.

"You can read more about their professional credentials in this June Conference program." She held it up. "But I hope they'll excuse me for relating a few personal tidbits. They were roommates at Columbia sixteen years ago when I taught archeology there. Other students referred to them as Starsky and Hutch, given their differences in appearance and temperament.

"Malcolm was an orator who always measured his words like a natural politician. Hal showed a caustic wit. Malcolm seemed never to wear the same sweater twice. Hal wore the same sweatshirt, week in, week out. Their only similarity—I hope they'll forgive me for saying this—is that they've both been unable to get along with a woman for very long. But I love them both, so please give a warm welcome to Malcolm Edwards's presentation and Halop Bogikian's response."

Malcolm approached the podium and peered out at the crowd. At six feet two inches with his wheat-colored complexion and wavy blonde bangs, he looked like a handsome, beefy Roman senator.

He spoke about US power and the Middle East: "The era of hit-back foreign policy is over. Some Americans are trapped in old Western movies, eager to channel Gary Cooper in *High Noon*. But shooting is the last refuge of those not brave enough to fight for peace."

Phoebe picked up the knitting she had carried everywhere since her husband's death. Her double-pointed needles clicked softly as she finished a baby hat. Malcolm continued: "Let's be pragmatic: We are a rich, capitalistic country, used to our luxuries and unwilling to risk all for the sake of abstract principles that never transform reality as we wish they might."

The progressive solution, Malcolm concluded, was to "develop ties with Islamic progressives and strive to bring social justice to our own society as they work to change theirs. Above all, we must not fight them, for if we do, they will win because they have less to lose."

When Hal, a lean five feet ten inches, stood up to respond, his dark hair bristled and so did his words: "According to the professor, we can work with the Muslim left. But I've interviewed some of their radicals. They're out to win the world for their god, and it's idiotic to think otherwise."

The audience became anxious as Hal disregarded polite academic blather and also diplomatic niceties. "We should just get out of the Middle East. We should push for energy self-sufficiency with small cars, oil drilling in Alaska, nuclear power—anything that will help us have no involvement with that whole part of the world."

In her chair at the front, Phoebe knitted intensely as Malcolm and Hal attacked each other. When some audience members criticized both options and proposed further US military involvement, Phoebe put down her needles and fiddled with her hair, twirling strands around her middle finger and flicking the ends.

When the show finally ended and the audience filed out bemusedly, Phoebe looked at both men and sighed. "That was quite a performance. Perhaps it was a mistake to have set this up, but I want my sons to be at peace. I'd give anything for you to stop your squabbling."

As they headed toward the door, Malcolm objected. "Phoebe, Hal and I just see the world differently. Hal thinks no two people can get along. I tend to see the silver linings. It isn't personal, at least not for me."

Hal punched the elevator button, thinking how Malcolm— silver spoon at birth, silver-tongued in college, cruising from silver lining to silver lining—always brought out the worst in him. He . . .

But Phoebe was speaking. "You both were so kind to me when Andrew died. Your memorial lecture, Malcolm, and your column, Hal, captured the husband who swept me into a world of riches and eight years of life in Turkey. Did you know I'm returning there a week from now to give a lecture?"

"Have a nice trip," Hal, still simmering, responded.

Phoebe continued as though he hadn't interrupted. "My assistant and I have planned it all out: We start at Istanbul where I speak, visit mosques and churches and ruins, see the modern clash of civilizations. After Istanbul we'll spend a week visiting Izmir, Ephesus, Antalya, and Antakya. I have tickets for two."

"You'll enjoy it," Malcolm said.

"Perhaps you will also. This antagonism you and Hal still have toward each other, and my fondness for both of you, gives me an idea: How about we go from two travelers to four? You'll each have ten days of vacation, and I'll pay for everything. Great historical sites, good hotels, good food. I would immensely enjoy your company."

Both Malcolm and Hal were tongue-tied, welcoming the vacation opportunity but not wanting to spend the time with each other. Phoebe persisted: "I know this is sudden, but I also know both of you. You're workaholics and don't take vacations. Hal, you'd get grist for some new columns. Malcolm, you're done with your teaching for the term. And from what I hear, perhaps this is a good time for you to get out of town."

Malcolm again wondered what she knew, but he recovered and came up with a diplomatic way to pass up the trip: "I'll check my calendar."

Hal was not so diplomatic: "I've never wanted to go to Turkey. As an Armenian, the thought of it gives me the heebie-jeebies. Like Jews going to Germany." He saw Phoebe's stricken face and tried to make amends: "I'll check with my editor."

Their eyes swung toward a beautiful young woman approaching Phoebe. "This is my assistant, Sally Northaway."

The reaction of both men startled Phoebe. Malcolm stared at Sally's bright smile and blonde shoulder-length hair, and his eyes immediately moved down her black, sleeveless shift. Startled into going beyond what he might normally say to his aunt's assistant, he murmured, "I dreamed about you last night."

Sally laughed. "Bet you say that about all the girls."

Hal stammered, "I'm surprised to see you here. I thought you worked at that church in Philadelphia."

Sally's eyes flashed at him. "No, it was my first time there. I volunteered to drive members of a Wilmington youth group to the rally."

Their conversation stopped as a middle-aged woman walked up. "Professor Edwards, you must autograph my copy of your superb book. It's wonderful. I keep it beside my bed and read a page every night before I fall asleep."

Malcolm said, "My pleasure. It's readers like you who make me want to write." He pulled a gold fountain pen out of his breast pocket and signed his name with a flourish.

Phoebe turned to Hal. "I didn't know you were there. What a terrible tragedy. And poor Sally in the middle of it."

Malcolm interrupted. "What happened? I was so busy yesterday that I never turned on the news."

As Sally described the shooting, Hal punched the elevator button again. No way was he going to come out of this looking good. He listened as Sally described the shooting. When she got to the part where she called 911 and fetched the pastor, the elevator door opened.

"So what was Hal doing while all this was going on?" Malcolm asked as he tugged on one of his French cuffs, with a flash of gold cuff link showing.

Sally looked at Hal disapprovingly. "I don't know. He ran the other way."

"I'm sure Hal had his reasons to leave," Phoebe said, as he stood there miserably. The elevator opened, depositing them in the lobby. "Since it's my birthday, I hope you will all come to lunch; I've made reservations. Shall we discuss our plans?"

They settled in at the hotel restaurant. Sally looked at the waitresses with an experienced eye. She thought about her last day on the job at Windows on the World, the World Trade Center's high-up restaurant. She remembered the manager saying, "You're doing great. Tomorrow you can move from breakfast/lunch to late-night dining. Much better tips, and after work we can go to my place."

Her reverie broke as Malcolm asked Phoebe, "How did you and Sally meet?"

With a quivering lip Phoebe responded, "When I went into Manhattan on September 12 to see if Andrew had possibly escaped from the eighty-sixth floor—perhaps had been hospitalized and unable to call—I met Sally. She had worked in the building and was volunteering to help obtain information."

Phoebe blinked back the tears as pictures played in her head. Chaos. Smoke and disaster, photos taped to walls: "Has anyone seen my husband?" Sally reached out a hand and patted Phoebe's.

They were silent. Malcolm after a while turned to Sally: "How long had you been in New York?"

"Not long. I grew up in San Diego and went to college there—business major, with lots of acting on the side. I came

East in June 2001, hoping to get on Broadway, but in three months I was offered only beds."

Phoebe added, "After that first meeting Sally and I kept in touch. We began talking. She was looking for a change, and I found myself overwhelmed trying to make sense of all the papers and investments Andrew left behind. I asked her to help, and she's been my assistant ever since."

Hal asked Sally, "Was that the change you were looking for?"

She regarded him coolly, but then her politeness kicked in. "In some ways yes. In college I lived on the beach. I never had to read anything but basic business textbooks. Traveling with Phoebe and doing research for the book she's writing has opened my eyes to a lot of things."

Hal looked at Phoebe with surprise. "You're writing a book?"

"Does that surprise you so much? I'm not yet a feeble-minded old woman. Don't treat me like one." Hal looked abashed. He had grown accustomed to thinking of his old professor as retired from creativity, especially since she had taken up knitting.

She went on, "Between losing Andrew and getting old, I'm thinking a great deal about death. The Turkey trip is not all pleasure: I'm writing about death in ancient cultures and our own, so I'm revisiting the archeological sites where I once worked."

Malcolm was polite: "I'd like to hear your conclusions."

"Thank you, but I fear that the only people interested will be those who are imminently dying." Phoebe turned to Sally and said, "I've asked Malcolm and Hal to come with us to Turkey."

Sally turned to Malcolm. "I hope you'll come. *Pragmatic Progressivism* is a wonderful book. It was one of the first books Phoebe gave me to read. She's very proud of you."

Malcolm stared at Sally and said, "I am definitely coming."

Hal stood and said he had to get back to work. Phoebe held out her hand: "I'll walk with you for a moment and then come back." She waited until they reached the lobby before speaking.

"What about this shooting yesterday? I know you're not telling us something."

"You're right, but I have my reasons."

She nodded. "I respect that. So will you come with us?"

"Look, Phoebe. I appreciate the offer. But Turkey? Besides, Malcolm and I would make you miserable. *He* makes *me* miserable. It would be like a trip through hell with a demon as my companion."

Phoebe laughed. "You exaggerate. You're both adults; surely you can behave."

Hal shook his head unhappily. Phoebe looked at him as she used to look at students, willing them to speak honestly, but he refused to give in. Finally she asked, "Does your reluctance to come have anything to do with the fourth member of our party?"

Hal wrinkled his brow. "Sally?" He tried to be nonchalant. "She seems very nice." Phoebe stared at him again until Hal finally grinned, "All right, you've got me. Did you see the look Malcolm gave Sally? He already has her wrapped up. On this trip three will be company, four a crowd."

Phoebe grabbed his hand. "I want you to come to Turkey for your education but also so you'll get to know Sally. I've wanted to introduce the two of you for some time."

"Really?" Hal looked up with interest before resuming his hangdog air. "I'll think about it."

Phoebe stared at him. "I've never known you to pass up a challenge. Come with us. I love Malcolm and think he will grow up some day, but he may need hard lessons. And I do think you and Sally have a lot to offer each other. Besides, you've muttered for years about writing a book on the Armenian holocaust. Perhaps a trip to the country you hate will force you to get it done."

———•———

When their June 10 flight to Istanbul left JFK, Sally had arranged the first-class tickets so she and Malcolm sat on one side, Phoebe and Hal on the other. After all, she knew Malcolm and Hal wouldn't last a twelve-hour trip side-by-side and, between the two of them, Malcolm seemed like far more pleasant company. Plus, he had cute hair.

As they settled into their seats, Sally knew she had chosen wisely. Malcolm in his red tie and black blazer, his shoes polished to a sheen, looked every bit the brilliant young professor. Across the aisle Hal slumped in his seat, his faded and frayed-at-the-collar oxford-cloth shirt looking as though he hadn't bothered to iron it. She tried to look beyond his indifference to clothes. Maybe his mournful expression and penetrating eyes made some women want to comfort him. Not Sally.

A stewardess came by and took Malcolm's coat. Sally watched the interplay between them. She recognized the attendant's flirty moves and waited to see how Malcolm would respond. He was polite, but his smile was reserved. Yet when he turned to Sally, he gave her the full measure of his charm. She felt herself melt before the onslaught, even though she knew what he was doing.

"Istanbul is a very romantic city," he whispered. She leaned closer to hear. From across the aisle Hal watched miserably as the seduction began. For the next hour Malcolm regaled Sally with well-told tales of Turkish history. *He has read a lot,* she thought. After two glasses of wine, Sally's guarded posture melted away and, before too long her head was nestled in the crook of Malcolm's arm as she slept.

Phoebe also slept, and Hal pulled out a book about the Armenian holocaust. He kept his head in the book, lifting it only to accept with grunts the steward's repeated offers of the Turkish brandy known as raki.

Later the attendants brought dinner. Malcolm urged Sally to take a glass of raki, in which he mixed water. When it foamed white, he said, "Turks call it lion's milk."

She took a sip and shuddered. "Are you cold?" he asked, wrapping a blanket around her. Sally took another sip of the brandy and snuggled down into the blanket. "Not now, I'm not." She smiled as her eyes fluttered shut.

CHAPTER THREE

Sally and Phoebe sat in the courtyard of the Royal Scimitar during their first morning in Istanbul. Phoebe drank tea and knit. She smiled and said *gunaydin* to hotel staff members who wished her a good morning in return as they walked by. Several guests recognized her and stopped by the table to tell her how much they had liked her late husband, the ambassador. Some lingered to gape at Sally, who wore a red blouse that matched her nail polish.

"What a gorgeous hotel. Did you stay here often?" Sally looked around at the deep casement windows and the golden honey color of the hotel walls. Pink roses and African violets filled flower boxes and spilled out of urns. Red and white geraniums in terra cotta set off the courtyard's lush green shrubbery. "I feel like we've suddenly come down in Oz."

Phoebe, draped in a long, shapeless grey dress, had dropped her big floppy hat on the chair beside her. She smiled at Sally's pleasure and said, "This is a garden amid wilderness. Still, I like living with the illusion that the world is filled with peace and beauty."

"It's stunning. Everything about it is beautiful. Look how the grass is cut alongside paths through the garden. The left edge is jagged, and the right edge straight. The gardener shows respect for geometry and at the same time shrugs it off. It's wonderful."

"I'm glad you like it." Phoebe smiled fondly at her assistant.

"You are both visions," Malcolm said as he walked up to the table and kissed Phoebe on the cheek. He put his hand on Sally's shoulder and left it there.

Sally blushed and shrugged her shoulder until his hand slipped off. She felt embarrassed that she'd fallen asleep on Malcolm's shoulder, although thinking about it made her stomach flutter. She looked up to see him smiling at her as though he could read her mind. She blushed again and hoped that Phoebe hadn't noticed.

Malcolm had dressed for an expedition. He carried a small REI backpack with a water bottle, suntan lotion, lip balm, and flashlight clipped to it, even though the plan for the day was merely to visit Haghia Sophia, the Blue Mosque, and several medieval churches with formidable frescoes.

"We'll be underway," Phoebe said, "as soon as Hal arrives. Where do you think he is?"

"Here," Hal said as he walked to the table. "I had to make a call to my editor. I made her mad last month, and she's asked me to check on a possible Istanbul story, so I thought I might bug out on these old buildings. Would you mind, Phoebe?"

Her face took on such a look of disappointment that Hal felt ashamed. He stole a glance at Sally, who glared at him. "Never mind," he muttered. "I'm on vacation. Editors can wait."

Phoebe arose and gave Hal a gentle push toward the door. They strolled on cobblestone streets to Haghia Sophia, the Church of Holy Wisdom, the famous domed cathedral that was a Christian wonder of the world for nearly a thousand years. "Such a glorious and sad story," Phoebe said as she guided them through the huge, dim interior, bigger than a football field.

Sally touched the huge slabs of marble as Phoebe explained, "Century after century from AD 537 on, the church added beautiful frescos and mosaics, but most are gone. When Muslims conquered this city in 1453, they turned the church into a mosque by ripping off crosses and destroying or plastering over the magnificent art. Now it's a drab museum."

As they climbed a switchback ramp to the gallery level, Malcolm took over from Phoebe and sounded like a veteran tour guide: "When he entered the building he had commissioned, the emperor Justinian is said to have exclaimed about Haghia Sophia, 'Glory to God who has thought me worthy to finish this work.'"

"And glory to Malcolm, whom God thought worthy to announce it," Hal muttered.

Malcolm led them through the north gallery, pointing out where Theodora, Justinian's wife, sat—far from the altar but with a perfect view of the dome with its jeweled cross on a background of stars. Hal interrupted. "Theodora—wasn't she the former stripper who sprinkled her pubic hair with grain, then invited geese to come and peck at the fragments? Sounds like someone just up your alley."

"Hal!" Phoebe's voice was sharp in the stone building. He muttered an apology before wandering off on his own.

Malcolm glued himself to Sally's side, pointing out items of interest and attending carefully to her ideas. She asked, "How do you know so much?" He shrugged modestly as he pointed out the huge wooden medallions that Muslim conquerors had hung at the gallery level. "I read a little Arabic," he told Sally in a way he hoped would sound casual, and pointed out medallions saying "Allah" and "Muhammad."

Sally held onto his arm. "It's amazing after so much strife that Christians and Muslims now share this building."

"Share?" Hal overheard Sally's last comment. "This building is not about sharing. The conquering Muslims didn't share: they destroyed. The Europeans sure didn't do much sharing even among themselves."

"That's the cynical view," Malcolm stated.

"It's true," Hal insisted, pointing to the tomb of Enrico Dandalo. He explained that Byzantine Christians partially blinded Dandalo in 1171 and that he took revenge in 1204 by leading an army of soldiers from Venice and elsewhere in an orgy of pillage and destruction.

Sally looked at Hal with surprise. Malcolm said, "Looks like you've been doing some reading. Here, I'll take a photo of the tomb for you." He pulled from his backpack a digital Nikon.

Hal muttered, "Looks like that cost you something."

"It's a marvelous camera with great resolution—eight megapixels. And I want to find the right lens." He reached into his backpack. Hal watched as Malcolm showed Sally his viewfinder and then shot the tomb.

"See way up there?" Malcolm pointed to a corner of the north gallery. "I remember reading"—he didn't say just two days before—"about that tenth-century mosaic of the man in full imperial costume. The inscription reads, 'Lord, help thy servant, the orthodox and faithful Emperor Alexander.' And look at that terrific eleventh-century mosaic over there: Jesus in the middle, Emperor Constantine IX on the left, Empress Zoe on the right."

Sally was impressed. "Those are gorgeous, Malcolm. I can't believe how old they are."

"Not so fast," Hal said. "Your glossy version of history is wrong. 'Orthodox and faithful' Alexander? He was a lecherous drunk who conspired to castrate his six-year-old nephew to knock him out of the line of succession. That sweet Zoe-Constantine mosaic? Constantine was the third husband, and artists substituted his head on the fresco for the heads of her earlier husbands. She probably poisoned her first. She certainly blinded and exiled her second."

"So history is full of ugliness," Sally said. "That's no surprise. But surely it's balanced out by so much beauty." She looked up at the great dome: "See what an achievement that is. Why wallow in the gutter when we could look at the stars?"

Hal shrugged. "Sorry, I've never been one for fairy tales. Give me the truth anytime. That dome you're admiring used to be covered by thirty million tiny gold tiles. Now they're gone, stolen by Muslims, and all that remains is propaganda from the Quran."

"'Propaganda?' Over a billion people believe it, and you dismiss it?"

"I've never been impressed by popularity."

Sally, exchanging glances with Malcolm, said, "I can see that."

Phoebe led them down to the ground floor gift shop and bought postcards before leading them across Sultanahmet Square to another huge domed building. At the crosswalks Turkish men ogled Sally, and she stepped closer to Malcolm for protection.

Phoebe tried to decrease the sparring between Malcolm and Hal by taking over the guide role. "This Blue Mosque, directly across from Haghia Sophia, was literally an in-your-face building project. A thousand years after the original, it's as if Sultan Ahmet was saying to Christians, 'Anything you can do I can do better.'"

She pulled two long silk scarves from her satchel, handed a red one to Sally, and said while demonstrating how, "Make sure it covers your face and arms." Inside even Hal was stunned by the vast, bright space surrounding two massive columns. Sally, enthralled by the mosque's wall tiles in cobalt blue, aqua, red, and white floral patterns, asked about their origin.

"Iznik, a little south of here," Malcolm was quick to say. "The year: 1616. This mosque includes fifty different designs and twenty-one thousand tiles. Look," he paused, "the red matches your blouse."

Sally smiled, but Phoebe whispered to Malcolm, "Stop your courting and watch." They observed Muslim men going through the ritualized prayer cycle in their individual places on a vast carpet: one bow, two prostrations, as they recited verses from the Quran. A few women huddled together at the back behind a screen.

They examined the elaborate *minbar*, the high pulpit from which imams gave their sermons on Friday. "Turkey has about forty thousand mosques," Phoebe said. "In each one an imam delivers the same government-written sermon."

Malcolm was enthralled: "That's power."

Phoebe spoke in Turkish to one of the mosque's muezzins and asked him to give a demonstration of his five-times-a-day call to prayer. When he assented and put his fingers over his ears, she explained, "It helps him to concentrate and listen."

Then he chanted, with Phoebe providing a simultaneous translation: "I witness that Allah is the greatest! I witness that Allah is the only one to worship! I witness that Muhammad is his follower and his envoy! Come to the prayer! Come to the prayer! Come to the salvation!"

The muezzin happily shuffled off. Phoebe walked with him, stuffing several bills into his hand.

Hal had pulled out a notebook and was scribbling notes in it when Malcolm joined him. "I thought you were on vacation."

"Just jotting down a few things so I don't forget."

"Like . . .?"

"OK, I wrote, 'It sounds like the muezzin was giving an order, not making a request.'"

"You're dead wrong," Malcolm snapped. "I've talked with American imams. They all emphasize what the Quran says: 'There is no compulsion in religion.'"

Hal tucked the notebook back into his pocket, recapped his pen, and insisted that he would not do public relations for Islam: "That may help you sell books, but I'd rather be right than rich. You know as well as I do that there's 'no competition in religion' whenever Islam becomes dominant."

Sally listened to Malcolm's response and tried to be polite as Hal turned to her and said, "I bet he's never even read the al-Tawba and the Anfal, the Quran's major war chapters."

She walked back to Phoebe. "Don't they ever stop bickering?"

"I hope they'll grow tired of it. Of course, they're preening in front of you." Phoebe thought back fifteen years to when Hal and Malcolm were both after the same girl. Malcolm won that competition, slept with her twice, then dumped her. She hoped that wasn't in Sally's future.

"I wish they'd stop," Sally said, bringing Phoebe back to the present. "It makes me uncomfortable."

"Then tell them that," Phoebe commanded. "Perhaps if you state it clearly, they'll stop. You'll find the right words."

Sally caught up to Hal and Malcolm, who had paused in front of the door. She looked nervously over to Phoebe, who was busy speaking in Turkish to an old woman.

"I wish you both would stop," Sally said. "We're in this beautiful mosque, and you're both arguing like children about who's read what."

She looked around and saw no one else nearby. "You two remind me of a visit I took to a nude beach. Guys outnumbered girls at least five to one, so you can imagine what happened when a couple of decent-looking girls lay down and took off their suits."

Malcolm and Hal grinned. Sally didn't realize that two Turkish worshippers had crept closer. As she talked, her voice rose: "Suddenly we were surrounded by lots of naked Frisbee-playing guys. That's what you remind me of, except you're exhibiting your brains."

They heard sniggering behind them. Sally turned and was appalled to see the two Turkish men grinning and elbowing each other. One said snidely, "I have studied English in school and would like to learn more about your American beaches." Sally stalked out of the mosque, trailing Malcolm and Hal in her wake.

Phoebe caught up to Sally outside. "Did you tell them?"

"Yeah," she muttered, "but I'm not sure they understood the point I was trying to make."

———•———

After a lunch of delicate crepes stuffed with cheese and spinach, they piled into a taxi to go to the Orthodox church complex to meet one of Phoebe's friends, the venerable Ecumenical Patriarch, revered by many of Turkey's several hundred thousand remaining Christians.

As they drove northwest along the waterfront, Phoebe pointed out the world's greatest natural harbor, the Golden Horn, explaining that the name came from the shape of the harbor and the legend that Byzantines threw their gold into it when the Ottomans captured Constantinople in 1453. Hal, half listening, wrote in his notebook about two skinny dogs fighting over a scrap of food, a man and a woman arguing, and a boy throwing mud at a sheet hanging on a clothesline.

When they reached the basilica, a priest took Phoebe to see the patriarch, so Hal shuffled around the sanctuary, jotting down specific details about icons and relics. As Sally strolled over, he commented, "I can't believe my relatives thought pictures painted on wood could make them holy."

"Did you ever talk with your grandfather about that?"

"He was a bitter old man, full of dismal tales of death and destruction."

"Look at the frescoes on the dome: The look in that man's eyes is so tender, so precious. Maybe they saw that and worshipped the idea behind it. Phoebe tells me they aren't actually worshipping the icons."

Hal shrugged. "OK. Give them one point for common sense." He realized that he and Sally were actually having a conversation, and he wanted to stretch the moment. He saw Malcolm talking with a black-robed priest. Probably trying to buy an icon, Hal figured. He turned to Sally, who was gazing intently at a picture of Jesus.

"My parents would hate this place," she said. " They had one way of thinking about God and hated anyone who saw things differently."

"But you're attracted to this?"

Sally suddenly looked sad, and Hal for the first time saw this lovely woman as needy. "I'm a pretty confused person," she said. "I'm like the people at the end of the book of Jonah: I don't know my right hand from my left. That's one of the reasons I like Phoebe. She knows what she believes, but she never tries to force it on me."

She put her hands on her hips and faced Hal: "And how about you? Surely there's more to Halop Bogikian than your notebook."

Now it was Hal's turn to laugh. "Yeah. I have a very hip wardrobe."

"I noticed."

By the time Malcolm rejoined them and said he had learned about the order of the icons at the front of the church, Hal was willing to follow meekly behind, even jotting down an occasional note. "Did you say Peter always comes first on the left?"

Malcolm eyed him suspiciously but could not ignore the chance to show what he had learned. Sally seemed genuinely interested, and Hal decided to put the feud to rest for a while. He listened as Malcolm pointed out how John the Baptist was portrayed in icons as having two heads, one on his neck and one on a plate.

Just then Phoebe approached with a short man in full black robes. The patriarch had a long white beard, a twinkle in his eye, and a greeting for each in turn. To Hal he said, "If there is hell, there is also heaven." To Malcolm he said, "If there is heaven, there is also hell." To Sally he said, "If there is no heaven and no hell, nothing matters." Then he gave each a small gold cross and departed.

Through the walls the mournful cry of the muezzin's call to prayer sounded, reminding all that this was Muslim territory. They walked out somberly, pausing before a door that was welded shut.

"Here's what happens when wisdom meets history," Phoebe said. "Almost two centuries ago Patriarch Gregory V encouraged Christians to overthrow Muslim rule. The Ottomans hanged him for treason. The door has been closed ever since in memory of him."

———•———

They returned to the Royal Scimitar where Phoebe planned to take a nap and Hal to catch up on e-mail: "You're on your own for the rest of the day," she said. Sally put on her swimsuit and a long cover-up that fell to her ankles. She grabbed her book, *The Second Coming* by Walker Percy, and carried it down to the patio, where she ordered a Coke. She was tired and felt as though she'd been pulled at like a bone between two dogs.

She was soon so absorbed in reading that she didn't see a young man with a black mustache watching her from across the patio, or even Malcolm approaching the table. "That's hardly vacation fare," he said, taking the book from her hand.

"No, wait." She grabbed it back from him. "Our time in the mosque and at the church made me think of this passage: Percy says the modern Christian is 'nominal, lukewarm, hypocritical, sinful, or, if fervent, generally offensive and fanatical. But he is not crazy.' Do you agree?"

"Yes to all that except for the last sentence. I'd say most are crazy, too."

"And do you agree with this?" Sally asked, as she read on: "The unbeliever is worse because of the 'fatuity, blandness, incoherence, fakery, and fatheadedness of his unbelief. He is in fact an insane person.'"

"Wait," Malcolm objected. "This is why I never liked Percy. He's an extremist. What's wrong if we eat, drink, sleep?"

Sally smiled and continued reading, "'The present-day unbeliever is crazy because he finds himself born into a world of endless wonders, having no notion how he got here, a world in which he eats, sleeps . . . works, grows old, gets sick, and dies.'"

"That sounds like Hal," Malcolm laughed.

Sally laughed nervously, feeling slightly disloyal and yet enjoying Malcolm's attention. She kept reading Percy's depiction of the person who "drinks his drink, laughs . . . for all the world as if his prostate were not growing cancerous, his arteries turning to chalk, his brain cells dying off by the millions, as if the worms were not going to have him in no time at all."

"There's some truth there," Malcolm acknowledged, "and that's why I like being at a university where we enjoy physical pleasures along with the life of the mind." He traced his finger along her arm.

She blushed and closed her book. After a final sip of Coke, she pushed away from the table. "I'm going to rest."

"Alone?" He smiled invitingly.

"Alone."

Malcolm watched her cross the café to the elevator, her hips gently swaying as if to music heard only by her. He rubbed his hand against his cheek before heading into town.

As soon as Sally returned to her room, she knew she couldn't stay. She was all keyed up and had been disappointed to find the hotel didn't have a pool. It did, however, have a Turkish bath. She read the hotel guide, which explained where it was and directed her to wear the hotel-provided white terry cloth robe and slippers. She took off her cover-up and put on the thick robe, then hurried down the hall to the Turkish bath, which unlike traditional ones was for both men and women.

Sally hung her robe in the ladies' dressing room. She put her slippers underneath and tucked her hotel key into the robe's pocket, then pushed open a dark wood door and looked upon a round, four-foot-deep pool surrounded by gray tile. Overhead a dome enclosed the pool chamber.

A man and woman and two young children floated in the pool, their voices echoing eerily off the dome. Sally slipped into the water until she was covered up to her shoulders. She closed her eyes and began to hum, switching from one tune to another and listening to how the steamy air transformed the sound.

When she opened her eyes, she realized that the family had left and a young man with a black mustache and lots of black chest hair was sitting on a bench, using a metal pan to splash himself with cold water from a faucet.

Sally turned her back to him, wishing he would go away or someone else would come in. She'd been in the water for nearly twenty minutes and was beginning to feel dizzy from the heat. But she didn't want to get out with him there. She glanced at him from the corner of her eye and saw that he was staring at her.

Sally nonchalantly made her way around the edge of the pool, until an expanse of water separated her from the Turk. She headed for the sauna, where she hoped to find a lock on the door. The man didn't move, and Sally began to feel silly and slightly paranoid. This, after all, was a major hotel, and just as ethnic screening at airports was improper, so was any tendency on her part to think ill of all Turkish males. Besides, it was only six o'clock.

Malcolm strolled through the cobblestone streets of Istanbul's tourist section, expecting—and hoping—to be accosted with offers from prostitutes, as he had the previous year during visits to Havana and Phnom Penh. Here, though, the come-ons were different: One child, bathroom scale in hand and trying to earn pennies, asked, "Want to get weighed?"

Most of the invitations came from carpet merchants: "Please enter my store." "My English is not comprehensible, no matter, you are buying rug, not me." "Please sit and have Turkish coffee. If you love it with your heart, you will love my rugs!"

After a while Malcolm stopped at a little café. A student wearing a University of Bosphorus shirt approached his table. "May I join you?" the young man asked. "You are an American?"

Malcolm nodded. "Yes, a professor from Columbia University."

"Ah, that is a fine university. It is a pleasure to meet you. My name is Zubeyir Uruk. I am studying international politics. What is your name?"

"Malcolm Edwards."

"The author of *Pragmatic Progressivism?*"

"Yes." Malcolm smiled. "How do you know that?"

"My professor assigned that book to us in the spring. He said we need more Americans like you."

Malcolm took that as a compliment. "And what do you think?"

"I agree that you are useful," Zubeyir smiled. "What are you doing in Istanbul?"

"Some friends of mine and I are visiting here for a couple of days. Then we'll go south to Izmir and beyond that spend a week visiting ancient sites."

"How many of you are here?"

Malcolm thought that question odd but responded, "Four in all."

Zubeyir suddenly straightened up and seemed tense with excitement.

"Why do you ask?"

"Oh, I've spent the past couple of days practicing my English by talking with every American I see."

"Your English is very good."

"Thank you. I've found that Americans almost always come in large groups and ride around in tour buses. Your way is much better. If I may ask, who are the other members of your group?"

"Certainly you may ask. It's a distinguished group. You may be too young to remember Phoebe du Pont, wife of the former US ambassador to Turkey."

Zubeyir seemed even more excited. "One of my professors last term often talked about Mr. du Pont and how American influence was changing Turkey."

"He died when the terrorists destroyed the twin towers in 2001."

"We watched that on television. It was amazing that a handful of men could destroy the symbol of American capitalism."

Malcolm nodded. "The Washington journalist Halop Bogikian and a young woman, Mrs. du Pont's assistant, are also traveling with us."

"I would like to meet them and learn more about America."

"Good. You should come to Mrs. du Pont's lecture tomorrow at six at Istanbul University." The student was eager to leave. Malcolm watched him wind his way through the narrow street, around tables of leather goods and rugs.

Sally opened the sauna door and slammed it shut. She reached out to lock it but then withdrew her hand, thinking she was being stupid: *So he's Turkish and has a hairy chest. Is that any reason to treat him like a rapist?*

Although she shamed herself into leaving the door unlocked, she couldn't stop herself from glancing nervously at it from her place on the slatted wooden bench. Gradually she relaxed: the Turk who had been eyeing her was not coming in. He was probably a businessman, maybe even an imam. The thought made her laugh, and she let her mind drift off to memories of being a girl lying on the sand of Mission Beach.

Suddenly the door opened and the young man entered, his black chest hair standing up. Sally stood up to leave, but he blocked the door. She would have had to squeeze by him.

"Do not be alarmed."

Sally sat down, not wanting to be rude, and the man sat next to her. "You are an American?" he asked.

She nodded nervously.

"What do you think about your country's imperialism?"

"I'm not here to discuss politics." Her voice trembled, and she again rose to leave.

"Not so fast," he said, moving quickly to lock the door. "I know what you are here for. You are an American woman without a ring on your finger. You are wearing a provocative swimsuit before a man who is not your husband."

"Let me out of here," Sally demanded.

"I've seen your movies. I know how you American women like to declare your innocence while all the time you can't wait to have sex with a real man. You came in here when the others left and waited for me. Now I will give you what you want."

He pulled down his trunks and grabbed her. "No!" she yelled as he pulled at her suit. "Let me go."

"You Americans are rapists and murderers. It's your turn to feel what my people feel."

———

Across the city Zubeyir was reporting to Suleyman that he had found a group of four potential victims. "The ambassador's wife, a leading American professor, a Washington journalist, and a young woman."

"You have done well," Suleyman said. "And the young woman, what does she look like?"

"I could find out tomorrow. Mrs. du Pont is giving a lecture. Why don't we seize all four of them afterwards?"

"Others in our group are still in Antakya, and I haven't heard from your classmate Aktas. We must be patient. But you will go to the lecture and learn more about the Americans' plans."

———

At the hotel Hal had answered his e-mail. He put on his white robe, meandered into the Turkish bath, and began to sing, enjoying the sound of his voice echoing back against the sloped ceiling. One of the echoes came back higher pitched than he expected. He heard the sound again. Coming from the sauna, it sounded like a muffled scream.

He slipped his way across the wet tile and pushed on the door, but it was locked from inside. He heard another scream that was quickly muffled. He shouted but received no response, so he backed away and charged the door. It flew open, revealing a naked man with thick black hair leaning over Sally. She lay on a bench, her hands tied under the bench and her mouth gagged, her eyes full of tears.

When the man turned his face toward Hal, Sally kneed him hard where it would most hurt. He cried out and put his hands down. A second later Hal hammered his chin. The man fell back, hit his head against the wooden sauna bench, and lay still.

"You OK?" Hal asked Sally as he removed her gag, untied her hands, and looked away. Sally, trembling and fighting back tears, pulled up her swimsuit and shivered, hugging herself and rocking. "I'm so glad you came. I didn't think anyone would come. Thank you, thank you."

Sally fell silent as Hal regarded the prostrate man. "We've got to get security. But I don't want to leave him. Can you go?"

She nodded. When he began to speak, she brushed him off. "I'm fine. I'll be fine."

Hal sat on the bench and nudged the man with his foot, hoping for some stirring so he could punch him again. Hal had seen many things as a reporter. He'd shot one man recently and another years before. But he'd never wanted to kill a person like he did now. He closed his eyes and wished he could make the episode go away. Then he heard footsteps and looked up to see a local policeman standing in the door.

The officer cuffed the would-be rapist, who was now awake and complaining. Hal asked for a translation. The American woman had provoked him, and the American man had beaten him. But the cop didn't seem to be buying it: he slapped around the perp.

Hal grabbed his terry cloth robe and headed upstairs to find Sally and the security manager. He found him reassuring her: "We take very seriously a sexual attack. You put up resistance and cried out. Even if he knows America only from movies, even if you were dressed immodestly, he should have stopped when you protested."

Hal objected. "What does her swimsuit have to do with it? He attacked her."

"This is not America," the security manager replied. "Since you are in a part of the old Roman Empire, do what the Romans do."

Sally, with her adrenalin ebbing, had moved from fear to anger. "You Turks! I'm almost raped and what I wear is to blame? Go to hell."

She stalked from the room. Hal followed. Outside in the hall he said, "I'll walk you back to your room. Maybe it would help to talk."

"You can go to hell too," Sally retorted, storming down the hall. Hal waited until she had entered her room, and he heard the lock turning before going to his room.

Sally wanted to knock on Phoebe's door and tell her what had happened but thought it would be better for the older woman to rest. She climbed into bed and looked up from her pillow. The words of a long-forgotten song, one her mom had often sung before they quarreled, came to her: "Climb, climb up Sunshine Mountain, where heavenly breezes blow. Climb, climb up Sunshine Mountain, faces all aglow."

"You're sunshine," her mom would whisper as she smoothed her hair away from her forehead. "Your smile is so pretty. You warm up a room." Sally smiled as the song floated through her memory, blocking out for a while the Sultanahmet mosque's call for prayer.

Phoebe heard the call too. She was reading the work of Sabahattin Kudret Aksal, a Turkish poet and playwright she had met just before his death in 1993. She read:

It's the crow that keeps his loneliness alive
On the asphalt, all by himself . . .
The crow that rings the night's doorbell
Will draw circles of light in the dark.

CHAPTER FOUR

When Sally entered the dining room the next morning, she saw Phoebe sitting alone at a table in front of a large window overlooking a patio, books arrayed before her. Sally smoothed out her linen skirt and took a deep breath before crossing the room. She dreaded telling Phoebe about her narrow escape.

She was aware of—or maybe she imagined—knowing looks sent her way by the waiters. She imagined that lurid stories had swept through the hotel, starting with the security officer and spreading to every man who worked there. They'd all be looking at her, ogling her, imagining doing to her what had almost been done. An involuntary shiver raced down her spine.

Phoebe looked up as Sally approached the table. "What a pretty dress," she said. "That blue is perfect." But she thought her assistant looked tired.

Sally smiled and pulled out a chair. She ordered juice and coffee as Phoebe asked, "What's wrong?"

Sally shook her head. "Something happened last night, and I couldn't sleep at all. I don't want to worry you, but I guess you'd hear about it eventually."

Phoebe began to twist her hair nervously, a reaction Sally had come to expect—and even count on. It seemed so normal.

"A man tried to rape me in the sauna. Hal saved me." Sally looked down at her plate. Even saying the words made it all come back to her. She blinked back tears. "You'd think I would have been grateful." She looked up at Phoebe. "But I almost bit Hal's head off. I don't know what I was thinking."

Phoebe reached out and took her assistant's hand. Sally felt it tremble birdlike against hers, the dry skin like paper. Sally gathered herself, determined not to burden Phoebe with her troubles. She smiled and squeezed her hand in return. "I'm fine now. Really. Nothing happened, and I'm fine."

"I'm glad you're taking this so well. I would be traumatized." Phoebe, grateful that Sally was strong, didn't press for details. Instead she looked up and waved at Hal, who came in dressed almost the same as the day before, his khakis and shirt both needing ironing.

"You know the hotel has laundry service," Phoebe said.

"It's expensive."

"I'm paying for everything."

"It's still expensive."

Phoebe smiled. "Come look at this book about the places we'll visit."

Sally and Hal were both grateful for the distraction. They glanced at each other, but both felt awkward after an intimacy neither had wanted. Sally was glad she didn't have to make conversation or pretend anything. She sipped her juice and didn't even notice Malcolm's arrival until he bent over and kissed her on the cheek. Then she blushed.

Phoebe gathered her books. "This morning we'll make two stops that will show you what I'm speaking about this evening."

They slid into a taxi at the hotel entrance. Hal sat in the front seat, the other three in back. Even though the front windows were cracked a few inches, the taxi reeked of cigarette smoke. The driver zipped through narrow lanes, sped down alleys, and roared up hills. Once he reached the top of a hill only to discover a truck coming up the other way. Since the street was too narrow for two vehicles, he had to back the taxi down the hill and wait for the truck to pass.

Finally he pulled up in front of Fatih Mosque. Phoebe asked him to wait while she led the group inside one part of it.

Sally looked around the undecorated room, puzzlement written on her face. "Of all the mosques in Turkey, why this one?"

Phoebe smiled: "You're right. It's not the most beautiful place architecturally. Its significance is historical. The burial church for Byzantine emperors once stood on this site, but in front of you now is the sarcophagus of Mehmet, conqueror of Constantinople in 1453. It symbolizes the Ottoman Empire at its strongest."

Malcolm protested: "This tomb is too simple to exhibit power."

"That *is* its power," Hal said, catching on. "It's like Mount Vernon: unostentatious."

They wandered through the graveyard just outside where stone turbans and fezzes topped the headstones marking the burial plots of officials. They walked out to the street and spotted their taxi driver sitting at a café table playing chess and drinking a Turkish coffee. Hal walked over, glanced at the board, and smiled.

Sally came beside him and asked, "What's funny?

"Oh, just something in the position on the board."

Phoebe, now alongside, heard that comment. "You see a checkmate sequence, don't you?"

Hal smiled again. "Chess players don't like kibitzers. It would be rude to say anything."

"We have to leave now anyway," Phoebe said. "I'll ask the driver." She said in Turkish, "It's time to go, but my friend here has a suggestion for you." Phoebe translated the response: "He says, 'I don't know what to do. He should make his suggestion.'"

Hal, with Phoebe translating, pointed out a three-move sequence that would leave the driver's opponent with no alternative but to resign. Both chess players looked, smiled, and shook Hal's hand. The driver then took a final drag on his cigarette, threw two bills on the table, and trotted over to the cab. Malcolm helped Phoebe into the taxi as Sally waited next to Hal.

"Wow, you really know chess! And I like it that you weren't looking to show off."

Hal smiled. "I played too much as a kid."

They were silent for a moment. Then Sally smiled back. "By the way, I'm sorry about last night after you saved me. I was rude."

"Don't worry about it. You had been attacked, and it was dumb of me to suggest talking about it. That's the last thing you'd want to do."

Sally climbed into the taxi thinking, *He isn't as clueless as he seemed.* But Phoebe turned her attention to their next stop: Dolmabahce Palace, home for the sultans from 1856 until the Ottoman Empire fell after World War I. A little smile played on Phoebe's lips: "I'll be interested in your insights."

Phoebe bought their tickets, and they strolled through the ornate reception room. Sally stopped in front of one of the room's four fireplaces and said to Malcolm, "This is wonderful. Absolutely gorgeous. Can you imagine living here?"

"He'd have to write more best sellers," Hal said as they examined a collection of gold dinner, tea, and dessert services. "I doubt if Columbia pays its professors enough to afford those."

Malcolm smiled as he walked from one room to the next and then pointed at a chandelier in the ballroom: "The heaviest in the world," he said, reading from the brochure.

Hal looked up: "How many people had to die or be enslaved to pay for this?" Sally had been running her hand along the banister of a glass staircase made of Baccarat crystal, but she yanked it away.

"You're asking the right question," Phoebe said. "The Ottoman Empire had moved from hard simplicity to soft decadence. The less there was to be proud of, the more pride the last sultans displayed. They tried to buy love and respect and ended up with neither."

As they looked for their taxi, a busload of schoolchildren pulled up in front of the palace. As the children poured out of the bus, several ran up with shy grins, held out their hands, and said, "Hello. Pleased to meet you. Are you American? How do you like my English?"

When the Americans returned to the taxi after shaking all the hands thrust their way, Malcolm reached into his pocket for a small bottle of Purell hand sanitizer. Hal was about to make a comment when Sally caught his eye. She seemed to dare him to keep quiet so he satisfied himself with a knowing smile and let it go.

By the time they reached the hotel, Phoebe's face was gray with exhaustion. "I need to rest and think through my lecture a bit more," she murmured.

Hal said, "I need to write a column." When Phoebe gave him her pointed classroom look, he quickly added, "I'm addicted to writing. If I go without it for a couple of days, I get the shakes."

Malcolm turned to Sally. "I guess that leaves you and me. Could I order room service for both of us? You could relax either in my room or yours."

Sally took a deep breath. She didn't want to be alone. The hotel that she had seen as so beautiful now gave her the creeps, but since they were leaving the next day, it didn't seem worth changing. She didn't want to go out, and Malcolm would make the afternoon go faster. "My room," she said. "But give me a few minutes."

Malcolm walked out of the hotel and to a shop down the block they had passed in the morning. The prices were touristy but that didn't matter. Then he went to his room, put on a fresh shirt, brushed his teeth, and combed his hair carefully before scanning the room service menu and calling to order lunch. *This could be a memorable afternoon*, he thought. But when he asked that the food be delivered to Sally's room, he heard a quick intake of breath on the other end.

"To the American woman's room? You are a lucky man."

"What do you mean?"

A polite cough: "Please, take no offense, sir. Only the opportunity to comfort such a beautiful woman after yesterday's unfortunate assault. That's all."

Malcolm asked for more information and received it; the man was almost leering through the receiver. He jammed the key card and the tissue-wrapped package he had just purchased into his pocket.

—————

Sally opened the French doors that led to a balcony off her room where a marble-topped iron table and two chairs sat. It was warm, yet she almost started shivering. She had put last night's attack out of her mind as they visited the tomb and the palace, but now that she was alone in the hotel, it all came back to her.

She heard a knock and froze, but when Malcolm said her name, she flew to the door, flung it open, and began babbling like a fool. All the nervousness and tension poured out of her in a stream of silly remarks about the weather, the view, the lovely food. He'd think she was an idiot, the way she kept talking. Or maybe, now that he was in her bedroom, he'd use the opportunity to be aggressive as well.

But Malcolm did not. He took her hand gently and said, "I heard about last night. I'm sorry you had to go through that." Wanting comfort, she moved closer to him, and he gently rubbed her back until he felt her relax against him.

When room service knocked, Sally started. Malcolm whispered, "If they make you nervous, go into the bathroom. You don't have to see anyone." He waited until she'd closed the door before letting the waiter in. He tried to ignore the waiter's knowing look and eyes that roamed the room looking for the woman who, the story went, had brought on the attack.

When the waiter left, Malcolm knocked softly on the bathroom door. He pointed to the food laid out on the balcony table. "I hope you like *tarhana corbast*," he said, pointing to a soup made with tomatoes and red peppers. "Phoebe mentioned that it was a specialty."

Sally toyed with her food, shrugging apologetically. "I don't have much of an appetite," she said. Malcolm offered her amusing tales about famous professors. Somerset taught classes in his pajamas. Liptendirt became so nervous that once a month he threw up in front of the entire class. Blender was blind but used his seniority to grab an office with great views, saying it was for the benefit of his students, yet he never had office hours.

Then they sat on the balcony and looked out over the surrounding mosques. When the mid-afternoon sun came in under the overhang, Sally closed her eyes and let its warm rays bathe her face. She felt herself finally relaxing. *I could fall asleep*, she realized; and after not sleeping the night before, the thought was welcome. Soon she was dozing.

When she woke up, Malcolm was still there, reading Walker Percy. He smiled and handed her the present, watching as she unwrapped a hand-painted tile covered by a geometric design in shades of blue, green, and red.

"It's beautiful, just like the ones at the Blue Mosque." She moved her fingers over the tile's surface, tracing the pattern.

"Iznik tile," Malcolm said, pleased with her reaction. It gave him the courage to push a little further. "I do want to apologize for pushing too hard. Maybe I'm too used to New York life. You could remind me of what goodness and purity are."

Sally had heard lots of lines in her day, and most were better than Malcolm's, but he seemed yearningly sincere as he delivered his. Maybe he was a fixer-upper that she had the means to fix. "Malcolm, if you knew me better, you wouldn't say that, but I appreciate your staying with me and being such a gentleman."

"Thank you. I'll go now and let you rest more." He reached out, brushed back a stray strand of hair, and kissed her gently on the cheek.

Sally lay back in the bed, holding the tile and replaying in her mind the events of the last few minutes.

———————

At five p.m. they all met in the lobby to accompany Phoebe to her formal lecture, "An American View of Terrorism."

Hal came down to the lobby wearing his old blue blazer, which he had tried to iron after checking the prices for the hotel's dry-cleaning services. *It cost more than the coat's worth*, he thought. But when Malcolm arrived with his crisp, pin-striped suit fitting like it had been custom tailored, Hal had second thoughts.

Phoebe was distracted by thoughts of her lecture, but Sally, in a figure-hugging black shift that skimmed her ankles and a single strand of pearls around her neck, chattered girlishly. Malcolm entered into her new mood, saying, "Sally, you look stunning," as he offered his arm and led her to a taxi.

Hal trailed behind, feeling a bit like Pigpen, the *Peanuts* cartoon character who always walked amid a cloud of dust. Phoebe looked up from her notes and noticed his scowling face: "That expression is quite forbidding, Hal. Surely nothing so terrible has happened that would warrant such a wrathful countenance."

In the auditorium of Istanbul University's Beyazit campus, the warm introduction Phoebe received from Turkey's minister of culture surprised Malcolm and Hal. They had come to think of her as a kind and knowledgeable older lady but not one given great international respect.

Phoebe explained the radical ideology developed by Ibn Abdul Wahhab in the eighteenth century in what is now Saudi Arabia. She noted that Wahhabis received support in the nineteenth and early twentieth centuries from others who opposed the decadence of the Ottoman Empire. "Softness rightly upsets some people and leads them to toughen up. The founder of your republic, the great Mustafa Kemal Ataturk, acted in response to Ottoman softness." The audience applauded.

She continued: "Today's Wahhab terrorists, like Osama bin Laden, have chosen a destructive form of toughening up. Two of the September 11 hijackers wrote in their notebooks, 'The time of fun and waste has gone.' I could agree with that, but there is a better way to toughen up: Work hard to gain economic prosperity on your own. Help the poor to do the same."

Phoebe emphasized the Muslim tradition that considers terrorist attacks against civilians immoral and concluded by saying, "Turkey is right to fight your little bin Ladens, like Suleyman Hasan. I am glad that Turkey is tough, and I am glad to be a friend of Turkey."

The room erupted with applause led by the minister of culture. "Thank you for your honest and brave remarks," he said. "We welcome you and your friends to Turkey, and we offer you our protection as you continue your travels."

Among those crowding around Phoebe to shake her hand was Zubeyir Uruk, still wearing his University of Bosphorus shirt. He had taken copious notes during the lecture and pushed his way through the crowd to ask Phoebe a question. "What do you say to Turks who want to oppose the United States in the way our predecessors fought other great empires, such as Persia, Rome, and Russia?"

She replied, "You should understand one large difference between those empires and the United States. When American soldiers lose their lives in other countries, the only land we ask for is the ground in which to bury them."

"But what if you seize not land but our souls? What if you entice us?"

Hal eyed the young man darkly and began to move closer to Phoebe's side. She saw his motion and smiled, waving him off. He turned to see Sally, standing off a bit to the side, listening carefully to the conversation. Every time a Turkish man came close to her, she seemed to shrink within herself, clenching and unclenching a fist and occasionally tugging at a lock of hair. He tried to push his way toward her, but Malcolm grabbed her arm and led her just outside the door, so Hal turned back to wait for Phoebe.

"Let's wait for Hal," Sally said.

"Why?" Malcolm asked. "So he can study you for his story about reactions to attempted rape?"

"I'm attacked, and it's a story?"

Malcolm drew her close, smoothing her soft hair as if gentling a horse. "That's how Hal would see it. Once a reporter, always a reporter. I guarantee you, nothing happens that he can't turn into grist for his mill."

As Sally pondered that, a young man tapped Malcolm on the shoulder. "Professor?" Zubeyir said politely. "We met yesterday in the market. You invited me to come."

Malcolm introduced him to Sally. He stared intently at her and asked, "Are you from California?"

Sally nodded and eyed him quizzically. She supposed Turks knew California because of Hollywood movies.

"I grew up listening to one of your poets singing, 'I wish they all could be California girls,'" Zubeyir said shyly. "You are beautiful. I would be your slave. I would do anything for you."

Sally gave him a stiff smile and wrapped her shawl more tightly around her. "It's a pleasure to have met you." Then she turned to Malcolm and said, "I'm going to find Phoebe," not waiting for him to follow.

Zubeyir followed her with wolfish eyes. "Are you having success with that woman?"

Malcolm smiled. "One must be patient."

The student laughed. "That's what the leader of my study group says." He gave Malcolm a slip of paper with an address on it. "If you want action while you are patient, you could come to this house and enjoy a Turkish beauty. You will have to pay, but I assure you the experience will be unique."

"Don't men always end up paying in some fashion?" Malcolm grinned.

Zubeyir seemed in no hurry to go although the crowd had thinned and Malcolm could see Phoebe and the others beginning to make their way toward him.

"Tomorrow night you are in Izmir? Where do you stay, if I may ask."

Malcolm took from his pocket an itinerary: "The Hilton. Why do you ask?"

"Very nice hotel. You will see the best of Izmir there."

In a crowded neighborhood of winding stone streets and two-story houses crammed together without room for lawns or trees, Suleyman sprawled on a soiled couch, waiting for Zubeyir to return. From below he heard music, muffled voices, and occasional laughter. Then footsteps quickly tapped up the stairs and the door flew open, letting in the pungent odor of perfume and incense. Zubeyir closed the door and waited for Suleyman to address him.

"What do you have for me?"

"I saw three of them—maybe the fourth. The ambassador's wife is an old woman, wrinkled from the sun, though she is clearly intelligent and well-respected by those in the room."

"And the others?"

"The professor smelled of wine. He told me they go to Izmir tomorrow, where they stay at the Hilton."

"Good work," Suleyman said. "You've done better than your Bosphorus roommate, that fool Aktas. He tried to rape an American at the Royal Scimitar last night."

"A blonde from California?"

"That's what my friend at the police station said. How did you know?"

"She's Mrs. du Pont's assistant. She is magnificent."

Suleyman twisted his mustache. "Then it will be even more of a pleasure to meet this group of four. Let what happened to Aktas be a lesson to you: Control yourself. We must be disciplined and committed. Don't let sex keep you from accomplishing the mission."

Phoebe and Sally chatted as they stepped out of the cab, while Hal and Malcolm were absorbed in their own thoughts. Suddenly they saw a man pointing a gun at them. He yelled, "Americans!" Malcolm pushed down Sally, and Hal moved to protect Phoebe, as the man pulled the trigger.

CHAPTER FIVE

On the hotel roof for a celebratory dinner, Phoebe ordered grilled bluefish, red mullet, and bonito for all, along with a cold dish of eggplant stuffed with chopped tomatoes, onions, garlic, and parsley, stewed in olive oil.

"It's called *imam baytldt*," she explained, "It means 'the imam fainted' because the concoction was so tasty."

"I almost fainted when I saw Police Director Kuris shooting blanks at us," Sally said.

"That was a cheap stunt," Hal said. "You're lucky no one had a heart attack."

"It was necessary," the policeman said stiffly, unused to criticism of the sort Hal was throwing out. "You Americans are much too casual about security. You think, *'It can never happen to me.'* I wanted to show you just how quickly it can happen to you. Turkey is one place where your American citizenship does not guarantee privileges."

Dinner at first was an awkward affair. Hal's anger smoldered. Was it the Turkish cop with his ramrod straight posture who was setting him off, or was it Malcolm, who was so attentive to Sally's unspoken requests?

Hal watched from across the table as Malcolm took every opportunity to lean close and whisper into her lovely ear. He couldn't figure out Sally. Was she encouraging Malcolm or merely tolerating him?

Gradually the mood at the table changed. After a leisurely dinner and several bottles of wine, everyone was calling Kemal by his first name, including Hal, who discovered the police director had an interest in history.

"We are grateful that the government assigned Kemal to us for security throughout our trip," Phoebe observed. "It should make the rest of the trip much more relaxing." She nodded reassuringly at Sally.

Malcolm signaled to the waiter for baklava and raki as Kemal bit into a strawberry and read a just-issued State Department advisory for Americans: "Terrorists in Turkey show an increasing willingness to attack Western targets. Americans should exercise caution and good judgment, keep a low profile, and remain vigilant."

Hal scraped his piece of watermelon down to the rind and joked, "We're Americans. We throw caution to the wind."

Malcolm downed his raki: "Danger is our middle name."

Kemal was firm. "Our chances of encountering trouble are small, but this is still a serious matter, more serious than I thought when Phoebe and I talked several weeks ago. That's why I'll travel the rest of the way with you. Now let me give you some practical guidelines. Don't go off on your own."

Malcolm sneered, pointed to his raki, and barked at the waiter, "One more. Eat, drink, and be merry before the policeman"—he loaded the term with derision—"forbids it. And I'll drink a *shalgam* also. That mixture of beet and carrot juice should keep me sober." He grabbed the waiter's arm.

Kemal scowled at Malcolm: "My assignment is to protect Mrs. du Pont, but the rest of you should not wander. Terrorists in Turkey may find your group a tempting target, and they do terrible things to those they see as enemies. Do not toy with them, for they will not toy with you."

Sally twisted her pearl necklace around her finger. "What else can we do?"

"Be alert to your surroundings."

Malcolm raised his glass of raki in a sour toast. "I don't think the *shalgam* is working."

Phoebe yawned. "We're leaving Istanbul at seven tomorrow morning. I suggest we retire."

<hr />

Malcolm stood outside his door, fumbling with his keycard. Put it in. Red light. Put it in. Red light. Where's the green light? He dropped the card to the floor and almost fell over as he bent to fetch it. He looked up and down the corridor and saw no one. *Sally. She'll help me, though I don't want her to see I'm too drunk to get in my door. Maybe she'll feel sorry for me, want to fix me.* The thought brought a loopy smile to his face.

He stumbled to Sally's door and knocked.

"Who's there?" Sally's voice was nervous on the other side.

"Iss Malcolm. Let me in."

"Go away, Malcolm. You're drunk."

He pounded again until he heard the lock turn and saw Sally's fresh-scrubbed face peeking around the door. God, she was beautiful.

"Malcolm, you'll wake up everyone. Go away."

"I can't. My key doesn't work. Besides, I need you." He pushed his way into the room and reached clumsily for her. She wrapped her robe more tightly around her waist and avoided his grasp.

Sally shook her head. "You're drunk. You don't know what you're saying."

"I know I love you. I want you. I need you." His voice took on a pleading tone.

Sally softened toward him. In his now rumpled clothes he looked less like the self-assured professor and more like a needy child. She told herself that she could help this famous person. She turned him around and pushed him gently toward the door. "I'll see you tomorrow, Malcolm."

He bent down to kiss her. She turned her head so the kiss landed sloppily on her cheek. He stumbled down the hall past Phoebe's room.

Inside Phoebe was reading four chapters of the Bible as she did every night, with a photo of her late husband propped up on a table beside her bed. She heard the footsteps as she sat in her room, thinking about the applause she had received. Then she looked at her photo of Andrew. "I'm so lonely," she told him.

Malcolm stumbled to the front desk. He reached into his pocket for his key card and grabbed it along with a slip of paper. While he waited for the desk clerk to recode his card, he opened the piece of paper. It contained an address in Istanbul. Malcolm tried to remember where it had come from. Right: the student at the lecture had given him the address of a whorehouse.

Malcolm first thought, *That's not right.* But then he asked himself, *Why not?* He had the money. Everything would be consensual. A grin spread across his face. He thanked the clerk for his key and weaved through the lobby. He was heading out for a taxi when Kemal called, "Going somewhere, Mr. Edwards?"

"Yesh. My business."

"No, you're drunk, and even if you were sober, I would not want you to go."

"Iss a free country."

"No, it's not. This is my country, and if you don't return to your room, I will arrest you for disorderly conduct."

"Fascist."

"I hope you never meet terrorists who would be glad to entertain your corpse."

Malcolm headed upstairs, muttering under his breath, "You win this time—but only this time."

As Sally bit into a juicy apricot early the next morning, Phoebe rejoiced that her assistant looked rested and buoyant once again. She also eyed Hal fondly as he approached her table. "Is that a new shirt, Hal? The color becomes you. What do they call it, periwinkle?"

He acknowledged the compliment with an embarrassed grin. "That's what the man in the hotel shop called it. In my neighborhood we just call it blue."

Malcolm stumbled into the restaurant, his eyes mere slits and his brow furrowed with pain. Then Sally spotted his shoes: one brown penny loafer, one black. Her eyes met Hal's in an instant of shared amusement before she caught herself. *Hal's not your friend,* she reminded herself. *You're only the subject of a story.*

Phoebe's voice betrayed a touch of irritation as she told her nephew to hurry. He grimaced and gulped two cups of coffee.

———————

As the ferry took them south across the Sea of Marmara, Sally breathed in the sea air and watched the city disappear behind them. "You'll burn," Phoebe walked up behind her. "Do you have a hat?"

Sally pulled her hair into a ponytail and dragged on a Phillies cap. Impulsively she turned and hugged the older woman. "Thank you for bringing me. It's going to be great. I know it is."

Phoebe smiled. "I hope so. I love this land so much. Andrew and I had many good years here. It's always felt like my second home, so it's a delight to share it with you all."

Kemal drove off the ferry with the roomy Opel that would be their traveling home for the next week. Hal and Kemal struggled to fit the luggage into the trunk as Malcolm stood off to the side and watched. Phoebe pursed her lips disapprovingly and told him, "Kemal is not your servant. I expect you to treat him like the professional he is." Malcolm accepted her chastisement and pitched in.

They settled into the car, Phoebe in the front with Kemal, the others in the back, with Sally sitting in the middle. As they drove south, they entered rural areas where fields spread before them like patterned Turkish carpets in shades of gold and green. Groves of fruit trees marched in straight lines up and down small hills.

As the day became warmer, farmers broke from their work, resting under their wagons or straw-covered structures in the middle of fields. Women wearing long skirts and scarves trudged along, hunched over from the weight of the bundles of sticks they carried on their backs. Malcolm put on his Oakleys.

In the front seat Phoebe worked on a baby hat, never looking down at the pattern. Sally leaned forward and asked her how she did it. "I pick out soft yarns in bright colors and always use these six-inch needles. If you'd like, I'll show you how to cast on and knit."

"Please," Sally said. "I'd like to learn."

Above the modern town of Bergama, white marble ruins rose above the acropolis of Pergamum. Despite two millennia of destruction and the carting away to Berlin a century ago of highlights like the altar of Zeus, referred to in the book of Revelation as "the throne of Satan", they could see how it was at its apex a shining, glistening, and apparently impregnable city on a hill.

But that glorious Pergamum had long since disappeared. Sellers of goddess figurines and temple trinkets pleaded for business near the entrance to the ruins. "Cheaper than Target," one yelled. "Cheaper than Wal-Mart," another added. An ice cream vendor lifted his voice: "Better than Baskin-Robbers. I suc-ream, you suc-ream, we all suc-ream for ice ca-ream."

They walked past the scattered pediments where pride had once reigned. A thin woman in a pink blouse sat by the pathway ahead, selling squares of hand-crocheted lace. A gold scarf covered her hair completely, leaving only her eyes uncovered.

"How exquisite," Sally exclaimed, as she fumbled through her purse for some lira.

"I'll show you how to bargain," Hal said. He picked up the lace and asked coldly, "How much?"

The old woman understood those words of English and said, "Ten lira," which was about seven dollars.

Hal shook his head. "Too much," he said, ignoring Sally's frown. He held out a five-lira bill and two ones. The woman shook her head. He added another one-lira bill and she accepted it.

Hal handed the piece of lace to Sally with a small bow. She accepted it uncertainly. "It's beautiful, but I feel bad that you bargained for it. That extra $1.40 means a lot more to her than to you."

Hal was crestfallen. He pulled his reporter's notebook out of his pocket and waved at Kemal. "Would you do some translating for me? I'll pay her."

"She may not answer. As you can see from the scarf, she's an observant Muslim. She'll be glad to take your money, but her husband is probably resting nearby, watching her. Let me ask."

He did, then turned back to Hal. "She'll answer a few questions, but she says if she talks to you, she can't be crocheting."

"Of course," Hal said, holding out two five-lira notes. The woman nodded, and Kemal and Hal squatted down before her. Phoebe, Sally, and Malcolm listened to Hal's questions and Kemal's translations of the woman's answers.

"She's a widow with six children, she says. Some days she sells many pieces—especially when a bus comes. Other days she sees no tourists. She's not afraid sitting here alone. What are her choices? She has to feed her children. It may take her two or three hours to make a square."

Hal scribbled rapidly in his notebook, interrupting occasionally to ask another question. Finally he was finished, and told the others as they walked away, "I learned a lot."

Malcolm frowned: "Take her story skeptically. She sees a group of rich Americans and knows exactly how to play us."

An emaciated mutt headed toward them, dull plaintive yelps coming from her throat. Hal took from his pocket a roll he had saved from breakfast for an afternoon snack and tossed it to the dog.

Sally watched Hal wander off, his new friend trotting hopefully at his side.

———

Greetings, brother." Suleyman hugged Trafik as they met in a rundown house on the highway to Izmir, with the green Ford van parked in front on a patch of dirt. Two chickens, hobbled together to keep them from running away, ran around the vehicle. "Zubeyir has found the foursome. Have you been training the others?"

"Yes, as you instructed. Scimitar, pistol if necessary, no attack rifles: old school."

"Good. This mission will be a good team-building exercise for us between the bombings. Those are necessary but inartistic. This will be a small but classic effort." They clicked bottles of Efes beer.

———

Before leaving Pergamum, the Americans climbed up the ancient, ten-thousand-seat stone theater, the steepest in the Roman Empire. From the top they looked out over the valley where the call for prayer had begun. Below, the undulating cry went from mosque to mosque, not in unison like a choir but in overlapping bursts so the calls sounded like attacks rather than melodies.

They stopped for a late lunch of *mezes*—olives, a tomato-onion-pepper mix, eggplant soufflés, all fresh and light—before heading south again to the big city of Izmir. Huge factories loomed on one side of the highway, and rubble from brick manufacturing lay in heaps along the other. "Look at those chickens hobbled together," Sally laughed, as they passed by a ramshackle dwelling with a van parked in front.

"We call those types of places *gecekondus*," Kemal said sadly. "You could translate that as 'shantytown,' but it means literally, 'built in the night.'" He pointed to shacks made of scrap and corrugated metal next to piles of garbage that almost buried a little stream. "Peasants from the countryside have moved in there. They are our new poor."

Sally asked Malcolm, "Isn't there a poem that goes something like, 'Hold fast to dreams/for if dreams die/Life is a broken-winged bird—' I can't remember the rest."

"Langston Hughes," Malcolm said. "It ends 'that cannot fly.'"

"I knew you'd know," she smiled. "Doesn't it make you wonder what dreams the people who live there have?"

Malcolm nodded. "I know I'd do anything to avoid being poor. It seems to me that if you can't afford the finer things, life's hardly worth living."

Phoebe objected. "Malcolm, you don't know ordinary Turks. Many are poor, but they love poetry and have a romantic view of life. With a little help they can build businesses and create hope for their families. When Andrew was ambassador, he used to talk about how we could help them develop micro-enterprises."

Malcolm nodded, "If I can help in that process, Phoebe, let me know."

"I'll tell you later about a way you can," she smiled. "I'm glad that's your attitude."

The discussion drifted away, and after a while Hal could see Phoebe's head nodding gently, the clicking of her needles silenced. He stared out the window at the lush fields and orchards passing by.

Suddenly Sally put her hand on Hal's arm. It tingled all over. She whispered, "You mentioned your grandfather once. What was he like?"

Hal turned a little in his seat, so that he could see her face as he talked. He gave no indication that the question surprised him.

"I remember that we played chess on the porch. He must have been eighty-six, and I was about seven. He had married and had children late. My father said it was because he was so wrecked by the Turkish massacre of over a million Armenians when he was young. He made a game of horror: Every time I learned a good chess opening, he told me a scary massacre story."

"Strange reward for studying chess."

"I loved the stories, and he wanted me to be tough. The day I learned the Ruy Lopez opening he told me about the 1890s prelude to the Armenian holocaust. He was a small child when Turkish troops burned his village and killed many men. Finally the Turkish commander announced that if the villagers gave up, they would be unharmed. They were trusting, like you."

Phoebe woke up and overheard Hal's story. She interrupted, "It seems in retrospect that they were naïve, but how could they know? The century of genocide was still in front of them."

"My great-grandparents weren't naïve," Hal retorted. "They hid out with my granddad and somehow survived. But when the others surrendered, soldiers seized the priest, gouged out his eyes, and taunted him by saying, 'Where is your Christ now? Why doesn't he save you?' The Turkish soldiers separated men from women and raped the women. The next day they bayoneted all the men in earshot of their wives."

Sally gripped Hal's arm tightly. Malcolm smirked: "Pleasant talk for relaxing travel?"

"Shh," Sally said. "I want to hear this."

"I don't think you really do," Hal said. "Malcolm's probably right."

"No!" Sally insisted, looking at Hal with eyes wide open. "Tell me!"

"All right. When noon came, the soldiers prayed to Allah. Then they took children and placed them in a row, one behind another. They fired bullets down the line to see how many could be killed with one bullet. They impaled several babies and ripped open pregnant women. They kept some of the raped women to be their slaves. Those who survived told the story."

Hal eyed Sally to see how she'd taken his story. She was quiet, and he worried that he'd said too much. They were all relieved when Kemal drove them into downtown Izmir, which was familiar yet foreign. Men heading home wore three-button suits with short-sleeve white dress shirts and square-toed shoes. But women's clothes varied enormously, from tank tops to beige *charshafs,* long coats that covered a woman from her head to her ankles, leaving only her eyes uncovered.

"If you want to see the conflict of cultures within Turkey," Kemal offered, "look at how women dress."

At the hotel restaurant a pianist mixed Broadway hits from the fifties with songs from the Carpenters. Hal ate little and the women had salads, but Malcolm moved through an entrée of *firin kebabi,* an oven-cooked greasy lamb leg served on pita bread with onion, and asked for more. "Not all of us are stoics like Hal."

Hal replied, "You feed all of your appetites."

Malcolm sneered, "You don't know how to enjoy life."

Kemal, seeing the argument growing, excused himself to check in with his office: "I spend much of my time at Ankara headquarters directing many operations around the country, so it is a pleasure for me to get outside for a time. Yet I must keep in contact."

Despite Phoebe's pleading for peace, the two warring sons jawed at each other some more until Malcolm announced, "I'm going to my room." He strode away, but a blonde sitting alone at a table by the restaurant door brought him to a halt. She was drinking Turkish coffee and reading *Pragmatic Progressivism,* with the book propped in front of her so that the back cover was visible to anyone walking.

Malcolm asked, "What do you think of that book?"

She looked up and did a double take: "You're Dr. Edwards. What a coincidence!"

He smiled. "Are you reading for business or pleasure?"

"Both. I am researching my dissertation on radical Islam in Turkey."

"For or against it?"

"If it can serve as a counterweight against American Christianity, I'm for it."

"Your English is very good, but let me guess. You are Dutch?"

"Of course."

"I admire your country. So progressive in your laws, so uninhibited in your lives."

"Is that what you Americans call a come-on?"

Malcolm smiled. "Would you like to come to my room and discuss further your work and mine?"

She smiled. "I always enjoy higher education."

An hour later the naked Dutch woman opened the door and beckoned to Zubeyir, who had been waiting in the corridor. He came in, kissed her, and went through the pockets of Malcolm's flung-aside coat and pants as their owner sprawled on the bed, asleep.

"Yes!" Zubeyir said. "Complete itinerary. Let's go."

"No," the woman said. "Copy it and put the original back in his pocket. I want to be here when he wakes up. A few things he and I talked about make me think we could get even more out of Malcolm than we hoped for."

CHAPTER SIX

The next morning Kemal drove his charges east to Sardis, past tethered goats grazing in cut hayfields and wooden grape arbors that formed roofs over patios and balconies. He told them he had talked with his intelligence division in Ankara and that no signs of terrorist activity were evident, but they should remain vigilant.

As they traveled, Phoebe talked about Croesus, the fabulously rich ruler of Sardis at its sixth-century BC high point. "Once he went to Solon, the famous Greek leader, and asked who he thought was the happiest man on earth. Croesus, of course, thought his money would induce Solon to pay homage to him. He expected Solon to say, 'You are the happiest, oh mighty Croesus,' but Solon instead named a man who had died valiantly in battle. When Croesus asked for a runner-up, Solon offered the name of another deceased. When Croesus objected to his answers, Solon explained that we should call no man happy until his death."

"Why?" Sally asked. Hal liked that about her: she wasn't afraid to ask questions, even when among those who were older and probably seemed smarter—or at least better educated.

"Because happiness depends on the sum total of a person's life. Until the end, how can we know what the next moments will bring and whether they will increase or decrease happiness?"

Kemal eased the Opel into a spot under a fig tree, and they wandered through the ruins. All that remained of a glorious city were tall marble pillars so thick that the five travelers, arms stretched wide around a pillar, would have needed a sixth to make an unbroken circle. Birds nested in the pillars where chinks of stone had been worn away by the years and elements.

As Phoebe and Kemal examined the pillars, Sally asked him, "What's in your backpack?"

"Stuff." Kemal, realizing he'd answered harshly, smiled and pulled out a camera. "This is what I plan to use today."

The wind whistled through the trees as Malcolm and Hal wandered among the ruins, with Kemal grabbing a vantage point from which he could take photos and also see anyone coming. Phoebe in her floppy hat and Sally in her Phillies cap sat and watched a woman herding sheep over the mud-streaked stones.

The woman impatiently gestured at her small son who was hanging back, hoping the Americans would give him a treat. He stood obstinately until his mother stalked off to catch up with the herd.

The boy turned his back on his mother and began to follow Hal, holding out his hand and wheedling, "Gum, please."

Hal pointed at the woman, who had almost disappeared in the distance: "Go there." The boy stopped following but didn't return to his mother. Instead he sat on a rock and began to draw in the dirt with a stick.

Hal stopped about ten yards farther on and waited. He was curious how the Turkish mother would respond to her son's disobedience. Some of the mothers who lived in his building would be filling the air with colorful curses—and pity the child who came within reach of their open palms. Hal took out his notebook and began to write, looking up every once in a while to see whether the boy or his mother would act first.

As he watched, a snake slithered out of a hole at the base of a temple marble near the child. Hal tensed. Was it poisonous? He didn't even know if Turkey had poisonous snakes. Why wasn't that in the tourist guides?

As the snake slithered toward the boy, Hal began to advance, moving slowly so as to startle neither serpent nor child. His eyes scanned the ground for a weapon, but none was immediately available. By this time Hal's shadow fell over the boy, who looked up, a grin of delight on his face. He figured he'd get his gum. Suddenly Hal lunged towards him. The boy's grin twisted into a scream, especially when he saw the snake flailing around, twisting in the air as it tried to strike Hal, who held it in his right hand.

Hal's hand trembled as he backed away from the boy, afraid to speak and afraid that the boy might, in his terror, stand and put himself in reach of the snake's bared fangs. When he'd reached a safe distance he spun around, flinging the snake into a pile of rubble.

By now the child's screams had reached siren volume. Hal scooped him up and jiggled him on his hip, but the cries only grew louder, finally attracting the attention of Malcolm, who held out a piece of gum. The boy grabbed it and abruptly ceased crying. Then shouts came from the hillside as the mother ran toward them. She grabbed the boy's hand and dragged him off in the direction of her flock, drowning out his indignant screams with what sounded like a string of Turkish curses.

Hal shrugged, looked down, and walked off, afraid that if he spoke he'd give away the terror he had felt. He told Phoebe and Sally, who had watched the whole episode, "No one ever accused me of being good with children." Then he hurried toward the car.

On the road from Izmir to Ephesus, Suleyman complimented Zubeyir: "Due to your able work, everything is going according to plan."

"What about the police director with them?" Zubeyir asked.

"He is an able man. I have had dealings with him in the past, so we must be careful with him. We will wait for a time when he is not with the Americans so that we can capture them easily. We will have patience."

Trakik reminded Suleyman, "You wanted to tell the students about Aktas."

"The fool attacked the blonde American woman in her hotel. He will languish in prison unless we hear that he is giving information to the government. Then we will kill him. But his action raises a good question for our students: What is the most important difference between jihadists like us and the fool?"

Fadil tried: "He showed the American fascination with sex?"

Suleyman pulled on his mustache and laughed: "Do you think any men could not be interested in sex? No, Zubeyir says the American is a beauty. I pledge that all of you will see her nakedness."

Zubeyir said: "He was caught?"

"A good thought, Zubeyir, but let's go deeper."

Sulhaddin tried: "He fell into the trap of American individualism, going on his own rather than working together as we do."

"Ah, much better. Sulhaddin, you will have the pleasure of shadowing the American beauty this afternoon, but you're still not right."

"Then what?"

"Did the fool's actions contain even the smallest amount of artistry? He was a brute, but I will teach you to be poets and dramatists. We will not rush. We will find the right backdrop for our play, and you will all have a turn on stage. I pledge you that as well."

Kemal drove the Opel over serpentine turns to Ephesus, past craggy green mountains and dusty gray hills dotted with dark pines struggling for footholds. The misty blue Aegean was sometimes visible off in the distance. As they approached the city, they drove by the ruins of the arena. Phoebe said, "Kemal, could you stop here for a minute? There's not much to see, but I want them to get a sense of the arena's size."

Kemal pulled over on the road's shoulder and let them out. He stood near the car where he could keep an eye on traffic and the Americans.

"Two thousand years ago the games would begin with the slaughter of wild animals," Phoebe began. "The killing reassured the audience that even beyond the boundaries of the city Rome was in control. At noon came the executions of people, showing that the city as well was orderly."

"Depends on your definition of *orderly*, " Hal joked.

"That was only one kind of execution," Phoebe continued as they looked at the mounded earth outlining the arena. "Burning and crucifying the intransigent were others. And then beheading: that was a privilege reserved for senators, soldiers, and top officials since it brought the least pain of all the options."

Phoebe said that awaiting beheading must have been awful, but the condemned were, like gladiators, supposed to show the triumph of valor over fear as they contemplated the inevitability of death. Each spectator was supposed to come to terms with his own vulnerability.

"Was it as solemn as it sounds?" Sally asked.

"No, these were feast days of great celebration, with the spectators thankful that they were not among those sentenced to die."

Despite the sun and the day's warmth, Sally shivered. She was glad to climb back into the car for the short ride to the ticket booth and restaurant.

Kemal paid for their tickets, and the group filed through the gate into the ruins of Ephesus. Although the remnants of impressive structures were now filled with the sounds of doves cooing, crickets chirping, and locusts humming, Sally could imagine a day when the city would have throbbed with the sounds of people and horses, as hammers and chisels echoed against the stone streets and buildings.

They strolled past pillars and explored the remnants of once impressive homes and courtyards, Kemal following thirty feet behind. Phoebe pointed out the evidence of sophistication and comfort, showing how aqueducts and copper cauldrons provided hot water for baths where increasingly soft men could sit and talk about the dangers of barbarian invasion.

As Hal watched a skinny dog watering a walkway, Phoebe translated the Greek inscription on one wall: "'Whoever urinates here, may the wrath of Hecate fall upon him.'" She showed the communal latrine where Ephesians, instead of crouching, could sit on slabs of stone with well-situated holes, and water running alongside and underneath.

"What happened to these people?" Sally asked.

"They became dependent on servants, fine food, and drink. They reacted poorly when challenged by barbarians."

When they reached the massive outdoor theater, Phoebe led them up the stone stairs until they were standing at the top, from where they could see the surrounding city and imagine the plays on stage.

Phoebe stopped to catch her breath. Then she said, "Those of you familiar with the Bible will remember how the angry Ephesians gathered here and screamed at the apostle Paul and his companions who were disrupting the idol-makers' business."

Sally shook her head. "I remember that story from Sunday school but never imagined it like this. I can almost hear the shouts and imagine the people flooding in." She trotted down the stone steps, two at a time, trying to absorb the theater's size and imagining it filled with hostility. *How had Paul's companions felt, knowing they might be stoned or beaten?*

She'd almost reached the bottom when she bumped into a thin young man wearing thick glasses and a Dokuz Eylul University shirt. Startled, he blurted, "Excuse me, Miss Northaway."

Sally said, "My fault. I wasn't watching where I was going." Then she frowned. "But how did you know my name?"

"Uh, the guard at the gate told me about visiting Americans."

"But . . ." Before she could finish, the student ran off, disappearing through the theater's entrance. When Kemal joined her, she said, "That was funny. The student knew my name."

Kemal frowned. He ran over to the entrance, but the student had disappeared among the ruins. He returned and pressed Sally for a description, but she hadn't noticed much besides his shirt.

"I can't call the local jandarma with only that information," Kemal said bitterly.

The group was subdued as it made its way out to the Opel. When they passed the ticket booth Kemal questioned the attendant, who shrugged and shook his head. "He knows nothing," Kemal said.

From the car's window they had one last view of the once famous Artemis temple, where now stood only one forlorn column, topped by a nest filled with three baby storks, straining their necks and squawking for dinner.

Phoebe dozed off, and Sally cast a worried look at her. "She was so looking forward to this trip, but it's physically hard on her."

Malcolm took a sip from the bottle of water clasped to his pack. "She's a tough old bird. I wouldn't be surprised if she outlives us all."

"She'd probably live longer if she didn't have to worry about you getting drunk," Sally said, wishing she could snatch the words back the minute she'd said them. He'd think Phoebe

MARVIN OLASKY 73

had been complaining about him, and Phoebe would never do that. Yet Sally had seen the older woman's worried frown when Malcolm lost control.

"Maybe with your help I can improve." Sally didn't want Malcolm to see that's exactly what she herself thought, so she decided to change the subject by turning toward Hal. "Could you tell me more about your grandfather?"

Hal closed his eyes to conjure up the memories. He was aware of Sally's eyes resting on him and the excitement he felt under her gaze, but he tried not to let that knowledge affect him. He'd tell it like he was writing a column.

"My granddad and his parents survived 1895. He was in his twenties during World War I when the Turkish government set up and paid special squads to kill Armenians. The Ministry of the Interior gave instructions to exterminate all males under fifty, all priests, and all teachers, and leave girls to be Islamized."

"I never knew that," Sally said.

"Nor did I," Kemal said, "but I can see why our schools would not teach about it."

Hal explained that the history largely was suppressed or forgotten. "Adolph Hitler knew that and figured he could get away with anything. He said in 1939, 'Who speaks now of the annihilation of the Armenians?' I'm sorry to say it, Kemal, but the Turkish army developed techniques later used by the Nazis, such as piling those to be killed into train cars—ninety in a car with room for thirty-six—and leaving them locked in for days, starving and terrified."

"Those were the Ottomans," Kemal insisted. "The Republic of Turkey emerged only in 1923. Different leaders, different capital: Ankara, not corrupt Istanbul. Maybe it is good that textbooks do not teach the history. That way it can be buried, forgotten."

Hal looked out at the olives and peppers competing in the fields and the vineyards reigning on the slopes of gentle hills. "Do you just bury and forget your family members?" he asked.

"But if you dwell on such awful things . . ." Sally's voice rose in a question that remained unfinished.

Hal said, "I don't buy the implication of your unspoken question. You think if I don't remember the past, I'll have a cheerier outlook on life. I think knowing of these atrocities gives me an accurate view of reality."

Malcolm went on the attack, saying that Hal's view had made him completely cynical about the hopes for human progress: "If you had been king of the universe, the United Nations, or at least the hope that it represents, would still be an idea on a drawing board."

"Is that supposed to be a bad thing? Do you think well-intentioned diplomats could have stopped the slaughter of Armenian women in 1915?"

Hal turned to Sally: "In 1915 Turks lured the women onto a death march by telling them they'd be taken to their husbands and that they should bring their valuables with them. That should have been the tip-off, but the naïve women made baklava to celebrate their impending marital reunion."

"I can guess what's coming," Sally said.

"Of course you can," Hal replied. "Some six thousand women went out on foot or in oxcarts. After five hours they stopped at a place known as Three Mills. There, in the name of holy jihad and by government order, the killing began. The dead piled up, just as they piled up in ancient times."

They stared out the car window at greenhouses constructed of curved wire frames covered with plastic so they resembled large white caterpillars on the march.

"We've made progress," Malcolm insisted.

"Sure, in science and technology. But in this time of pragmatic progressivism, bodies have piled up in European concentration camps, in the gulag, in Rwanda, in Cambodia, in lots of places."

Sally didn't know what to say. She felt young and naïve. She had no experience to put against Hal's and no way to counter his argument. She stared out the window at the red tile roofs clustered on the hillside above green and amber checkerboard fields. She murmured, "Why can't we just be happy for the sun, the wind, this landscape?"

"Is that all there is?" Hal asked. He fumbled through his backpack and pulled out a CD. "I'm tired of talking. Could you put this in?" Kemal reached back, grabbed the CD, and slipped it into the slot. The car filled with Patty Griffin's voice:

> A whole lot of singing that's never gonna be heard
> Disappearing every day without so much as a word
> I think I broke the wings off that little songbird
> She's never gonna fly to the top of the world.

They passed Adaland, a water park boasting a Disneyland-like castle with slides, and headed toward the sea. Soon they stopped in the resort town of Kusadasi at the Kismet Hotel, a favorite of Phoebe's for its gardens and private beach.

Malcolm said, "I've bought a new condominium and want some good carpets. I resisted the Istanbul tourist traps, but a friend told me of a good store just down the street, Oriental Treasures." He turned to Kemal and asked obsequiously, "Director, may I go?"

"Yes, I know the place. No harm will come to you there."

"Anyone want to go with me?"

Phoebe demurred: "I'm fully carpeted."

Sally said, "Yes, that would be fun."

Phoebe turned toward Hal, but he said, "I'll catch up with my e-mail."

As Malcolm and Sally headed off, Phoebe spoke sharply to Hal. "Why aren't you fighting for her?"

"I know Malcolm."

The Oriental Treasures manager, a stocky man with slick-backed black hair, wore a double-breasted blue suit with a starched white shirt. He greeted Malcolm and Sally as they entered his establishment.

"You have come to the right place. I will show you step-by-step how we make the most prestigious carpets, those once made for sultans only."

He whirled them past tanks of silkworms munching on mulberry leaves. "Like my parents' chicken farm but much easier," Sally said. She peered into a room of young women squinting at the intricate patterns they were to follow, their hands moving like hummingbirds as they knotted wool or silk.

The manager escorted them to a showroom and pointed to prize results exhibited on a wall: "Look at this ten-inch by twelve-inch silk carpet segment, produced by the thin fingers of talented Turkish women: twenty-five hundred knots per square inch."

"How much would that tiny trophy cost?" Sally asked.

"Three thousand dollars," the manager said proudly, "Now I will show you large carpets in silk, wool, and combinations. You will fall in love with these carpets and marry them, until death do you part."

He clapped his hands and assistants appeared. Tight knit shirts with banded sleeves displayed their muscles. They thrust each rug forward, dramatically rolling it out so the ends fell inches from where Sally sat.

"Here, let us serve you lion's milk, raki," the manager said. Servers immediately appeared as the rug thrusters kept unrolling new carpets, one over the other.

Sally sipped the liquor and exclaimed about a carpet with brilliant gold hues, "It's like the sun coming from behind a cloud."

"Each carpet," the manager proclaimed, "no, each sunburst has a government seal of authenticity." She saw a small rug she liked but suspected she could not afford. Neither it nor any of the others had a price tag. "We discuss cost after you have consumed more raki," the manager laughed.

Malcolm downed another raki and went wild. "It's time for me to invest the royalties from *Pragmatic Progressivism*," he told Sally.

As he negotiated prices for three large carpets, Sally wandered the building. She asked one salesman what the average carpet weaver was paid. The answer: $300 to $500 per month.

Malcolm arranged for his large purchases to be shipped to him in New York, but he carried one brown paper package with him as he rejoined Sally, weaving slightly. "This is for you," he told her.

Sally opened it and saw that it was the small rug she had praised. "Malcolm, you are so generous." Then she checked herself: "But I can't take this."

"Yes, you can," Malcolm responded. "All part of the bargaining. When I bought the large carpets and did not bargain to the walk-away point, the dealer threw in this one to stay in my good graces for further sales and recommendations to friends. He succeeded: I'm happy. I hope you'll be happy too."

"Malcolm, thank you." Sally hugged him and kissed him on the cheek.

They returned to the hotel without incident, Sally holding Malcolm's hand and keeping him walking in a generally straight line. Malcolm said, "See, all I have is a slight buzz. How about a swim?"

"Is that safe for you now?"

"Sure, and you'll be with me."

Sally agreed and minutes later she and Malcolm were walking barefoot on the hotel's soft grass, past an apricot tree and big pines surrounded by pachysandra. They rounded a corner and stepped onto a wooden dock. Sally took off her cover-up and jumped into the pleasantly cool water. She swam easily while Malcolm in his Speedo swam smoothly enough to a rock that thrust out of the sea.

When he returned, Sally was floating comfortably on her back in the blue Aegean, her blonde hair and tanned thighs complementing the palette. Malcolm felt erotically charged but knew he had to proceed cautiously. He lightly asked, "Are you ready for a race to the dock!"

"Sure," Sally said, and she was off. By the time Malcolm caught up to her, she had already climbed two rungs of the ladder and thrust her head over the dock, but he pulled her back into the water, laughing. She came up sputtering but amused.

"I told you I'd try again," he said, tracing her cheek with his finger.

Sally began to speak, but he put a finger to her lips.

"Shh. Don't say anything. If you think too much, you'll never do anything." He bent forward and kissed her gently on the lips, tasting the salt that lingered there.

Sally pulled away and raced off to the rock. This time Malcolm caught her two yards before she reached it. He hugged her, pinning her against the rock.

"Don't tease," he said. He began to kiss her shoulders, and she became rigid.

───── ◆ ─────

Hal, e-mail done, sat on the veranda. As night approached he saw lights twinkling in the water's ripples, with the gentle hillside on the other side of the bay slowly fading from view. Houses on a nearby island were lit up like luminaria. The castle at the island's crest looked like a birthday cake with one candle—an illuminated Turkish flag—askew.

Suddenly Hal heard Sally's voice break the night silence: "How could you think that?" She stomped onto the veranda and into the lobby without seeing him. Trailing behind her came Malcolm. When he saw Hal, he quickly put on a broad smile and said, "Normal ups and downs of romance."

Sally knocked on Phoebe's door. "Come in, dear," she called out. When she saw her protégé's tears, she asked, "What's wrong?"

"I could say Malcolm, but it must be me. He didn't respect me, but why should he?"

Phoebe hugged Sally. "Forget Malcolm for the moment. Remember: You're not that person anymore. Would you like to pray with me for strength to continue?"

Sally shook her head, so Phoebe said nothing more.

After several minutes Sally asked, "What would I do without you? You make me believe in second chances."

At that moment Malcolm by phone was asking Provost Samuel Brewster whether he could have a second chance.

Brewster complained, "Ten, count 'em, ten students are ready to go public with their statements about sexual harassment, and it won't be a 'he said, she said' because of your secretary's taping and record-keeping. I can ask them to wait until you return next week, but I hope you invested your royalties: You may need them for living expenses next year."

CHAPTER SEVEN

Over the next three days, as the Americans and Kemal wound their way toward Antakya, Phoebe taught what became a traveling archeology and thanatology seminar. She showed how the Greeks built stadiums into the sides of hills, but the Romans, arrogant and affluent, built in the middle of plains. As they drove east across sprawling valleys with rolling fields of grain in swathes of yellow and green, Phoebe told them about the thousands who died in battles there.

Phoebe wore her knowledge lightly, showing it when needed to prevent an error. When an offer to buy ancient coins at bargain prices tempted Hal, Phoebe warned against it. "Some sellers mix modern coins with cattle feed. They harvest the coins after they've passed through the cattle's digestive tracts. By that time they look old."

Phoebe wanted them to visit in Aphrodisias the best-preserved stadium in the ancient world, one almost three football fields long. Sally quickly reached the field. "We've been cooped up in that car for a long time. Anyone for a race? One end of the field to the other?"

Hal agreed, but Phoebe said she wanted a word with Malcolm. Hal and Sally lined up near one end with a breeze in their faces. Phoebe, laughing, said, "On your mark. Get set. Go." Sally was off fast, her hair waving behind her, beckoning Hal. By the time he reached the end, Sally was already sitting on the grass laughing.

"You're mocking me," he grinned and tackled her playfully. They rolled over and looked at each other.

"Thank you for the history lessons."

"Thank you for listening."

They lay quietly next to each other, watching the clouds scud overhead.

At the other end of the stadium, Phoebe was asking Malcolm for advice. "I'm glad you have sympathy for the Turkish poor. I'm not sure we ever talked about this, but it shouldn't come as a surprise to you that when I die almost my entire estate—really, it's Andrew's—will go into a foundation set up to fulfill his dream of starting micro-enterprises in Turkey and around the world."

Malcolm said, "That's wonderful," but it did come as a surprise to him. He had expected that at least several million dollars from the childless couple would come his way: Phoebe had called him her favorite nephew.

Phoebe asked him his opinion of several economists who might serve on the foundation board, but Malcolm was having a hard time concentrating. Phoebe's news, on top of what the provost had said, led him to remember nineteenth-century novels in which a previously successful man could only repeat a dire word: *"Ruined. I'm ruined."*

The approach of a short, dark-haired woman who recognized Phoebe from a previous visit saved Malcolm from the need for any more conversation just then. But his eyes narrowed as he saw Hal and Sally walking back toward him from the other end of the field.

"You're awfully quiet," Sally was saying to Hal. "Do you regret coming on this trip?"

"I was nervous at first." He stopped and faced her: "OK, I'll tell you the truth: I get nervous around beautiful women." He looked away. "But Phoebe convinced me that I didn't need to be."

Sally laughed: "I had the same worry about intelligent men, and Phoebe told me not to worry. She's pretty convincing that way, especially when she's reshaping your life."

Hal laughed with her and took her hand. They started walking again like happy children, swinging their arms, until Hal peered at the woman with whom Phoebe was chatting.

"You look like you've seen a ghost." Sally's brow furrowed with concern.

"That woman," Hal replied as they reached Malcolm. "I swear she looks like Aurora Mardiganian. She made it to Ellis Island in 1917 after the Turks killed her father, mother, brothers, and sisters."

"Have you been telling her Armenian horror stories all this time?" Malcolm protested. "You're obsessed. Sally, aren't you tired of this?"

"Shh," Sally said. "I want to know. Let him talk."

Hal pushed on: "Aurora told awful stories. The worst was about killing squads planting their swords in the ground, blade up, at intervals of several yards. Turks on horseback each grabbed a girl, rode their horses at a controlled gallop, and tried to throw the girl so she would be impaled on a sword."

Sally shuddered. "What if they missed? Did the girls go free?"

Phoebe and Kemal walked over. Hal said, "I should stop. You've heard enough."

But Sally protested. Somehow she knew it was important to hear these stories and let the horror wash over her. She pleaded with Phoebe, who asked Hal to continue.

So he went on, making his voice as expressionless as possible, as if to reduce the savagery of the tale. "If the killer missed and the girl was only injured, he scooped her up and tried again until she was impaled. Aurora survived by apparent accident, and Hollywood based a silent film, *Ravished Armenia*, on her account. Authorities in London allowed the film to be shown there only after a scene of Armenian women being crucified was deleted. The Brits said it was inaccurate."

"Was it?" Malcolm asked.

"According to Aurora it was," Hal said. "The scene showed women being crucified on large crosses with their long hair covering their nude bodies. Aurora pointed out that the Turks didn't make their crosses like that. Are you sure you want me to continue?"

Sally bit her lip and nodded.

"They made small pointed crosses."

"You mean . . ."

"They stripped the women and raped them. Then the Turks made them sit on the crosses, with the points penetrating their vaginas. Aurora said the Americans had made a civilized movie because they couldn't stand to see such terrible things, let alone experience them."

When Hal finished, no one spoke. The silence stretched on until Sally thought she couldn't bear it any longer. "How do you live with all those miserable images seared into your brain?"

Hal shrugged. "I write them out. It helps."

Phoebe's face took on a sad cast. "Turkish people have done wicked things, but they also have created and preserved much that is beautiful. Hal, you can't forget those terrible events, but you should not hold every Turk responsible for them. That would be as unjust as holding every American responsible for the evils of slavery."

"I'll try, Phoebe. But it isn't easy."

"Worthwhile things seldom are."

Late in the afternoon they stopped at a regional museum that displayed a figurine Phoebe had found during an archeological dig four decades before. The museum director greeted them and began what sounded like a practiced spiel, listing the ways that Turkey could easily outdo any Six Flags theme park in America: "We have had at least twenty flags over Turkey in the past four thousand years: Pithana, Anitta, Egypt, Hattusa, Urartu . . ."

"We don't care," Malcolm whispered, but the director was on a roll: "Syria, Pergamum, Ontus, Bithynia, Commagene, Arsacid, Bagratid . . ." He then insisted on guiding them through various exhibits: "West pediment of the temple . . . small figurines . . . this is the oldest piece of hammered metal that we have."

Phoebe and Kemal listened closely, but Hal's mind wandered. He noticed that Malcolm was staring intently at the display case the director was discussing. Then Hal looked beyond the case and saw that Malcolm was paying attention not to the small figurines in the case but to the fetching figure of a dark-haired woman wearing the curious combination of a Muslim headscarf, a bikini top, and tight jeans. Trying not to seem obvious, he listened in on their conversation.

"Thank you for correcting my pronunciation," Malcolm was saying. "I've only been in Turkey for a few days. But could you tell me about your clothing? You cover your head, but other beautiful parts are visible."

"You get straight to the physical," the woman replied, returning Malcolm's stare. "I was told that a rich American like you would say something like that. My name is Kazasina. Do you like Turkey so far?"

"My friends and I have seen lots of old ruins," Malcolm replied, "but I'm beginning to have a taste for something young and modern. Any suggestions?"

"Yes. My friends and I will be glad to meet you." They walked out of the museum, with Hal following. He watched as they headed to the parking lot.

Kemal came running outside, followed by Sally. "Where's Malcolm?" he yelled. Told what had happened, the policeman was furious. "Irresponsible. Immature. Reckless. Potentially dangerous." He raced to the parking lot but was too late.

Waiting for Phoebe to bid farewell to the director and Kemal to return, Hal and Sally sat together on a stone that overlooked the ruins. They listened to the loud, wailing call to prayer by the muezzin of a nearby mosque.

"I don't like just sitting and listening to that sound," Hal said. He walked over to three ancient columns on which birds had made their nests.

When he came back, Sally was lying on the stone, looking at the cumulus clouds overhead. Wordlessly, he put his hands under her head, giving her a pillow from which to watch. She leaned back, looked up, and turned her head to smile at him.

———————

The next morning Malcolm sat quietly at breakfast, drinking cups of Turkish coffee. Kemal berated him: "I have informed my colleagues that I cannot be responsible for the safety of this group if you go running off like this. One more episode, Malcolm, and—how do you Americans put it—I'm out of here."

Malcolm was obstinate. "Kemal, is your major worry security or sex? This woman also had a beautiful mind, unencumbered by bourgeois hang-ups. We could talk about life and politics with a shared vision."

"What vision?" Hal asked.

"Peace in the Middle East. She also had good advice for us for the rest of the trip: She's from Antakya and said we should be sure to see St. Peter's cave church and the Vespasian-Titus tunnel."

Hal was half indignant, half impressed. "Malcolm, I don't know how you do it. You walk into a museum, and it almost seems like this beautiful woman was waiting for you. What's your secret?"

Malcolm grinned: "Wish I could bottle it and give it to you, sport." Then he turned to Kemal and said, "I do regret bugging you, but as a professor I try to pay close attention to students, and as a traveler I want to spend time with people I meet, not just see the sights. Can you blame me for that?"

"I blame you for putting this whole group in danger."

———

That day they rode in the Opel past long-needled pines and fields of purple heather, goldenrods, and occasional orange poppies, past greenhouses overflowing with tomatoes. They opened the windows and smelled wild oregano growing near rock ruins. Sally once again felt joyful, pointing out beauty as they motored by: "Look at those orange-blossomed pomegranate trees. Look at those grapes growing in clusters and those gray-green olives. This whole area is bursting with life."

When they stopped in Antalya, Sally enjoyed walking through the old city with its twisting six-foot wide alleys bordered by three-story houses with red-tile roofs and peeling stucco. As they meandered through the alleys, avoiding the drainage ditches in the middle, children ran after them yelling, "Hallo, hallo." They surrounded Malcolm with his camera, vying to get their pictures taken.

One man brought out his own camera and asked a friend to photograph him standing next to Sally. Kemal muttered to Hal, "He'll talk for days about the American blonde he seduced." Other men stayed in the doorways, sullen expressions plastered on their faces. Kemal told Sally, "I don't like this," but surrounded by children, she had trouble sharing his concern.

Curiously juxtaposed against the stone and wood houses was an old billboard for New Camel Exotic Blends featuring a semi-dressed woman with a come-hither look. Malcolm was eyeing the billboard when an empty bottle of Efes beer whizzed by his head and broke harmlessly against the wall. The thrower ran down a side alley.

"Walk out quickly," Kemal told his four charges. "Tight formation." They weren't sure what a tight formation was, but they scurried away with Kemal bringing up the rear.

"Why did he throw that?" Malcolm asked.

"Why not?" Hal answered. "We're Americans. I'm glad it wasn't a grenade."

When they reached an open plaza, they slowed down and took a breath. Sally remarked, "It's sad to think that these sweet children could grow up to be those angry men."

By the time they arrived at their hotel, the sun was setting. The lobby of the modernistic Hillside Su by the sea looked like a futuristic movie set, with its high gloss white floors, white walls, and white foam furniture.

Malcolm loved it. "It's not like that ancient city with its teeming culture and hatreds. Here everything starts fresh. We all step onto a naked canvas and make our own history."

Hal shuddered. "We don't start fresh," he protested. "If we forget the past, we lose ourselves." He pointed to the hotel's omnipresent mirrors, which even skirted the white cement swimming pool by the hotel's back entrance. "We only see ourselves."

Phoebe explained, "This is how the Turks think of America, as a blank slate without cultural richness. They think we remake ourselves at will, usually responding to our immediate urges. Is that a fair summary, Kemal?"

"Yes."

They passed by a lounge with a wall-sized television that at the moment showed a man in black leather with a black glove on one hand singing to panting women. Kemal became their guide: "See, look at this program on KRAL, which is our imitation of MTV. But here, I'll change the channel. Look, it's an Islamic religious program. See the women in their black *charshafs*; everything is covered but their eyes."

"You have even more of a culture war than we do," Hal observed.

"That's true," Kemal admitted, "but some television shows become hugely popular by playing to the middle." He clicked the remote: "Ah, this is our most-watched comedy, *Don't Let the Children Hear*. See, the man argues with his wife in the kitchen.

The show's name comes from their attempt to cover up their arguments."

They watched for a while, with Kemal explaining: "The husband is forty but he has no mustache. That is our traditional Turkish sign of manliness, so he is, how do you put it, henpecked by his wife, with her dark eyebrows and dyed blonde hair."

"Turkish gentlemen prefer blondes?" Hal asked.

"And not just gentlemen," Sally muttered.

Kemal watched a young man in a coat, tie, and tense expression eyeing them. With one eye on the young man and the other on the TV, the policeman said, "Let's channel surf. That's how you say it, yes? Ah, here's one of our shows like your *American Idol*. It's called *TurkStar*." The show flickered on, showing two dyed-blonde, scantily clad hostesses.

"What do you think of these shows?" Phoebe asked.

"I worry that Turkey is getting soft," Kemal responded, keeping an eye on the young man who was edging closer.

"Enough," the young man said. "I tell you that people like me are not soft. We are looking for a leader who loves justice and will fight for it."

"And who are you?" Kemal asked.

"My name," the student said proudly, "is Fadil. I am a student in . . ." He hesitated for a second. "Konya."

"What are you doing here?" Kemal asked. "Konya is a good drive north of here."

Fadil hesitated. "Er, a research project." He added hurriedly, "But I must go." He smiled shyly and said, "Until we meet again," and then walked off into the whiteness of the lobby.

"A strange young man," Phoebe said, "but his protest is telling. Turks historically respond to poets willing to lead them into battle."

Kemal agreed. "I grew up on poems by Koroglu. In the fifteenth century he championed help for the downtrodden and resistance to government control. When a Turk combines action with poetry, he is a force."

They all slept well in their icy-white bedrooms, but as they rested, Suleyman and his terrorist troupe drove. Trafik whined, "Tomorrow the Americans will be driving along the coast. The next day in Antakya will be their last before they fly back to the United States. Our students along with Kazasina have had opportunities to snatch them, but we wait and wait. Why?"

Suleyman smiled and counseled, "Patience, patience. The difference between failure and leadership is impetuosity. Yes, we could have taken them in Ephesus or Antalya, but that would have been brutish, not poetic. We would have had to shoot our way past that police director. He is not an easy mark."

"But he's always with them," Trafik said.

"Know your enemy," Suleyman responded as the kilometer signs whizzed by. He asked the students, "What have we learned about our adversaries?"

"That the professor is a typical American, consumed by sex," Fadil said.

"Very good," Suleyman responded. "We can use that."

"That the police director is angry with the professor for his selfish American individualism," Sulhaddin added.

"Very observant," Suleyman said. "We will use tomorrow to prepare. The following day we will use the professor's infantile infatuations to provoke the police director's irritation and allow us a bloodless capture. Wait and see."

The next morning Kemal drove for long stretches along the coast as the Opel headed toward Antakya. Both Hal and Malcolm felt they had nothing more to say to each other; Hal read a book on Armenian history and Malcolm one on how clever lawyers cross-examine witnesses. Phoebe taught Sally more about knitting.

At one point Kemal mentioned that he had grown up in Antakya, and Phoebe said quickly, "I know a visit to your home town is bittersweet for you, but I trust the pleasure will outweigh the pain."

"Yes," Kemal said, "let us trust." He then was silent.

When they stopped for a lunch of *inegol koftesi*, meatballs with raw onion rings, Sally took Phoebe aside: "What do you mean about Kemal's pleasure and pain?"

Phoebe replied, "He suffered a family tragedy several years ago. Kemal had a sister. He no longer does."

"What happened?" Sally asked.

"That's a story that he can tell you when he wishes," Phoebe said.

When they reached their hotel at the end of the afternoon, Kemal said he had asked his parents to meet him and Phoebe there. "They want to thank Phoebe for her kindness in the stressful situation we had," but he added no details and did not invite the others.

Sally said she would swim in the Mediterranean, and Malcolm quickly announced, "I'll swim too."

"In the pool, I hope," Sally retorted. "Or find a different beach." Malcolm shrugged and headed to his room. Sally and Hal walked on the smooth stones of the beach onto a dock, then climbed down a ladder into the cool water of a brightly lit cove. Sally's strokes were smooth and Hal's functional, but he had trouble coordinating his crawl stroke and his breathing.

Fifty yards out Sally in blue turned to making easy side-strokes, while Hal, in baggy red trunks and uncomfortable in the water, dog-paddled furiously beside her. She watched him and murmured, "You work so hard. Can't you relax, close your eyes, and enjoy this sun, this sea?"

Hal grunted, "Every time I close my eyes, I begin to sink. Besides, I'm supposed to be protecting you."

She giggled at his awkward dog paddle: "Here, you're moving your arms too fast." She reached out and took his hands. "Slow, gentle. The salt will keep you up. Relax."

Hal smiled, not wanting to let on how stimulating her touch was. "You know, this is almost the story of my life. I'm the fish out of water, never completely comfortable. It gives me an edge in my line of work. But look at me, I can hardly stay afloat."

"It must be hard going through life expecting people to behave badly, looking for corruption."

"That's what journalism is. Besides, only fools go through life expecting feel-good stories every day."

"Sure," Sally said, "but don't you think there's more good than evil in the world?"

Hal replied quietly, "If everyone were like you and Phoebe, I would." They were both quiet for a time, until Hal said, "It looks like I have to hit the dock. Even with your tender loving instruction, I'm getting tired."

"Race you," Sally said, and she was off. She was already on her elbows, lying on the dock, as he climbed the ladder.

She lifted herself on one elbow and watched him. "Why did you run in Philadelphia? I thought you were afraid or out to get a story, but I don't think so now."

Hal shook his head and tried to change the subject.

Sally said, "It was really chaotic in that sanctuary."

Hal agreed, "It would have been worse had the lights been on." As soon as Hal spoke, he realized he'd said too much. He stared at his feet. "Or at least that's what I read in the newspaper."

Sally sat up and put her hands on his shoulders. "Please, look at me." He did. "I saw what you did with that snake when the child was in danger."

"Anyone would have done the same."

"No. And I know only two people who would risk their lives standing up to a gunman in church: Pastor Carrillo and you."

"Now wait."

"I'm already late in seeing it. You shot him. Why didn't you say something? Why did you let me think you ran away?"

"I had my reasons."

"And I want to know them. I want to know you. Your Armenian stories have opened my eyes. You're changing me." Sally's eyes welled up. "Can't you let me into your life?"

"I'll try." He pulled her close, kissing away the salty tears.

———·———

When they returned to their rooms after dinner, four chocolates—two dark, two white—awaited each of them on bedside tables. Malcolm ate them one after another. Sally ate a dark chocolate and left the rest. Kemal, irritated by another sign of softness, threw them over the balcony. Hal wrapped up his carefully and laid them aside to use as an energy supply the next day.

Phoebe ate two slowly as she read the four chapters of the book of Ruth, looking at the photo of Andrew and wishing he was there to share them with her. "It's so long since you left," she murmured. "And now I look forward to more long years. Will I ever find joy again?"

CHAPTER EIGHT

On the road to Antakya the next morning, Kemal hummed as he drove. "My staff in Ankara has no reports of any terrorist activities. And our last two days have certainly gone well. Good weather, no incidents, no more dangerous liaisons—right, Malcolm?"

"Dangerous? *Everyone* has been friendly to me, starting with the student who questioned me my first day in Istanbul and came to Phoebe's lecture."

Kemal was suddenly at attention. "What were his questions?"

"All friendly. How many of us were traveling, where we were staying in Izmir."

"Sounds like an interrogation."

"Nothing of the sort. He said he was thrilled that the widow of the ambassador to Turkey was here. It was polite of your government to have you accompany us but unnecessary."

They watched on their right the gentle waves of the Mediterranean. Kemal pondered, then responded, "You are probably right, but did anyone else ask about your travel plans?"

"The woman I met at the museum did, but it was all in the context of a friendly discussion of international relations and ideologies."

"It's easy for policemen to be paranoid," Kemal said lightly. "But I haven't forgotten about that young man who knew Sally's name at Ephesus. And I've seen three times on our route a green Ford van with a license plate beginning in 34, which means that it came from Istanbul. Next time I see it I plan to stop it."

"What do you think you'll find?"

"Nothing, I suspect. Some Istanbul residents vacation by the Mediterranean. Perhaps I do not wish for this educational journey to end. Tomorrow I will be back in Ankara, with a mountain of paperwork on my desk."

"I can't wait to get home," Malcolm said. "Bills to pay—and not just telephone bills but alimony. More speeches to give."

"But you like hearing yourself talk," Hal said.

"When I am charged up about a subject, yes," Malcolm replied with melancholy, "but I've said the same thing so many times, and with such fierce conviction, that I almost parody myself."

Their first stop in Antakya was the mountaintop site that made Simon Stylites famous early in the first millennium when the city, then known as Antioch, was the Roman Empire's third largest. Kemal drove the Opel up the steep slope, and Malcolm then led the way up stone steps, the flashlight on his daypack clicking against his water bottle. Hal grabbed Sally's hand, and they followed closely behind. When they reached the top, they stared out over the blue sea.

"No wonder Simon Stylites chose this spot to build his tower," Hal said. "Prime real estate."

Malcolm mused, "He wanted to isolate himself from sin and temptation.

Phoebe replied, "That shows he misunderstood the problem: it comes from within. You can't hide, even in plain sight. What's inside will bubble up." She seemed reluctant to leave, but in the early afternoon they headed down, stopping at a seaside restaurant for lunch. There the elderly woman waved off the menu: "I'll have the sea bass. It's very good here."

Two cats prowled under the tables, waiting to feast on cast-off fish bones. Normally at lunch Phoebe contented herself with bottled water, but she insisted on ordering wine for the table. Malcolm raised his glass in a salute: "To my aunt, still my favorite and most influential teacher."

Sally said, "To many more years of good work and good health. I hope to enjoy them with you." Then she looked closely at the older woman and was surprised to see tears that Phoebe tried to hide by reaching down and fondling the cat that had wrapped itself around her chair leg. Sally took Phoebe's other hand and looked at her inquisitively.

"Andrew and I ate here on our twenty-fifth anniversary," Phoebe mused. "We stretched out in the sun on the dock after enjoying magnificent grilled bass."

She paused, then spoke up: "I want to say something that you, Malcolm, with your penchant for temporary attachments, should particularly take to heart." She blushed but looked him straight in the eye: "Andrew and I made love that night. It became even better, more tender, as we grew older." Malcolm looked away.

"His death was hard," Phoebe said slowly, "but how can I complain about my carriage becoming a pumpkin not at midnight of the first day but over a quarter-century later? My only regret was that I married late and we had no children." She smiled: "But Sally now is like a daughter to me."

They all listened to the soft lapping of the waves.

———

As they approached Antakya's archeology museum, Hal followed Phoebe and Kemal inside, but Malcolm grabbed Sally's hand.

"I know I was a lout the other day. I understand why you're still angry. But I've thought about what Phoebe said. I saw her marriage to Andrew, and I know what it meant to both of them.

If I had a woman like you, I know I could change." He studied Sally's face for an indication of softening. "Give me some sign that I haven't completely destroyed hope. Won't you?"

She looked impatiently at the door to the museum and pulled her hand away. "You have so much going for you, but you're racing to throw it away. You want me maybe for a night or a week, or even a month, but not for life, and that's what I'm looking for. Sorry, Malcolm. I really am sorry."

"Then I'm sorry too. You leave me no choice."

"What do you mean?"

But Malcolm didn't answer, and after a moment Sally hurried to catch up to the others. Phoebe, brightening when Sally approached, began pointing out items of interest.

Malcolm lagged behind in the first room as the group moved into the second, his attention captured by a young jeans-clad woman with dark eyebrows and bleached blond hair. They peered together at a mosaic showing a god eager for sex. Malcolm whispered to her, "Interesting, don't you think?"

The woman looked at him: "You are an American."

"I am, and your hair makes you look American. You could be a student in one of my classes. What is your name?"

"Fatima Hasan," she responded. "I study art. What do you teach?"

"I teach politics and sociology at Columbia University."

"So you are the one."

Malcolm looked around to see whether they were being overheard. "Yes, the one for you? Tell me, in your art classes, do you draw male nudes from life?"

"From life? My English is not good. What do you mean?"

"You have models in the studio who take off all their clothes?"

"No. Our professors would not think that proper."

"How, then, could you paint what this mosaic shows?"

Fatima blushed. "Should I do a study from life?"

"My thoughts exactly."

"And you will be my model?" Fatima asked.

"Yes," Malcolm agreed. "Do you have a studio?" They walked hurriedly out of the museum.

Kemal, standing close to Phoebe in the last room of the museum, looked around and didn't see Malcolm. He raced back through the rooms and hit the front door just in time to see him heading off in the front seat of a Fiat.

When the others came back, Kemal was punching a wall and swearing in what Phoebe told them was vivid Turkish.

"I am sorry," he said. "I should have been watching, but Malcolm made this liaison quickly. I have put up with the antics of Malcolm for the last time. I will not be a pimp, enabling him to meet Turkish women who find America and money more attractive than virtue."

"But you only have to be with us until tomorrow morning," Sally protested.

"Exactly," Kemal said grimly. "That is why I can find a local officer to take my place. It is the end of your trip, and you will be safe."

"Wait," Hal started, but Kemal was already on his cell phone giving orders.

"Let him go," Phoebe said. "I know the Turkish police. It's a matter of honor for them."

Kemal turned back to them. "It is arranged. A police inspector I know from a previous investigation volunteered to meet us at the cave church that is next on your schedule."

They rode in silence until they arrived at a small dusty parking area in which half a dozen cars sat. "We'll wait," Kemal said. "The inspector said he would be here shortly." The atmosphere in the car was strained, although Phoebe did her best to fill the silence. Kemal fumed in the front seat, his jaw working furiously as he gripped the wheel.

"He's put me in a most uncomfortable position. I am sorry to leave you this way, but I warned him that I could not tolerate his total disrespect for my position. If I thought that I was endangering you, I wouldn't go. You understand that."

He spoke gruffly, and Phoebe must have sensed his professional turmoil. She nodded her assent. "My nephew is entirely to blame. I don't hold you at all responsible."

At that moment a little Suzuki careened into the spot next to them, and a muscular man with a potbelly climbed out. Kemal climbed out to greet the other officer, letting his door slam shut before speaking. They took several steps away from the Opel and began to talk. Kemal punctuated his words with choppy jabs of his arm and frequent turning and pointing at the car where the three Americans sat and watched. The fat man nodded sympathetically before turning toward them and gesturing for them to get out.

"I will take care of you," Mustafa said in his high-pitched voice.

Kemal awkwardly accepted Phoebe's embrace, answering it with a tight military bow. He turned to Hal and Sally and shook their hands before climbing into Mustafa's car and heading off. The Americans suddenly realized their vulnerability, and as the silent Mustafa watched them, his face expressionless, his arms crossed over his chest, he seemed more intimidating than comforting.

But St. Peter's Church, Christianity's first church structure, in use for almost two thousand years, stood in front of them. It was formed from a natural cave on the western slope of Antakya's Mount Silpius. Its ancient presence exuded peace and calm.

Phoebe gathered herself and assumed her role as tour guide, filling the uncomfortable moment by explaining how, according to the ancient tradition, the Gospel writer Luke had owned this property and made it available for preaching by Peter, Paul, and other apostles. They stepped into the cave's gloom and examined its limestone interior, fissured from erosion and dripping water.

"Those were times of hope and treachery," Phoebe said. "See the escape passage, useful in times of Roman persecution?" They peered up into the tunnel, now largely blocked, and could still see a small opening leading up and away. The mountainside above the church was honeycombed with such passages and tombs.

They stood for a while and solemnly took in the flavor of the cave, under the watchful eye of big Mustafa, who paced nervously outside.

"They hid but did not run," Phoebe said. "They stood out in a rich society becoming so selfish that people would not sacrifice for others." She looked at her watch: "Time to go." They walked slowly but resignedly toward the Opel, the only vehicle remaining except for a green Ford van now parked next to it.

Hal stopped at the entrance of the cave and stared at the van. His face hardened. "It begins with 34. That's an Istanbul license plate. Didn't Kemal say he'd seen one before?"

A Turkish man with a jet-black mustache stepped out of the van. "Mrs. du Pont," he called, "since this is the end of your tour, we want to remind you of some of the highlights."

"Who are you?" she asked, peering at the stranger.

"No, the proper question is, 'What are *you*?'" A young man holding a Beretta came out of the van. "Do you remember Zubeyir Uruk, who asked you questions in Istanbul after you gave a lecture full of lies?"

"What do you want with us?" she asked, looking anxiously for the police inspector, Mustafa.

"You know what we want," Suleyman said. "It will just take your brain a while to catch up to that sick feeling growing in your stomach." A second young man, also armed, stepped out of the van. "Do you remember Fadil Bayancik, who watched with you the program and commercials by which you corrupt Turkey?"

"You are kidnapping us," Phoebe said, still surprised that what was dreaded had turned real.

"Bravo," Suleyman said sarcastically. "I'm glad that one of you knows what is happening. Miss Northaway, do you remember Sulhaddin Timur, who blurted out your name in Ephesus?" A third gunman appeared.

"And you are right to be insecure about your security detail. Mustafa, join us, please." The perspiring inspector came alongside Suleyman. He held a revolver as well.

"You can't do this," Hal sputtered. "We're American citizens."

"Can't?" Suleyman exclaimed "CAN'T?" he roared. "Ah, let me introduce the students' tutor, Trafik Kurban, with his favorite weapon, an AK-47." Another man stepped out. "We also have a guard down below to make sure no one interrupts our family get-together here."

"Other police will be here any moment," Sally said, in a shaky voice.

"Ah, you've watched some of your American movies. I like their showmanship also. But since I don't want us to have a failure to communicate, here is my first order: get in the van now." The three student gunmen came alongside the three Americans and gestured with their weapons.

Hal lunged at Fadil, grabbed his wrist, and tried to yank away his gun, but as they wrestled, Mustafa knocked the American out with a blow to the head, then picked him up from the dust and tossed him into the back of the van as he would a log. Trafik roughly pushed Phoebe and Sally inside.

Sally tried to suppress the panic that engulfed her. What if Hal was dead? His motionless body resembled a corpse. She knew Malcolm would raise the alarm when he returned to the hotel and found them missing, but that could be hours. The thought of Malcolm gave her a place to set her anger. Never would she forgive him. Never.

Following many twists and turns, the van finally reached its destination. Hal awakened and felt the lump on his head. No blood. The back door opened and his captors dragged him out, shoving him in the direction of the women, who were huddled together in the doorway of an old stone farmhouse. Mustafa unlocked the outer door and shoved the three Americans toward and then through an inner door, where he tied them up before slamming and locking it.

As their eyes adjusted to the dim light, they saw Malcolm tied-up sitting near Phoebe. His face registered relief followed quickly by regret. "I'm sorry," he said. "That woman who lured me is the wife of the terrorist chief. You can't scold me more than I've scolded myself. But what happened to Kemal?"

"You happened to Kemal." Sally spat the words. Bitterly she described the policeman's decision to leave, making clear through her words and expressions that she blamed Malcolm for their trouble.

He apologized profusely but then commented, "I've had some time to think and I suspect that our position is better than it seems. Our captors seem to be radical Muslims, yet that doesn't make them terrorists. The leader seems sophisticated. He's obviously Western educated. He might listen to reason."

Just then Suleyman pushed open the door, with Fatima and Trafik behind him. He spoke buoyantly: "Yes, I am Suleyman Hasan, a reasonable man, hard on Turkish traitors but hospitable to foreign dignitaries." He crowed that his band had displayed patience: "You think we could not have swiped you, Miss American Beauty, at Ephesus?"

He smiled at Sally and stroked her hair, but she yanked her head away. "Mr. Edwards, we could have seized you when you were with our comrade Kazasina. But it was fated for you to act as you did because your chasing after women irritated the police director. You kept us from having to shoot our way past him."

Malcolm said, "But we are still unarmed, innocent civilians. How, according to Quranic teaching, can you justify yourself?"

"Hmm, how do I hate you? Let me count the ways. Mrs. du Pont, a member of a mighty capitalist family, spread lies about Turkey. Mr. Bogikian's writings show no respect for Allah or even Christianity. And you, Mr. Edwards, think you are our friend, but did you ever hear the Turkish saying, 'Pray to Allah every night, or the devil will steal your clothes?' Did you think you could steal your sexual treats without the devil giving you your due?"

Suleyman laughed and shook his head. "I am always amazed to see how you American innocents abroad expect us to feel blessed as you shower your dollars upon us. In your overconfidence you were blind. We declared war on you, and you thought you were at peace."

"Could we have some water?" Malcolm asked.

"Tomorrow. Perhaps I can teach you patience. Tomorrow we will talk again, for as our Turkish poet Ulku Tamer wrote, 'Dueling you will strengthen my character. . . . If your bullets hit my chest, like the leaves of a plant I have long forgotten about, what does it matter?' Until tomorrow."

PART TWO

TRUTH AND RUTHLESSNESS

CHAPTER NINE

Outside the farmhouse window a rooster crowed. Malcolm, stirring, saw through slit eyes the first rays of light. He licked his lips, parched from lack of water, and tried to sit. One arm had been tethered to a pillar, making any movement difficult and some movements painful. With his free hand he rubbed his eyes and looked around him.

Tied to the same pillar was Phoebe, who was curled tightly in a fetal position. Without makeup, her face flaccid with sleep, she looked as though she'd aged a decade in the past half day. Malcolm regretted putting her in this danger, but he was confident that she would be ransomed: wealth had its privileges.

Across the room and tethered to an identical pillar were Hal and Sally. Malcolm thought bitterly of Sally's rejection: If she hadn't turned her back on him, maybe this wouldn't have happened.

Hal groaned and rolled over. He struggled to a sitting position, saw Malcolm staring at him, and asked, "Are you satisfied now?" Before Malcolm could respond, Suleyman, Mustafa, and Fatima, all armed, unlocked the cell door and entered.

Suleyman boomed out a wakeup call for the women. "Phoebe du Pont," he barked, "you do not have your servants here to wake you gently. Now you are in the hands of those you have oppressed." Phoebe sat up stiffly, frowning.

Sally heard a distant voice breaking into the remnants of her dream but didn't yet move, so Suleyman stooped and patted her on the back. She stretched, smelled garlic, opened her eyes, saw Suleyman's face, and closed them quickly. Then she reopened them and shuddered.

"Ah, you are scared, Miss American Beauty," Suleyman said, standing up. "You have nothing to fear. Allah, the all-compassionate, has good things in store for you."

Malcolm approached Suleyman as a man of reason: "I would like very much to hear your legitimate complaints. I have a reputation and platform from which to air any reasonable grievances you might have."

"You hear that?" Suleyman said, turning to his wife and smiling broadly: "He says we have 'legitimate complaints.' How kind he is, yes?" He turned back to Malcolm: "Here is my reasonable grievance in two words: American imperialism. Your businessmen steal our oil. Your soldiers steal our peace. And most of all, you steal our souls. You tempt us with your luxuries and your perversities."

A rat skittered across the room. Mustafa, quick for a big man, dove for it and caught it, then snapped its neck. "It will be good for the Americans' dinner," he said.

Suleyman orated on: "You tempt our young men and women to desert the teachings of Muhammad, peace be unto him, and you expect us to offer peace to you? That is my legitimate grievance."

Sally felt sick. She wanted to calm herself by looking outside, but all she could see was a patch of blue sky and the branch of a tree. A bird carrying a twig in its mouth flew down from the branch and settled on the windowsill before swooping through the bars and lighting on a nearly empty grain bag. The bird dropped its twig and rustled in the folds of the burlap, searching for seed.

Suleyman spoke again. "Don't you know that *Islam* means both 'submission' and 'peace'? We cannot be at peace until the whole world submits to Allah."

Sally tried to change the subject: "You speak English well. Did you study in America?"

Suleyman laughed. "I know what you are thinking: *Change the subject, get him talking about himself, a few words from the game show contestant.* Maybe I will humor you later, when we give you the dinner Mustafa will prepare."

"Could we have some water?" Phoebe croaked. Suleyman shook his head, but after Fatima whispered to him, he boomed out a laugh: "My wife is kind. She will bring water for all of you."

Fatima returned with bottles of water and two empty pails, then left. "A good sign," Malcolm said as he drank and then poured some on his head, slicking down his hair. He looked around at the others, waiting for their agreement. "I suspect he'll hold us for ransom."

Phoebe stared out the window and said, "We have no way of knowing that." She shook her head sadly. "This may sound strange, given our circumstances, but I've enjoyed every bit of the journey. I liked being a teacher again. Thank you for being such good companions, and I do apologize to each of you."

"Stop, Phoebe." Sally's voice broke the silence. "You sound as though you're saying good-bye. Please don't give up."

Hal reached into his pocket and found the four pieces of chocolate from the hotel, crushed within the napkin but still edible. With his free arm he tossed one each to Phoebe, Sally, and Malcolm. Silently they nibbled together.

Hal swept the room with his eyes, taking note of details as if he would later need to describe them in a story. Even though they'd taken away his notebook and pen, they couldn't keep him from the habits of journalism practiced over so many years. Maybe he could find a way out. He turned to Malcolm. "You came before us. Did you notice anything distinctive about this place?"

"They blindfolded me. They must have driven a half hour or so. Smelled a lot of manure."

Hal passed by the opportunity for a jibe. "You've spent time with Fatima, and you've seen her with Suleyman. Tell us about that relationship."

Malcolm scratched the stubble of beard with his free hand and said, "Suleyman is clearly the boss, but once Fatima disagreed with him about something—I don't even remember what—and he raised his arm as if to strike her."

"Maybe we can work on Fatima," Hal said. "And how about Suleyman? What's with all this poetry?"

Phoebe nodded. "Suleyman seems to be one of those Turks with a deep love of poetry. He's clearly a romantic, motivated not only by ideology and Islam but a particular ideal of Turkish manhood."

Hal asked her, "Did you note that when he declared each of us guilty he didn't say anything about Sally? What do you figure that means?"

"I don't know."

———————

When Kemal dropped by Antakya police headquarters before heading back to Ankara, he told himself that he had made a mistake in letting moral indignation overcome watchfulness. He decided to swing by the hotel to say good-bye to Phoebe and the others before they headed to the airport.

He was alarmed when informed that they had not checked in. "*Gunaydin*," he said when a sleepy sergeant answered his call to the jandarma, the local police post. "I must speak immediately to Inspector Cavus, who should be guarding the visiting Americans. When did he last check in?"

When the sergeant told him Mustafa had not checked in, Kemal became furious. "We must find him." The sergeant searched Mustafa's locker and found a note he had left there: 'Brothers, I have made my decision. Like you, I have viewed torture films and become angry. But now I see the need to direct my anger against the Americans. I hope you will join Hezbollah alongside me.'"

Kemal moaned, "We should assume the worst: he has kidnapped the Americans. Put out a special alert. Here are descriptions."

He drove to the dirt lot where he had handed off his charges to Mustafa. Fifteen hours had gone by, with other cars and trucks coming in and out. He examined footprints and tire treads, but who could say which were significant? *Good for detective novels but probably of no use here*, he thought.

Kemal prepared to call his Ankara office. He dreaded the conversation with his superior, who would have to contact American officials. They would demand the head of the dumb Turkish cop who had abandoned Phoebe du Pont.

He looked at his watch and knew he'd wasted enough time. He had given up smoking but found a cigarette in a desk and lit it as he called to set in motion what would surely end his career. By the time he hung up, Ankara had begun to monitor cell phones in the Antakya region and was preparing to send a specially trained hostage rescue squad. For the time being Kemal could do little else.

———••———

Time dragged without the terrorists making another appearance. Suleyman was increasing the tension, as he had for Zeliha Kuris and many other victims. The four Americans stewed as the hours crept by, their stomachs growling. Eventually emergency replaced modesty, and they relieved themselves in the empty buckets Fatima had left behind.

Hal and Sally both became increasingly agitated. Sally said, "I'll go crazy if we have to be here much longer." Hal tried to joke, "My kingdom for a laptop," but reality was biting.

Malcolm, though, continued to seem eerily optimistic, and Hal jumped at him. "Can't you come to grips with reality?" Malcolm surprisingly held his tongue, and Phoebe decided that this might be the time for one more attempt at reconciliation. She smiled and said, "Since we don't know what the next hours and days will bring, let me suggest that we talk."

"Talk?" Hal protested. "Talk about what?"

Sally smiled mischievously, thinking of a way to break down barriers. "Let's play Truth or Dare. I used to play that game at sleepovers. And this looks like the mother of all sleepovers."

"Truth or dare?" Phoebe asked, genuinely confused. "What do you mean?"

"One person starts by asking another, 'truth or dare?' If the other person answers 'truth,' you can ask a personal question that the person has to answer honestly. We used to ask, 'If you could kiss anyone in the world, who would it be?' or 'What do you dislike the most about her?'"

"What if the person answers, 'dare'?"

"Then you can ask him to do something embarrassing. We had tense games, hoping that we wouldn't have to reveal a secret crush. But since we're all grownups here and don't have much freedom of movement, I assume we'll have more truth than dare."

Phoebe volunteered to go first. "Fair enough," Hal said. "Phoebe, tell us the truth about something or accept a dare."

"I'm too old for dares. I'll tell you the truth."

"Since this is a high school game, tell us what you regret about your high school years."

Phoebe's hand flicked nervously at a strand of hair at her crown. "I had a crush on a boy in my class, but he never asked me out. Ten years after graduation I went back to my hometown and saw him playing basketball, so I said hello. He took a break, and after we talked some, I asked, 'Would you have gone out with me?' He said he wanted to ask but thought I'd say no."

"Boo, that's tame," Hal said. "Did you go out with him?"

"No," Phoebe smiled. "It was too late. But that's high school life. So many things left unsaid." She stared pointedly at Malcolm and Hal. "Same thing sometimes with college roommates. Hal, it's your turn: will you tell us the truth?"

He shifted uneasily but nodded.

Sally regarded him carefully. "What do you regret most about your life?"

Hal thought for a minute before responding. He began with bits from a speech he often gave that touched on the joys of journalism, the feeling that accompanied winning the Pulitzer, and the commitment and sacrifice required by his job. A reproachful glance from Sally caused him to stumble. "Why are you looking at me like that?"

"Because we promised truth, and you're giving us happy talk like I used to give."

Hal looked at her respectfully. "OK, I'll tell you the truth. Every time I've come close to a woman, every time it's been time to commit, I've backed away. I've chosen career over love, the story over commitment."

"Maybe you need to ask the Wizard of Oz for a heart," Malcolm said.

"You know, if I could, I would," Hal murmured. He couldn't resist shooting back: "And maybe he could ask him for courage."

———

At the other end of the farmhouse, the terrorists sat around a table and congratulated one another. "A successful snatch," said Trafik, puffing on one of the New Camel Exotic Blends, "but what do we tell the world?"

"Yes, what are our demands?" Suleyman said with a smile. "Let's hear from the students."

"Imperialists out of Palestine," Zubeyir responded.

"And Iraq," Sulhaddin said.

"And Afghanistan," Fadil added.

"Ha ha!" Suleyman exulted. "Those are excellent demands, brothers. But are they a bit general? Do you think we should ask for specific steps that the Americans might indeed take?"

"You told us the old woman is rich," Zubeyir said, "so why don't we demand a certain amount of money? I've seen that in American movies."

"You are observant," Suleyman responded, stroking his mustache, "but what types of people seize the rich to obtain money?"

"Lowlifes. Selfish scum," Zubeyir replied.

"Are we that type of person?"

"No."

"You are right. We will not do the obvious. To meet our political objectives it will be better to offer the Armenian journalist for ransom. If other Armenians or journalists pay up, fine. If not, they will have shown greater concern for money than for life, and when we kill him, it is their fault, not ours. Either way, Hezbollah wins."

Behind the locked door, Sally groaned. "Am I the only one who's going nuts in here? My arm is asleep; my scalp itches; I want a shower."

"At least we're together," Phoebe said. "If we were alone, time would move more slowly."

Hal waved his wrist, a white strip of skin showing where his watch had been, and displayed the twig with which he had amused himself. "No watch, but I can write a column in the dirt. One step up from muckraking."

"Shall we play more truth or dare?" Sally asked.

Phoebe smiled apologetically. "I don't know how much of that I can take just now. Perhaps we could touch on lighter topics. I was thinking of my favorite movie, *It's a Wonderful Life.* What film has stuck with you?"

Malcolm thought for a moment and said, "I like *The Godfather* and *Miller's Crossing*. Crime, violence, the American way."

Sally said, "I'm embarrassed, but my mom watched *The Sound of Music* again and again."

Hal jumped in: "Nothing to be embarrassed about. I'll confess to my low-class favorite: that old Western, *High Noon*. Comes from my granddad; I guess he wasn't only a ghost with macabre stories. He taught me to love Westerns: 'Clean pictures with red blood,' he called them. As he learned English, he became a repository of odd sayings like 'politics is the crookedest bone in the human body.' And he knew how to make money."

"That's not a crime," Phoebe said.

"No crime," Hal agreed, "but he had one passion. He drove a horse and wagon through the streets of Boston, picking up used mattresses to recondition and sell. He found bits of gold on streets paved with cement. He gripped every penny tightly, opened a furniture store, and bought his own home."

"You should be proud of him," Sally said. "That's the American dream."

"Yeah, he made a good living. But nightmares from the past loomed over him. In his forties he married my poor grandma. Sometimes he took a buggy whip to their children, but those hurts healed. The psychological scars passed on to the third generation, including me."

They were silent for a time until Malcolm spoke. "My father set my course. He graduated from MIT, made money in electronics, and broke away from Grandfather's primitive faith. My father created and worshipped his own god and encouraged me to do the same."

"Who were you supposed to worship?" Sally asked.

"Myself," Malcolm responded. "Or maybe it was a trinity: me, myself, and I. My earliest memory is of my mother showing off to Phoebe and my uncles how, when I was three, I could recite the alphabet backwards and add two-digit numbers in my head."

"I remember," Phoebe said. "You were cute."

"Of course I was cute," Malcolm said. "My mother made sure of that. Dancing lessons, elocution lessons, outfits from Saks. But maybe Hal is right: I didn't learn about courage. I remember one time a friend was climbing a chain-link fence to get away from children who were chasing him. His pants cuff caught on the top of the fence. He flopped back, head pointed to the ground, helpless as the bullies threw mud at him. And I, I'm ashamed to admit, didn't defend him. I threw mud at him too."

"That's awful," Sally said, stifling laughter as she imagined the scene. "I shouldn't laugh—after all, you're just telling the truth—but you have to admit it's a funny picture."

"My friend didn't think so."

Hal said, "At least it sounds as though your parents were well matched."

"They were both comfortable with money, if that what's you mean. But my father became greedy and put almost all the money into some high-tech stocks. When that bubble burst, he lost almost everything, and my mother decided they weren't well matched."

They were all quiet for a while. Hal leaned back against the pillar, his shoulder touching Sally's. Though he didn't look at her, he was keenly aware of her presence.

Hal said, "My dad tried to escape Granddad's money fixation by becoming an English teacher."

"Not a crime," Phoebe said.

"No, but then he married my mom. She thought he'd become a high school principal and earn some decent money. Instead he moved to a private school that offered him freedom to teach the way he wanted in exchange for less money."

"But isn't she proud of him?" Sally asked. "I wish my parents knew about books, or at least any book other than the Bible."

"She was more disappointed than proud. She nagged him to get a higher-paying job. He learned to ignore her and escaped by playing chess. The more he played, the more escape he needed since his chess playing bugged my mom. Not until last year did he find a way out of the trap."

"How?"

"Died of a heart attack. He left me all his portraits of Armenian leaders."

They were silent for a time, until Sally said, "Listen to us. You'd think we didn't have one happy memory among us." She looked fondly at her mentor: "Except for Phoebe, of course."

The door opened and Fatima spread two plates of kebab, flatbread, and yogurt before them. Hungry as he was, Malcolm eyed the meat suspiciously: "Lamb or rat?" Fatima ate one piece to show it was good.

Suleyman appeared in the doorway, grinning broadly. "Bogikian, I just heard you talking about your father. I'll tell you about mine by reciting for your pleasure a poem by a Turkish poet I admire, Ozdemir Ince:

> They killed him every day,
> Sometimes at a clerk's desk
> Sometimes at the grocer or the café,
> They killed my father every day. . . .
> My father lived by dyin.
> Dying he lived long.
> I'm a dying son too."

"Was your father a clerk?" Sally asked.

Suleyman didn't answer. Instead, he let his eyes slide over her, lingering on her breasts. Sally shivered at the attention and turned her face away, hoping he would go away. Next to her Hal shifted, so that his body partially blocked Suleyman's view. Sally felt a rush of gratitude at his unexpected sensitivity.

Phoebe decided to be direct: "What do you plan to do to us?"

"Ah, my comrades and I will discuss that more tomorrow morning. You can all be sure that you will be treated exactly as Allah the all-compassionate would have you treated."

CHAPTER TEN

The next morning Phoebe seized the opportunity offered by one of Suleyman's visits. "You can see we aren't going anywhere," she said in Turkish. "Must you keep our hands bound? It is very difficult for us . . ." Phoebe pointed at the bucket. "Miss Northaway and I would appreciate more privacy."

Suleyman fondled his mustache and looked about the room. Its single window was eight feet off the ground and securely barred. Finally he nodded.

Phoebe smiled gratefully before making a second request. "I knit hats for babies," she told him, "and, truthfully, I also do it for myself. I like to keep my hands busy. Could you give me my knitting bag?" When he looked doubtful, she added. "You'll see its contents are harmless."

Suleyman's laughter boomed out: "Harmless? I looked. Your knitting needles are short, but they have sharp points and could be used as weapons. No. But you, Miss American Beauty, may have your little bag with its soaps and creams inside. I want your face to be radiant."

"Don't bother," Sally muttered. Hal pinched her, and she realized that she was in danger of antagonizing a man with life-and-death power over them. She forced herself to look at him and smile. "Thank you. That's very kind."

"Very good," Suleyman regarded her approvingly. "You are learning. And I will answer your question about my father. He still lives, and he is rich, but he is dead inside. He is an engineer for a company that does business with you Americans."

He scowled and walked out but said before closing the door, "I will send Fatima to unbind you." She did so and had a look of sadness in her eyes as she released Phoebe, who was drooping against the pillar. Once they were untied, Hal stood up, stretched his legs, and stooped to slip an arm around Phoebe. "Let me help you up. You have to walk."

"My legs are asleep, and I feel lightheaded. Why don't you exercise and let me be?"

"Nope. I'm staying at your side, and you're walking. Come on, stand up." Together they hobbled around the room: ten paces one way, ten the other. "Twice around and then I'll let you rest."

Sally stood on tiptoes under the window. "Malcolm, come here." When he reached her side, she motioned for him to bend over so that his back formed a platform about two feet off the ground. "Do you think you can hold me?" she asked.

She climbed onto his back as he pretended to buckle under her weight. Carefully she planted her feet and stood up. Her head just reached the sill. "How lovely," she said wistfully. "Our little farmhouse is next to a corn field. In the distance are mountains. I think I see a minaret, but I haven't heard the call to prayer. We must be too far."

Hal helped Phoebe sit down before joining the others by the window. "Do you see anything that would be helpful to us?"

"Like a ladder and crowbar located conveniently within reach?" Malcolm asked.

"Who knows? How many cars do you see?"

"Just the van and a little Fiat."

Sally hopped down, and after that time passed slowly. Phoebe spent more time on the floor, dosing frequently. Hal made sure the older woman made her circuits around the room.

Sally heard some rustling overhead as two sparrows swooped into the room and landed on the seed bag. She watched them pecking at it, and as she drew nearer, they flew onto the sill. From that perch they scolded her. She eyed the bag as an idea formed. Kneeling down beside it, she shook it out. A few seeds fell to the floor. Several roaches skittered into the corner.

After a moment's hesitation she began to gnaw on a corner of the bag until she had formed a small tear, from where she began to unravel the bag and form the rough strands into a ball. When it was about two inches in diameter, she held it up and said, "Play ball!"

Hal's face lit up when Sally tossed the ball to him. "Wait," he said. "Could we make strips out of the rest of the bag?"

A half hour later a pile of two-inch strips lay on the ground where the bag had been. "I don't see what good they'll do," Malcolm said.

"Neither do I," Hal agreed. "But the choice is keep busy or go crazy."

Sally watched as the two men, their animosity momentarily forgotten, argued over rules for the game they seemed to be inventing on the spot. She realized after a few minutes that it was a variation of a game they had both played as kids who were often left alone to fill great periods of time. The ball did not have much bounce, but that didn't bother them. They merely factored it into the rules and talked between innings.

Sally sat next to Phoebe, putting her arm around the older woman. "It's funny how these circumstances have actually brought those guys together. Look at them."

They listened for a moment to Hal's chatter about watching the Red Sox play at Fenway Park and Malcolm's sad response: "When my dad's patents made us rich, we became more fearful. He became so afraid I'd be kidnapped that he never took me into big cities."

Phoebe nodded, but her mind seemed far away. Sally looked at her with concern: "Are you OK?"

"I've had better days," the older woman said. "But I'm not afraid."

"I wish I could say that," Sally said. "As long as I'm moving or listening, I can keep myself distracted. But these long periods of silence—that's when I feel overwhelmed by fear."

A shout from across the room broke the silence. Hal was sprawled across the dirt, and Malcolm stood triumphantly over him. "I win. Yes, the joy of victory."

"I've known defeat," Hal acknowledged ruefully. "My dad looked at chess as life or death and baseball as a waste of time, so I never got to play until I was twelve. Boy, did I stink."

"Me too," Malcolm agreed. "I missed gaining a sense of teamwork or even cheering for someone else. Never even saw the Red Sox play."

"I go to games now when they come to Baltimore. Hey, I think Boston's in next month. If—when—we get out, come to the first game of the series."

Malcolm hesitated and had such a strange look in his eyes that Hal asked, "What's the matter?"

"Just wistful for a moment. But you're right: we'll both get out. I'll see you there."

———•———

At the other side of the farmhouse, Suleyman was showing off as he sat at the head of the round table and commanded his team: "Think. We want to make demands that seem reasonable but at the same time are impossible for the Americans to grant."

"Why not demands they can agree to?" Sulhaddin asked.

"You deserve the truth, so I will be honest. America has a big lead on us economically and a system that allows it to maintain its advantages. Even if Muslim West Asia becomes rich, Americans will become richer."

"So we can't catch up?" Zubeyir asked.

"I have been in America. Parts were so beautiful that I cried. Things worked so well that I cried. No matter what we accomplish, as long as America is moving ahead, we will never catch up."

Zubeyir again was puzzled: "So what do we do?"

"We cannot beat them economically, but we can beat them politically. Some rich Americans sit on what their parents accomplished. They feel guilty. They think others should be handed prosperity as well."

Fadil caught on: "So we play on guilt?"

"You are a fine student."

On the other side of Antakya, Kemal went over reports with a local police inspector, Abdul Aleman. Tire tread and footprints at the scene of the abduction: nothing. Local police had gone door-to-door near the bottom of Mount Silpius: no eyewitnesses. No one could identify the woman who had departed from the museum with Malcolm.

Kemal told Abdul, "We must know more than we think we know. We raided the houses of known Hezbollah sympathizers. Nothing. Inspectors in Ankara and Istanbul vigorously interrogated two captive terrorists from southern Turkey. Nothing."

"No communication from the kidnappers yet," Abdul noted. "Maybe they weren't even Hezbollah."

"We will hear from them. Let us think. The women with whom Malcolm cavorted—no information about them. Wait— that student in Antalya who came from Konya. His first name was . . . Fadil. He probably was not registered at the Hillside Su, an expensive place, but we might as well try. Work on that."

———— · ————

At the farmhouse the sun was beginning to set. Phoebe dozed on the floor under the window. Sparrows pecked at the seed in the corner. Hal turned to Sally and said, "Your turn: truth about where you come from, or dare."

"Dare, and it better be something good."

"When we get out of this, I dare you to come with me to the July 4 celebration in Washington and sit as close as we can to where the fireworks go off."

"Agreed."

Malcolm interrupted. "And I want to ask you a question too. Truth or dare?"

Sally smiled: "Since I can guess what your dare would be, I have to tell the truth."

"Then I'll ask what Hal asked: I'd like to know some Sally history."

"Fair enough. Your ancestors, Malcolm, were Puritan divines. Yours, Hal, were Armenian peasants. I really don't know where I come from. I just know the hippie parents who produced me in San Francisco in 1980. They went to a Billy Graham crusade as a joke and somehow—I don't understand how it works—decided to give up drugs and become fundamentalists."

"Christ, the ultimate high," Hal snorted.

"Guess that was it. I won some gymnastic awards as a kid, but when I was eleven, I had to choose between normal life and doing that intensely."

"Same thing that happened to me playing chess at sixteen. Would have had to spend hours every day going through books of openings, middle games, end games. Not for me."

"Nor for me," Sally assented. "I desperately wanted to be normal. But my parents didn't want me to watch movies. Didn't want me to dance. Thing is, my dad was right to see the dangers out there, but his rules were so tight."

"Did he let you do anything?"

"Ran track in school. Nothing else. Instead of letting me become more independent little by little, he held me so tight that I had to break away."

"Repeating your parents' lives?" Malcolm asked.

"Sounds like we all do it," Sally responded, her sentences becoming clipped as they became painful: "Became a beach brat. OK, truth: I hate even thinking about all the stereotypes I was filling, in stereo. Nineteen years old. Knocked up. Guy took off. Didn't have an abortion, didn't want to be a single mom: I chose adoption, which was sad but good. Graduated and moved to Manhattan."

The key rattled in their cell door. "Here come Suleyman and Mustafa, your efficient and charming hosts," the terrorist chief boomed. "I have come to tell you our demands. We are not after petty things," he said. "But we ask for concessions that will be good for Muslims and good for America."

He went on to announce a series of demands, to be met within forty-eight hours, mostly having to do with appointing Muslims to the American judiciary. To Hal all the demands sounded ridiculous, the product of a mind out of touch with the American system, but he figured he might as well ask: "If you get a positive response, will you let us all go?"

"You are an Armenian joker," Suleyman declared cheerfully. "I will let one of you go. You should understand that we are men who follow rules, not anarchists."

"Rules you make up as you go along?"

"Hardly. The rule I follow was propounded by my ancestor Abu'l-Hasan al-Mawardi, al-Ahkam as-Sultaniyyah, peace be unto him. Before he died in Baghdad in 1058, he told of four possible ways to treat captured enemies: release them, hold them for ransom, enslave them, or kill them. There are four of you. My plan is to use all four methods. That means one of you will die."

"That's barbaric!" Hal exclaimed, as both Sally and Phoebe blanched.

"Truly, Mr. Bogikian?" Suleyman asked. "Letting three of you live is highly civilized, I think."

Mustafa ordered them to stand together while he fiddled with the camera. Then he looked at Suleyman, waiting for him to give a signal to start filming.

"Smile for the camera," Suleyman ordered.

The Americans glared at Mustafa, refusing to give him that pleasure. Suleyman, seeing they would not bend, promised payback later. "You must work harder to please me," he said. "Oh, and I will make one further offer to all of you: The first one to videotape a statement to the world explaining why America is evil and Islam is great will go free. How's that for a game show prize?"

"You started out saying you want truth," Hal replied. "How then can you ask us to lie to save our skins?"

"I am not asking you to lie," Suleyman responded. "I am asking one of you to tell what you know deep down is the truth: That Allah is all-powerful. I am giving you a taste of that by showing how I am all-powerful over you in this house."

"Dictator Suleyman," Hal said sarcastically.

"No, I am a poet. Here is one of my favorites, by Ataoi Behramoglu: 'Some day we shall triumph for sure, I tell you, loan sharks of old! You geese! You grand vizier!'" Suleyman scrunched a cockroach with his shoe.

"Doesn't seem very poetic."

Suleyman scowled. "I leave you with one story, about the son of a horse trainer employed by a tyrant. The tyrant, disappointed with the looks of a particular horse, gouged out the horse trainer's eyes. The son vowed revenge and took the name Koroglu, which literally means 'the blind man's son.'"

"Kemal mentioned Koroglu."

Suleyman gazed out the window as though the scene he described was there, just beyond the confines of the room. "And did he mention that Koroglu took loving care of the ugly horse until it became strong, swift, and beautiful? Then he rode that horse to the mountains, where he recruited a rebel force to fight against the lord."

"I see that you identify with Koroglu," Hal replied, "but yesterday you admitted that your father is a rich engineer."

"You miss my point: Koroglu was a poet, and we poets develop our own truths. The tyrant assembled an army armed with rifles. The rebels had only bow and arrow. Koroglu proclaimed in a magnificent ode, 'We were faced with legions of the enemy. On our brows appeared dark words of destiny. Rifles ruin bravery.'"

"What happened?" Sally asked.

"On that day rifles did not ruin bravery. People in nearby villages brought their pickaxes and shovels. The tyrant, frightened, retreated. The poem celebrates the victory: 'The hero holds fast, cowards flee.'"

Hal was intense: "You're not the poet standing alone against a prosaic world. You're like a million others who see themselves alone as right, as brave, as representing unrecognized genius. You're deluding yourself. In reality, you feed on the hearts and flesh of others."

This time Suleyman was not smiling as he left. Mustafa and Trafik made sure the cell door was locked and relocked.

Suleyman regained his composure as he conducted a seminar for his three students on how to deal with hostages.

"Why forty-eight hours?" Fadil asked Suleyman.

"Good movie of that name. Eddie Murphy. Nick Nolte. I was supposed to study engineering at the University of Texas. I spent most of my time watching movies."

"Ah," Sulhaddin said. "That's why you know so much about America. Your demand to have Muslim judges appointed could produce a great step forward."

"Oh, the Americans will not meet our conditions," Suleyman said confidently. "Their politicians will denounce us before the cameras. But we are injecting an idea: why not Muslim representation? Some of their journalists will carry it forward. So will their professors, particularly in the programs our Saudi brothers have funded."

"You think ahead," Fadil rejoiced.

"Of course," Suleyman said. "I played chess too, like that Bogikian. Perhaps it would be amusing to play a game against him."

CHAPTER ELEVEN

The next morning Malcolm woke up deciding it was time to act. He would walk away from captivity by accepting Suleyman's offer to make a videotaped anti-American statement. He knew that it would hurt his reputation among moderates while gaining him new popularity on the academic left, but regardless of those calculations, the important thing was to get out.

He didn't want the others to scorn him, so after a yogurt and flatbread breakfast, he said, "Sally, can you sing?" When she looked puzzled, he added, "Maybe a patriotic song like 'America the Beautiful'?"

Sally protested, but Malcolm crossed over and whispered, "Bugs," while pointing into the corners of the room and cupping his ear in imitation of someone listening.

"I learned 'The Battle Hymn of the Republic' when I was a girl," Sally said, and she started singing as Malcolm quietly explained his plan to the others: "If I get out, I'll be able to get help for you."

Phoebe protested, "You'll look like a traitor. Maybe you'll *be* a traitor." But she had to admit that it gave them a chance. Hal said Phoebe should be the one to gain release, given her age and health, but she said she would never make the necessary statement.

Sally carried on with the musical cover, and Hal discovered her lovely singing voice:

> In the beauty of the lilies Christ was born across
> the sea,
> With a glory in His bosom that transfigures you
> and me:
> As He died to make men holy, let us die to make
> men free,
> While God is marching on.

Charmed by her voice, Hal was less critical of Malcolm's plan than he otherwise would have been. "Given what you've already written and said," he told him, "you are the person Suleyman would believe. I wouldn't make a statement like that either, even though people will know it was made under duress. But if it's something you want to do, go for it."

"So, as I sacrifice my reputation, you'll play your part?"

"I'll be furious with you so Suleyman will be convinced you've joined his side and abandoned us. Of course," he grinned, "it's not hard for me to be furious with you." They shook hands and ended their huddle just before Zubeyir, entranced by the singing, came in and asked for more.

———

Across town Kemal was learning that two guests with the first name "Fadil" were at the Hillside Su the same evening Kemal and the others had been there. Neither of them had a Konya address.

One was from Antakya, and his address was a dormitory room at Mustafa Kemal University. Kemal rushed there, not expecting to find Fadil but hoping for some scrap of information.

Suleyman worried about the students he had recruited. He already had ordered the death of Aktas, the would-be rapist, when the fool seemed ready to tell all to the police. His other recruits, while slightly more disciplined, were still impatient. They had seen too many American movies with quick violence and quick sex: He had even caught Sulhaddin and Fadil trying to slip out to a nearby farm where a pretty farmer's daughter lived.

Mustafa had administered a sound beating, but Suleyman knew it was only a matter of time before boredom led to more mischief. He gave the students their next lesson in chess and told Sulhaddin and Fadil to study the most-used opening, the Ruy Lopez, and not to emerge from the side room until they had the major variations down cold: "When you do, you'll have a reward."

As Fatima brought the prisoners bottles of fresh water, Malcolm approached her. "Please tell your husband I have something to say. Do not tell the other Americans." He looked back at the others as though afraid of them. She bowed and stepped out of the room, carefully locking the door behind her.

Suleyman waited before responding. Finally he came with Trafik and said, "Professor, I hear you have something to say to me."

Hal glared at Malcolm, who told the terrorist chief, "I want to make a deal, but I can't talk here."

Suleyman laughed. "Come, professor, let us talk," he said, tying Malcolm's hands. Trafik escorted Malcolm into the kitchen and stood by with his gun ready as the American talked about how much he disliked America and disdained Christianity. He also filled his speech with talk about Islam's virtues, such as its early contributions to science and medicine, and his hatred for Western imperialism and American aggression against Muslims.

Suleyman watched the professor with brooding eyes, nodding his head at the American's indictment of his own country and praise for Islam. He stood up when the diatribe was done and slapped Malcolm on the back.

"Very good, Mr. Edwards. That is an excellent speech, delivered with grace and intelligence. I read some of your work on the Internet, and I see that this statement is consistent with your writing but takes it a step further. We can make use of your articulate denunciation of evil and acceptance of the truth."

"Good," Malcolm replied. "So you'll release me and ransom off Phoebe, I assume."

"We'll free you, but I've decided that we will not stoop to ransoming a rich lady. Our Saudi friends give us all the money we need, and we don't want Americans thinking we are—what's that expression in the movies?—gold diggers."

"That's not what I had expected."

"No, you thought we'd kill the Armenian and ransom off your aunt. Kazasina told me how your brain works, but you don't play chess. I do."

"Wait—you mean to behead Phoebe or Sally?" Malcolm felt like throwing up.

Suleyman smiled again. "Do the math, Mr. Edwards. And if you could enslave one of those women, which would you choose?"

Malcolm did throw up.

Suleyman patted him on the back. "Get it out of your system. Revolutionaries must swallow many bitter pills. You have not read our Muslim sages, but I suspect you are familiar with Vladimir Lenin. His revolution was not like the one we will have, but he once wrote that a revolutionary must crawl on his belly like a snake to accomplish a mission. Do you like snakes, Mr. Edwards?"

———·———

Kemal quietly picked the lock of Fadil Bayancik's room at the university's main campus, located six miles from the center of

Antakya. A bed, a desk, a chair. Nothing on the walls. A mouse pad—that meant Fadil had a computer, which meant his family was rich by Turkish standards and might have multiple homes. But his men had already checked out all homes in Antakya registered to Bayanciks.

Kemal thought he was facing another blind alley, until he spotted a photograph tucked under the mattress. Two elderly people dressed in peasant costumes. Grandparents?

He was already on the phone to his inspector, Abdul. "I need to find out the maiden name of Fadil Bayancik's mother."

When Hal whispered Malcolm's plan to Sally, she was angry: "Hal, you're too easy on him now. I don't care what the situation is, it's wrong to provide propaganda for Suleyman."

Sally stopped as she heard footsteps outside the door and then the turn of the key. Malcolm stumbled through, followed closely by Trafik, who carried a video camera, and Suleyman. Mustafa stood in the door with an AK-47.

Suleyman directed Trafik to set up the camera and called to Zubeyir to bring in a molded plastic chair, the kind seen on almost every Turkish balcony. "Sit here," he ordered the professor, who would become his star witness to American evil and Muslim marvels.

Malcolm, faced with the moment of becoming a public apologist for terrorism, wavered for a second before reminding himself that he was a social revolutionary who sometimes had to embrace odd bedfellows like Suleyman. Besides, the startling news that Phoebe would probably be killed made his action vital: he did not want her dead, and maybe he could get to the police and help her.

Suleyman now acted like the master of ceremonies introducing a keynote speaker: "Behold the man who will finally tell America the truth." Zubeyir slid behind Hal and watched him with his gun poised.

Hal ignored the student and said, "Don't, Malcolm! Whatever he's promised isn't worth betraying your country—and us."

Malcolm snorted. "Shut up, Hal. This isn't a Western where a white-hat hero rides to the rescue. We each know our limits, and I've reached mine."

Hal, playing his role fully, lunged forward, but Zubeyir's gun crashed down on his head, sending him sprawling to the ground. Blood darkened the dirt under his head. That satisfied Suleyman, who smiled at Malcolm and said, "Another way to tell a true revolutionary is by the enemies he makes."

He told Trafik to begin filming, and soon the captive's practiced voice filled the room with an attack on US leaders and "Christian-fascist America." Malcolm concluded with praise for his Muslim brothers: "The heroes of our age are men like Suleyman Hasan who show us the road to universal progress. I welcome their jihad."

Escorted by Suleyman and Trafik he left the room, and the door closed behind them. Sally knelt beside Hal, cradling his head in her lap, while Phoebe gathered the strips of burlap. "We'll use them as bandages," Sally said, as she washed the wound. As she bound Hal's scalp with the burlap, she sniffled, "Malcolm's a traitor."

"You shouldn't think badly of him," Hal said. "He despises much about America, and that's why his speech was over-the-top, but now he'll be freed, and maybe he'll come rescue us. Something's happening to me: I don't hate him anymore, and I'm actually hopeful." He brightened under Sally's touch: "Hey, that sounds like your type of optimism."

"Wish I still had it," she replied.

———•———

Suleyman tied Malcolm's hands, pushed him into the back of the Ford van, climbed in after him, and told Zubeyir to drive into the hills. "Kazasina was right," he said: "You are a flexible person, and I will keep my part of the bargain."

After a few minutes Suleyman stroked his mustache and said, "Now that our alliance is confirmed, I'd like to ask a personal question."

Malcolm was still not ready to celebrate his release. It was possible, he figured, for Suleyman to change his mind, shoot him here, and leave his body by the side of the road for the buzzards to eat. He had better not do anything to offend the terrorist. "I'm glad to be of assistance."

"You have sex with American female college students, yes?" Malcolm nodded hesitantly, and Suleyman continued: "When I spent my two years at the University of Texas, the coeds did not flock to me as I thought they would. Some seemed afraid of Turks. But that was fifteen years ago, and now I see on Web sites that many of your college women have become whores."

"Those are the bargains they make. It's consensual."

"I want to know about your bargains. How do you know for certain which students will have sex with you?"

"Here's the giveaway: They say, 'I'll do *anything* for an A, and they do."

"Then what happens?"

Malcolm's face clouded as he talked of the woman he married soon after graduating college: "Debi thought I would be with her only. Islam is wise to allow men to have four wives."

"Allah recognizes our superiority."

"True, but some women do not understand that. After Debi and I were married for half a year, I started looking around. In America wives get angry about that."

"Here too, sometimes," Suleyman admitted. "Fatima the other day said . . . No, you tell more of your story."

"I tried to placate Debi by telling her she could do the same."

Suleyman was startled. "Malcolm, my new friend, that seems cowardly to me."

Malcolm agreed and explained that although he said he didn't care, he ran twelve miles the day she left instead of his usual three and damaged his knee. Then the van stopped, and

Suleyman opened the back door and let Malcolm stand outside. It had started raining.

The ex-prisoner looked at the lonely landscape surrounding him and shook his head in disbelief: "You can't leave me here. I'll never find my way back. You might as well . . ." He decided not to complete the sentence.

Suleyman sneered. "Your knee is better, is it not?"

"Yes."

"Head down that goat path, and you will find a village in several hours. Be careful. Some of my countrymen are suspicious of foreigners."

"Could I have some water?"

"I'm thinking of taking Sally to a quiet house by the sea. How can I convince her to be like one of your coeds?"

Malcolm's mind swirled. Still angry that she had rejected him, he said, "Proceed slowly with her. Excite her with poetry. Take her to an unusual spot. She'll come around."

Suleyman's eyes gleamed. "Poetry? She must have the soul of a Turk." He untied Malcolm's hands and gave him a bottle of water. "Farewell. May Allah preserve you."

Suleyman jumped into the front of the van, and Zubeyir stepped on the gas, sending a spray of gravel into Malcolm's face. He was free, just as he had wished.

He felt a moment of panic.

———•———

Thirty minutes later Kemal led a four-man assault team toward the front entrance to the farmhouse, with two more men waiting at the back. Each assault team member carried an M4/A1 carbine and a pistol. Each wore an armored vest with steel plates front and back, a Kevlar helmet, goggles, and earplugs.

The team blew open the front door of the building and threw in "flashbangs," concussion devices that create what the word indicates. With light and noise disorienting the defenders they thought were present, Kemal and his men swept in, but no one was there.

That's because Suleyman, upon his return to the farmhouse, had discovered a panicked Trafik blindfolding and tying up the captives. "Praise Allah, you are back. We have word that the police director may know where we are." Fadil and Sulhaddin had then yanked Sally and Phoebe through the rain into the van, with Mustafa pinioning Hal's arms and slinging him into the back of the van.

So Kemal a few minutes later was left muttering, "We're too late. They must have been warned." He went through the papers scattered on the floor, hoping to find clues. At least he was finally on a warm trail. While his men searched the kitchen and the other rooms, Kemal entered the small room where the Americans had been kept.

He held a handkerchief over his nose and mouth to mute the room's fetid odor, a mix of unwashed bodies, illness, and human waste. Chains showed where the Americans had been bound. He knelt over a darkened patch of dirt. Carefully taking a plastic bag out of his pocket, he scooped up some of the dirt to send to the lab. It looked like blood but not enough to signify death.

He searched the trampled earth for writing, hoping the Americans had scribbled into the ground information about their captors. Near one of the pillars he found a series of scratches and a small twig, and even the beginnings of a word: SUL, he thought. But the rest had been rubbed away by the sole of a boot.

Kemal climbed wearily to his feet. They hadn't found bodies, and that was a good thing, but the blood was cause for concern. Kemal knew that once terrorists began abusing their prisoners, death was not far behind. With growing urgency, Kemal met his men: "What have you found?" he barked.

Not much, they reported. The farmhouse had not been a long-term headquarters, which explained the lack of papers or telephone. Kemal glared at his men: "It's not possible for this band of thugs to live here three days and leave no evidence. Find it or be prepared to find a new job."

By nightfall Malcolm had walked for hours, following the scrubby goat path as it zigzagged over rocky fields and up hills dotted with olive trees, their ancient trunks as gnarled and bent as Malcolm felt. His water was long gone, and Malcolm's hope to aid the release of the others, along with most of his self-respect, had evaporated. He recalled how Debi had told him often enough that he was worthless: she was right.

He wiped a trickle of sweat from his brow and plodded on until suddenly the chant of a muezzin broke the silence. As the discordant notes washed over him, he scrambled up a small hill and stared into the distance. There a squat cement building with a single, tile-topped minaret declared that he was in Muhammad's land. Malcolm laughed, never thinking that he would be so excited about seeing a mosque, because where a mosque was, could a police station be far behind?

He stumbled into the mosque, his face sunburned, his legs scratched and bloody. For frustrating minute after minute he struggled to make the muezzin, who had just descended from the minaret, understand him. The muezzin scratched his beard and finally brought him to the house of the imam, who knew a few words of English, and the attempt at explanation began again. Finally the imam drove him to the local jandarma.

The two policemen on late duty did not speak English, but they understood that Malcolm was an American in some kind of trouble. Nothing exciting had happened in their district for many weeks. Since they were short of toilet paper they used the numerous special alerts from headquarters as a substitute, and knew nothing of his situation. They did know that if they called Antakya headquarters, they would have to transport the American there and fill out papers, so they would not get to bed at their regular time. They put Malcolm in a cell and tried to make him understand that he should wait until morning.

CHAPTER TWELVE

Breakfast did not come the next morning for Phoebe, Sally, and Hal. They sat miserably shackled on the wet stone floor of a windowless room, guarded by Mustafa. They hadn't changed clothes in five days, and dampness added to their discomfort. The roof leaked and cockroaches scurried around. At least this time the captives had some sense of where they were: they could smell the sea.

In the main room of his new hideout, Suleyman felt triumphant that his gang had moved in time to evade the police. "This is proof that Allah is blessing us and that our friends at the jandarma protect us. We didn't leave anything important at the other house, did we?"

Trafik said they hadn't and added that the house had been a dangerous place anyway since it was traceable to Fadil's grandparents. He rejoiced that they now had an isolated house with stone floors and stockpiled food and wine: "The only problem is that I am short of cigarettes."

"Don't you know that cigarettes are dangerous? Haven't you read about secondhand smoke? Think of the students. You could kill them."

Trafik didn't like being reprimanded. He walked into the prisoners' room and sneered, "Get ready to die. At sunset, the forty-eight hours will be up." He kicked Hal and headed over to Sally.

"Would your master Suleyman like you treating us like this?" Hal protested. "Isn't he trying to show that terrorists are civilized?"

Trafik enjoyed his discomfort. "Civilized?" he laughed. "Mustafa, show them how civilized we are."

Mustafa grunted out his best English: "What you know about me? I show you: I do not use toilet paper. Toilet paper is for weaklings." He held up his left hand proudly. "This is what we do."

He saw Sally shudder: "Do you hate that? Why? Maybe you hate me. Is that it? If Suleyman says yes, I will do something that will truly make you hate me." He advanced toward her.

But just then Suleyman burst into the room with Zubeyir and Fatima at his side. "You are shackled because your police director forced us to change houses. He is the cause of your pain. You should also know that Malcolm is now a free man. He was the smart one among you."

"Smart traitor," Sally muttered.

"What was that? Are you feeling bashful? Don't. Your professor told me much about you." Suleyman ran his finger along Sally's arm as she tried to wriggle free. "Don't try to get away," he laughed. "And don't look at the Armenian here. He cannot help you. Submit to Allah."

Phoebe was weary, but she now roused herself. "Is it Allah's decree to commit murder?"

"Don't lecture me about the decrees of Allah, old woman. Muhammad, peace be unto him, ordered nine hundred men from the Qurayza to proceed to the market of Medina. They dug trenches. Allah's messenger ordered the men beheaded.

He watched as his men buried the decapitated corpses in trenches."

"And what of the women?"

"You think the women and children of those condemned by Allah deserve mercy? Muhammad, peace be unto him, had them sold into slavery. The best-looking became gifts for his companions. He chose the very best, Rayhana, for himself."

Suleyman stared at Sally and said half to her, half to himself, "Should I kill you or make you a slave? Or perhaps I will follow the example of Allah's greatest messenger and make you a second wife? I must make a decision. Mustafa, take the shackles off Miss American Beauty." He complied. "Now, stand up."

She bit her lip. "No."

"These Americans: They just say no. Pay attention: you are playing by my rules, Allah's rules now. Mustafa, pick her up."

Avoiding Sally's kicks, Mustafa lifted her. "Now you will see how a poet deals with you. A vulgar person would rape you right away, but I am civilized. Fatima, remove her shirt."

Sally yelled, "You slimeball!" She tried to bite the big man. Hal struggled against his shackles.

Fatima hesitated.

"Fatima, strip her to the waist and tape her mouth," Suleyman shouted. Fatima obeyed her husband, but she seemed sad. Sally stopped struggling.

"Ah, Allah be praised. Look, Zubeyir, and enjoy." Suleyman admired but did not touch Sally. "You see, Miss American Beauty, I am a poet who admires beauty, not a rapist." He called out, "Fadil. Sulhaddin. Have you gone through the major Ruy Lopez variations?"

"Almost," Fadil called back.

"Then you will have to see this show another day: work before play." He turned back to his audience within the room. "Now I will show you how strong I am: Today I just look. We go little by little. Later there will be more. And I will show you how civilized we are: Trafik, Mustafa, do not kick Mr. Bogikian again."

Suleyman and his troupe walked out, leaving Sally sobbing as she dressed. Fatima then shackled her, whispering, "I am sorry," as she did so.

Hal looked away. "I'll kill him," he muttered, letting the chain bite into his flesh, using the pain to stoke his anger.

Phoebe began to cough, a deep wracking spasm that shook her body. Hal stared helplessly at the older woman. His anger couldn't protect Sally or provide warmth to Phoebe. He had thought he understood powerlessness. He had certainly written about it enough. Yet he had always written from a position of comfort. Although he lived in a shabby apartment, he could afford better whenever he wanted. His voice had always been heard until now.

He yanked against his chains, crying out as the metal bit into his flesh and his shoulder muscles burned with the effort.

"No reason to kill yourself," Sally said.

"You're right," Hal said bitterly. "They'll do it for me."

Still without a good lead, Kemal back at the farmhouse reached for his cell phone and punched in the number of his superior. He took a deep breath and waited for the connection, dreading the call and knowing that his time in charge of the investigation was rapidly running out. Behind him he heard the sound of boots and breathless excitement: "I may have found something, sir."

Kemal cut off the call as Abdul thrust cigarette butts at him. "I decided to smoke one," he said, his voice trembling. "It's a special exotic blend. They're usually sold for only a short period of time, and those who like a particular kind commonly buy in large quantities, often going to the same tobacconist for years."

Kemal reached out for one of the butts, taking it carefully between his thumb and forefinger. He lit it, smelled it, and felt the lethargy and hopelessness begin to lift. He smiled at Abdul: "Good work. Now find Antakya's top tobacco specialist. We have lots of digging to do."

Again Kemal dialed the number but optimistically this time. He reported the find, confident that the enormous powers of the Turkish police could discover what kind of blend it was and which of the thousands of tobacconists in this cigarette-crazed country carried it.

"Once you get the brand, can you narrow the search?" the Ankara official asked.

"Yes, we are making great progress. We believe that one of the prisoners was writing the name *Suleyman* in the dirt at the first holding point. . . . Yes, he has evaded us for five years, but we hope to catch him. . . . A prisoner, now deceased, said Suleyman has a chain-smoking associate from Antakya, so the cigarettes probably came from here."

Happy about even slight progress, Kemal referred to his favorite American movie: "We'll round up the usual tobacconists." And then came more good news: Malcolm was found, and at a jandarma post out in the countryside! He would soon be at headquarters and ready to be interrogated.

Suleyman, with Mustafa and Trafik in tow, reported the countdown to his damp and miserable hostages. "Only eight hours to my deadline and no word yet from American officials. Malcolm's video is on CNN, but I am sorry to tell you that your president has not responded to my dare. Perhaps he is on vacation or sleeping?"

"Time for truth," Hal said. "You don't expect a response, do you?"

"Of course not. Time for truth: I have let one of you go, and that leaves one for enslavement, one for ransom, one for death." Sally glared at Suleyman as he examined her and declared, "Her eyes are a dagger, but her breasts make me stagger. You see, I am a multilingual rhymer." He left the room.

Sally wept, and the other two captives also were at their lowest point. Hal tried to do what Phoebe had done before in perking them up by eliciting pleasant memories. "Let's think about something else. What's your favorite ending to a book?"

Phoebe applauded his gambit: "Good idea, but you first."

"OK." Hal thought for a moment: "Fitzgerald, *The Great Gatsby*: "So we beat on, boats against the current, borne back ceaselessly into the past.""

Sally looked at Hal: "It is not often that someone comes along who is a true friend and a good writer. Charlotte was both."

Hal was puzzled. "That's from . . . "

"E. B. White, *Charlotte's Web*. I can see you had a deprived childhood." Sally smiled. "You're a good writer, and I think you are a true friend." She looked into his eyes, and Hal, in this coldest environment of his life, felt suddenly warmed.

Phoebe enjoyed seeing the developing bond. "I like the way the Bible ends: 'The grace of the Lord Jesus be with all. Amen.'"

No grace was immediately apparent as Mustafa came in to torment them, and Phoebe especially. "I will tell you how tough I am," he said in harsh Turkish, waving his muscular arms before the old woman and suggesting that he could readily reach out and throttle her with a bare hand. "I killed my wife with an ax. I struck her from behind, but the blade was dull, and her head did not drop off. It hung to her neck by a piece of skin. Then the skin broke, and the head fell."

Phoebe shuddered.

"What did he say?" Sally demanded.

Phoebe replied, "Dear, he said he is a widower." But her face was ashen.

Hal believed that Suleyman had made his decision and was now playing a waiting and tormenting game. He worried about Phoebe, who gradually sank into a sickly stupor. She coughed incessantly. Each rasping breath she took sounded as though it might be her last. Sometimes she was lucid, talking fondly of Andrew as though he were close by. In those moments she also talked about heaven and pleaded with the others to make their peace with God.

"She never talked like that before," Sally said.

Hal nodded. "It was always clear what she believed, but now there's an urgency." He thought he had to do something to bring Sally out of depression. When Trafik squashed a cockroach, he had an idea and issued a challenge: "Hey, roach killer, I can beat you at that."

"What?"

"I'll bet I can kill more of those bugs than you can." He used his shoe and bashed a cockroach that had paused in front of him.

Trafik was intrigued. "I'm bored. What do you have to bet?"

"If I win, get Suleyman to let us out of these shackles. If you win, you can kick me some more."

Trafik grinned. He placed his revolver on the floor near the door and unlocked Hal's leg irons.

"Let me stretch my legs for a moment." Hal walked back and forth, winking at Sally as he passed her. She had stopped crying. "I'd suggest these rules," he told Trafik. "Two-minute drill—Mustafa can time us. All the cockroaches on that side are yours to kill. The ones on this side are mine."

The contest began. Sally went from revulsion for roach-killing to cheering for Hal as he looked and dashed. Splat. Crunch. When the two minutes ended, Hal and Trafik were tied, 5–5, and the remaining cockroaches had escaped into the wall through small holes.

"Overtime?" Hal suggested. "We can go anywhere in the room after the next cockroach that dares to come out." Trafik agreed, and they waited until one ran between the two. Trafik lunged for it, but Hal lunged for Trafik. He knocked him down and raced for the revolver. His fingers were inches away from it when Mustafa jumped on him.

A minute later Hal was again in shackles but with aching ribs where the terrorists had kicked him. Worse psychologically was the contempt that Trafik spat his way: "Give me a break! Your pathetic escape attempt should make you ashamed even to live."

In the dining room Sulhaddin and Fadil announced that they had finished their chess studies and wanted their reward. Suleyman asked questions about the major variations and, when he was satisfied, told them that they would soon enjoy viewing the naked Miss American Beauty.

Then he convened his seminar: "Students and first wife Fatima: You have university educations to undergird your creativity. Tell me: who should die, and how?

"Death through beheading, of course," Sulhaddin said cheerfully.

"Yes," Suleyman agreed, "our good taste dictates that. But which one?"

Suddenly Fatima asked, "Why did you call me first wife? I am your only wife. Even if you make the American your slave, she is not worthy to become part of our family, is she?"

"That is a good question." Suleyman looked nervous. "But as Allah is merciful, should we not be merciful?"

"Of course," Fatima murmured, her eyes downcast, "but don't we want in our family only those truly committed to jihad?"

"Yes, but I will be the judge of true commitment. Do you understand?

"Of course, master. Your judgment is perfect."

Suleyman beamed and lifted up her face. "Students, this is the kind of wife you should have. She is also wise: Tell me, Fatima, what should we do with the old woman?"

"She has learned our language and studied our customs. Perhaps we should be merciful."

"I will consider that." Suleyman addressed the students: "I see that none of you is ready with an answer. Think hard about this while I toy with the Americans some more. I like to see them squirm."

Kemal at headquarters faced Malcolm across a plain wooden desk, not bothering to hide his contempt as he listened to the American's long, self-serving tale of woe.

"You talk about helping the others escape, but you have nothing to offer. Face it, you made a propaganda video for terrorists and chose your own safety over the lives of your countrymen."

Malcolm had convinced himself otherwise. "Suleyman suggested that he would kill Phoebe. This was my chance to get you information on her whereabouts. It's not my fault that your slow raid didn't do the job and just sent the terrorists scurrying to another hideout. Besides, you're the one who abandoned Phoebe, Hal, and Sally."

"Ah, but you provoked me," Kemal said.

"And you allowed yourself to be provoked. Face it, when put to the test, neither of us passed."

Kemal hesitated and then said, "You are right. So let's concentrate on what information you have brought us: Confirmation that Suleyman and Trafik are involved. First names of others. Suleyman's romantic self-image. He may have a place by the sea. He plans to kill one person. Anything else?"

———

In the cell room near the sea, Suleyman announced, "You can rejoice that I will behead one of you. As you learned at Ephesus, that was the Roman way of honoring the illustrious. I could crucify you, but that's for, how do you put it, small-timers? The Quran treats everyone with dignity. It says in Sura 47, 'When you encounter those who deny the truth, then strike their necks.'"

"I've watched some videos of beheadings," Hal said. "They seem hardly a kindness."

"You are right, Armenian," Suleyman said. "I have studied both the history and the art of beheading. I too criticize the aesthetics of some. For example, in 1930 a crowd led by a Turkish sheikh seized a lieutenant, Mustafa Kubilay, and quickly sawed off his head with a hacksaw. That wasn't right."

The journalist in Hal had to ask, "What happened to the sheikh?"

"The Turkish government put down the riot and hanged the sheikh. He deserved it for using a hacksaw rather than an elegant scimitar."

At Antakya headquarters, Kemal shouted threats at the officers. Someone, probably a policeman, had tipped off the terrorists. Several of them did little to conceal their contempt for him. *They fear the terrorists more than me,* he thought. The deadline loomed, and he still had no leads unless the cigarette came to something. The phone rang. "Director Kuris?"

"Yes."

"Maltepe Samsun, tobacco specialist. It looks as though these cigarettes were a limited edition, sold for a brief period of time. Here's the announcement: "New Camel Exotic Blends Sold only in December. Using Turkish tobacco. 'A fun and irreverent brand that offers adult smokers a flavorful and indulgent smoking experience with the flavor of New Year's spirits. Uncork the excitement.'"

"Ah," Kemal said. "My excitement is uncorked. Cigarettes sold six months ago. If one of the terrorists is still smoking these, he must have made a large purchase or stored them somewhere for future use. Now all we must do is talk with the tobacconists and see if any recollect such a big sale of pricey cigarettes."

"That's all?" Samsun asked. "Do you know how many tobacco shops are in Antakya?"

"Get me a list. My men will get started."

CHAPTER THIRTEEN

Despite his talk of patience, Suleyman was also growing weary of waiting.

True, the professor had come through; even though many discounted his condemnation of America as one made under duress, CNN promoted it throughout Europe and the Middle East. But the old woman, despite her feebleness, did not seem afraid, nor did the reporter, whose watching eyes seemed always to be plotting. And Sally: he could feel her fear, but he had hoped to ignite her desire.

He was in a foul mood when he next entered their cell. Fatima had just come in with yogurt and flatbread, but Suleyman kicked the dish to the side and said, "We have been treating you so well that we have not educated you properly." He leaned over Sally, breathing garlic on her and speaking harshly, as if with his voice he could bend them to his will. "You will listen as I tell you about one of my heroes, a true follower of Allah, an Algerian, Muhammad Madani of the Armed Islamic Group."

Suleyman paced the small room, fury infusing his voice, so that even his comrades backed away. "During the 1990s

Muhammad fought to make Algeria a strong Islamic land. He did not hesitate to set off a car bomb that destroyed an entire apartment block."

"Is that supposed to make us worship him?" Hal asked.

"Bow before his poetry. Once, in the village of Hamadi, he beheaded a man and a dog, then attached the man's head to the dog's body and vice versa. He killed one man by skinning him alive and left a booby trap in the corpse that killed the man's brother who came to mourn the traitor's death. The people he killed had made others suffer, so he made them suffer."

Phoebe roused herself and stared at Suleyman. "You make it sound as if you were in Algeria."

"I was. You might say I served my internship there. Our original goal was to kill the leaders who kept us from having elections, but the army protects them, so freedom fighters went after soft targets."

"Women, children—that's truly noble."

"If you harden some targets and leave others exposed, are we at fault because we choose the soft rather than the hard?"

"You still murder the innocent. Is that what the Quran tells you to do?"

Suleyman went off into an exposition of the Quran and its focus on war, not peace. He then observed that a corrupted country needs cleansing, like this room needed cleansing: "Feh, you Americans have bad odors."

Phoebe objected again: "You could clean with water rather than with blood."

"What you call murder is the true spirit of Islam. I heard Muhammad Madani say—I have never forgotten his words—'We are ready, in order to cleanse this country, to sacrifice two-thirds of the population to permit the remaining one-third to return to the ways of God.' We too are patient for that one-third."

"So much for your talk of elections. Why didn't you patiently study and then help your people by becoming an engineer?"

"That mundane work is not fit for a poet. My real education came in Algeria. They say you never forget your first killing.

I will tell you about mine, how ten years ago I slit the throat of the sixteen-year-old son of an official who turned his back on Islam."

Seeing Phoebe lean back, exhausted, Hal took over the questioning: "You're proud of that?"

"I had no choice. The official himself was a hardened target, so I had to kill the soft. But I learned from that experience. When I slit his son's throat from the front, blood spurted everywhere. The better way is to cut from the back, severing the spinal cord and avoiding the spurting."

"You're crazy."

Suleyman ignored him: "The official added police protection. His family stayed inside. We waited until one day his wife grew weary and decided to go shopping with a security guard. My comrade had to shoot her from a distance. I disapprove of that: we should execute with scimitars, the natural way Allah intended."

Hal was fascinated despite himself. "Did the official ever get vengeance?"

"Vengeance? That is for your Westerns. No, a year later we killed the man's second son. I learned the importance of patience."

———·———

Kemal, waiting for reports from his inspectors, fumed over how long the process of visiting tobacconists was taking. He paced the linoleum, up and down, back and forth, even jumping at times a couple of linoleum squares to keep from punching the wall. Where are they? What are they doing?

To fill in the time but with hope of gaining some edge on Suleyman, he asked Malcolm for more information about the terrorists' mannerisms and intonations. Malcolm offered impressions of Suleyman stroking his mustache and Trafik smoking that would have been amusing had the situation not been so desperate.

In the house by the sea, Suleyman changed his approach. "Miss American Beauty, I have been thinking of you," he said, running his hand through Sally's hair. She jerked her head away from him.

"Did you know that the sixteenth-century poet Baqi wrote poems about the conquests of Sultan Suleyman? Here's the beginning of one of them: 'Lord of the East and West! King whom the kings of earth obey!/Prince of the Epoch! Sultan Suleyman! Triumphant Aye!' That's how it once was and how it again shall be.

"Dictator Suleyman again," Hal cut in.

"For the glory of Allah," Suleyman insisted. "Here's what Baqi wrote about the sultan:

> Thy sword in cause of God did lives as sacrifice
> ordain.
> As sweeps a scimitar, across earth's face on every
> side
> Of iron-girded heroes of the world thou threw'st a
> chain.
> Thou took'st a thousand idol temples, turnest all to
> mosques;
> Their jangled bells thou made play out the call to
> prayers' strain."

He stopped and awaited applause: "Was that not a noble effort?"

To Suleyman's surprise, Sally seemed more belligerent after his recitation: "Do you expect me to feel warm about the scimitar slicing lives, about Sultan Suleyman turning churches into mosques?"

"I thought you liked poetry."

"Not grandiose songs of conquest." An idea came to Sally: "Why don't you write me a poem of your own in the style of

Baqi? I know that would take some time, but I would like to see whether you're not only a great warrior but also a great man."

Suleyman fingered his mustache suspiciously. "Are you trying to postpone the inevitable?"

She smiled her sweetest smile. "Perhaps. But do you accept a challenge?"

"I will write you one quickly." He hurried from the room, telling Fatima that she could now give the prisoners their flatbread and yogurt.

Stretching to his fullest, Hal could touch Sally's shoulder with his fingertips if she leaned his way. "That was smart," Hal whispered. "Maybe Kemal's close." He gestured at Phoebe, who was sleeping fitfully: "I don't know how much longer she can stand it."

Kemal was getting closer. His investigators fruitlessly visited almost all of Antakya's tobacconists until they finally found a shopkeeper who remembered a sale of the exotic blend, Midnight Madness. Kemal rushed to the downtown shop, located near the archeological museum.

The bowed, wizened seller recalled a thin man who bought out his entire stock, twenty cartons, "at three times the price of regular Camels. What a magnificent day that was."

"Magnificent, sir, but do you have a name? An address? Any records? Can you remember anything more? Time is short." Kemal's voice was harsh, his questions too fast. The old man reacted like a donkey, so the police director forced himself to gentle his tone. He reached in his pocket, pulled out a one-hundred-lira bill, and held it before the old man's greedy face.

"Maybe there's something . . ." His gnarled fingers reached for the bill, but Kemal snatched it away.

"It will be yours after you refresh your memory. I'll leave an officer to assist you.

The old shopkeeper sighed, "My old brain is too tired."

Kemal pulled Abdul aside. "Make the old fool some coffee and go through his records. Call me at headquarters when we have a breakthrough."

All too soon Suleyman returned with his poem. He called in Trafik, Mustafa, and the students for a proud reading but told Fatima to leave. He stood in front of Sally, looked down on her, and said, "I have named it 'American Beauty,' and have put your name in it."

> Bright 'midst captivity a slender tree doth shine.
> Your face is like its subtle thought—hard to divine.
> Your breasts as fair proportioned as my poetry
> sublime.
>
> Thy cheek, like limpid water, clear doth gleam.
> Thy pouting mouth a bubble round doth seem.
> And from your eyes I see of light a beam.
>
> My heart is full with the Sally-love I show.
> For thy lissome figure my excited organs glow.
> Suleyman, thy servant, O my queen, before thee
> lieth low.

He stopped and peered at Sally: "Well?"

Sally remembered Hal's admonition to play for time. "It's very elegant."

"You are moved by it."

"Uh, yes."

"I am glad. If you understand that, perhaps you are worthy of being my second wife." Suleyman gestured to Mustafa, who gripped Hal. Then he bent over, put his hands on the side of Sally's head, and kissed Sally hard. Gasping, she opened her lips and tried to squirm away, but he stuck his tongue in her mouth, and his spit ran down her cheek.

That was it. She bit his tongue and, as he was recoiling, slapped him as hard as she could. He slapped her back much harder and went into a rant: "If I were in your situation, Miss American Beauty, I would not insult the one who holds the power of life and death over you."

Mustafa kept his headlock on Hal, who was trying somehow to respond. Sally dissolved in tears, and Suleyman bellowed: "Do you know what I can do to you? I will tell you what happened in Blida, Algeria, in 1993. We killed two daughters of a traitor and grabbed the third, the prettiest, to give our men a taste of heaven. She serviced twenty men in our mountain hideaway for two years. Then one of the men became soft and helped her to escape."

Sally sniffed out, "I'm glad that a young woman finally defeated you!"

Suleyman quieted down to his normal loudness: "She defeated me? The following year she committed suicide. I can take your body and your spirit."

"You're proud of that?"

"No, I learned from that. The men became bored with having the same woman week after week. I had her toward the end of that period, when she was no longer pretty. We should have killed her sooner."

Hal shut his eyes in a vain attempt to block Suleyman's words and the images they conjured up. If they did not escape, Sally and probably the rest of them were doomed. Suddenly he understood his grandfather's bitterness and his inability to put the past behind him. Some things were too much for any man to bear. What kind of cruel cosmic joke was it that he, like his grandfather as a child, was helpless in Turkey?

He looked with anguish at Sally, ashamed that he could do nothing for her. She returned his sad look with a tremulous smile, as if she had read and understood his thoughts. But Suleyman walked over to Hal and kicked him.

"She's mine, Armenian. Don't look at her like that." Then he walked to the door as if intending to leave. He reached for the knob, paused, and said, "One last story," as if it were an afterthought—though Hal suspected it was a tale he'd always intended to tell. "I will tell you about our greatest achievement, which was also my graduation, so to speak."

Trafik interjected, "Ah, this is a terrific story."

"The leaders of the town of Ben Talha in 1997 decided to support the corrupt government, so on one glorious night, September 22, 1997, one hundred of us killed three hundred renegades with Kalashnikovs, firebombs, swords, and knives."

"Let me guess," Hal said. "You carried a sword for beheading."

Suleyman said that when the killing was over, he and his comrades took with them thirty-six teenaged daughters of the government supporters as a half-payment on the seventy-two virgins each would gain in paradise. "After we enjoyed those daughters of traitors, we slit their throats and tossed their bodies into dry wells. Yes, Miss Beauty, you are right to criticize us for keeping that one traitorous woman for two years. This way was much better."

"You're no poet. You're a beast!" Sally cried out.

"Wrong," Suleyman said. "If I were a beast, I would use weapons of mediocrity like Kalashnikovs. Would that I could use only a scimitar, but your Indiana Jones showed that swords can't beat revolvers, so we use .38s when we need to: not blasting away like your Clint Eastwood but just enough. We even choose smoke bombs over grenades. Beastly, Miss American Beauty?"

"Yes," Sally insisted.

"No!" Suleyman shouted. "We are not inartistic. We do not merely point and fire. We are revolutionary artists! And now we will see some more art. Zubeyir, Fadil, Sulhaddin, pull up that woman who says I am a beast."

Sally again kicked out, but the students unshackled her and pulled her in front of Suleyman. "This time, all the clothes off," he growled.

They stripped her and held her, trembling, before Suleyman. "Students, I promised you a look. I keep my promises. Armenian, I want you to see her too." Mustafa forced Hal's head to turn that way, but he closed his eyes. "Ah, you pretend to be a gentleman, but you will never have this woman. I will take her now." Suleyman unbuckled his belt.

"No," Sally pleaded, a tear trickling down her cheek. "I'd rather die."

"Be careful what you ask for," Suleyman roared. "Maybe you are the one I should kill. Trafik, the sword."

Suleyman felt the edge of the scimitar with his thumb. A crimson bead appeared, which Suleyman pressed against Sally's lips. "Here, taste my blood the way Americans have drunk the blood of Muslim children." Sally spat at him.

Suleyman held the curved blade over the back of her neck. "One downward stroke," he murmured. "Just one." Sally held her breath as Hal struggled ineffectively against his shackles.

———

At the tobacconist's shop Abdul yelled at the sleepy seller: "Lives are at stake! Now move, old man. Think!"

"I can't think any more." The old man's voice trembled. "I'll close up the shop and rest. Maybe while I sleep I'll remember whatever I can." Abdul threw up his hands in disgust. "A half hour. That's all."

———

At the house near the sea, Suleyman put the scimitar down. "No, I cannot kill this American beauty," he announced. "I love to ride a spirited horse. I must ride this woman. I will take her to a special place, a place of Caesars, a tunnel of love, and perhaps she will come to love my poetry. I will be a god to her."

Phoebe raised her head. "If Allah did exist, he would strike you down."

"Quiet, crone!" Suleyman yelled. "You think your god can save you? Even your police director cannot save you." As Sally glared at him, Suleyman said she could get dressed. "But then, Trafik, tie her up and have Fatima bring the camera. My patience is at an end. We must record what we do and why we do it."

CHAPTER FOURTEEN

Trafik set up the camera and began taping. Suleyman, picking up the scimitar again, stared into the lens. "I am Suleyman Hasan. I do not hide my face. I do not hide my name. I am willing to lead."

He tilted his head back and quoted from Turkish poet Kemal Ozer:

> I saw the crowd, surging from the side streets,
> Swarmed a public square as far as the eye could see.
> Its gaze was fastened on a single face
> Its ears propped to a single voice.
> I saw the crowd, ready in unison
> To shout a single word out of one mouth.
> Poised to shoot like a tightened bow.

Then came his appeal: "Fellow Muslims, we must act in unison, we must be that tightened bow ready to fire arrows at our enemies. That is the way to move beyond suffering. Only fury purifies. Only fury saves. I am the warrior-poet Suleyman Hasan, a Koroglu for the twenty-first century. All of us together can overwhelm these westerners."

From the corner of the room, a voice broke into his trance. Phoebe, gaining strength as she spoke, said in Turkish, "You quote poetry selectively. I have read Ozer, and I know what comes next in that poem. He confesses, 'This surge of spirit does *not* bring together so many arms like a fist.'"

Suleyman's face turned a mottled purple. "Shut up!" he screamed as he punched her. Hal and Sally strained against their shackles until Mustafa kicked them in their stomachs with his heavy-soled boots.

"Feel the fury of our fists and our feet," Suleyman snarled. "Now we will continue: Trafik, go back to the spot of the interruption, and then tape our prisoners, sitting there like the miserable, defeated rats that they are."

After the cameramen complied, Suleyman continued his oration: "These Americans are seducers. They entice us from what is good and right. They all deserve to die. But I have decided to kill only one, for all the world to see."

Suleyman swung the scimitar over his head, waiting for the Americans to cower. As the camera rolled, he paced back and forth, laying out his case against them. When he finished with Hal and Sally, he turned to Phoebe, who was no longer prostrate but had raised herself to a sitting position. She stared defiantly into the camera. Only Sally could tell what effort it took.

"This old American woman came to Turkey many years ago as an imperialist agent. She has learned our language and studied our culture so she can know our weaknesses and attack us from within. She undermines our fortifications." He leaned into the camera: "My verdict is clear: she is a spy, and for that she will die."

"No!" Hal cried. "You can't kill her." Such was his despair and frustration that he said and meant hard words to utter: "Take me. You must let her go. Kill me."

"Here again, Americans are saying 'must.' But I am in charge here. I am what I am, and I will do what I will do."

"You're right, Suleyman." Phoebe's voice was calm. "You have that power here. But will you give me ten minutes to prepare myself and say my farewells?"

Suleyman was about to say no, but Fatima leaned over and whispered in his ear. He laughed and said, "Now you Americans will see how I have respect for women. My wife asked me to consent to the request, so I do. You see how generous I am?"

"We see exactly what you are," Hal replied.

Suleyman left the room, leaving Mustafa and Fatima as guards.

As Suleyman withdrew, Phoebe sank against the wall. Her hand trembled. When Hal started cursing their situation, Phoebe shook her head. "I don't have time," she said. "Suleyman may be bluffing, just wanting to scare me. But if he is not, I want all of you to know that I've had a happy life."

"You told us about Solon's warning not to call a person happy until he dies," Sally said, tears flowing down her cheeks.

"He was wrong," Phoebe smiled. "If life has been good and we have confidence that it will not end with death—and I have that, Sally, I do—then no matter what happens, we can be happy."

Phoebe continued: "I want to talk to you as a dying woman to people who also will die someday." With effort she raised her voice so they could hear her.

"If Suleyman comes through on his threat, do weep for me. When his friend Lazarus died, Christ wept. For me death will be separation from what I know and separation from all of you. I know the sword will sting, but I believe the sting will be physical and not spiritual. The sword will kill my body but not my soul."

As Phoebe spoke, she did not know that the old tobacconist, awakened from his nap, was saying to Abdul, "How silly of me to have forgotten. The thin man who bought the exotic blend gave me his address so I could write him the next time we got the cigarettes in. It will take time to go through my records."

Abdul called Kemal, who roared, "Push him along! Speed is crucial. I'll have the hostage-rescue team in the car ready to go."

There's still hope," Hal insisted. "Maybe we can delay this somehow. Kemal might still come."

"Yes, there is hope," Phoebe whispered. "I remember this from the Bible: 'I know my redeemer lives, and at the last he will stand upon the earth. And after my skin has been thus destroyed, yet in my flesh I shall see God.'"

For several minutes Phoebe was silent, her head bent as though in prayer, and then softly the raspy voice said, "And though I walk through the valley of the shadow of death . . ."

Sally joined her in the psalm she remembered from her childhood. Her voice gave Phoebe strength, and though the younger woman often stumbled over the words, they ended in unison: "Amen."

The Americans heard footsteps outside the door. Fatima opened it a crack and slipped in. She glided over to Phoebe, put her arm around her, and whispered in her ear. The old woman paled further, and her lips began to move: "If God is for us, who can be against us?" Fatima slipped back out the door and locked it. Phoebe's soft voice continued. Moments later Suleyman barged in, followed closely by camera-carrying Trafik and all the others.

Phoebe seemed barely aware of their presence. Her lips continued their recitation but now so softly that Sally could not hear the words. Sally watched her friend, noticed her dignity and grace, and then turned her face away. She would not look.

Yet that did not satisfy Suleyman. "You will watch," he ordered, sending students to both Hal and Sally to hold their heads and point them toward his triumph.

Sally would have cried out, but Phoebe's calm countenance stopped the words in her throat. As they unshackled the older woman, Suleyman said, "Old woman, I give you one more chance. Allah or Christ?"

Phoebe's voice hardly quavered. She stared Suleyman straight in the eye. "When I have accepted such good gifts from God for sixty-eight years, how could I turn my back on him now? I am ready to greet Jesus and my husband."

Phoebe saw a flicker of indecision in Suleyman's eyes. In a flash she imagined him saying, "An honest woman—remarkable. If you had answered 'Allah,' I would have known that you were lying to avoid death; but since you tell the truth, I will spare you." Then came an even more surprising vision: Suddenly Andrew was beside her, and she felt herself in the presence of God, lonely no more.

But Hal and Sally saw none of that. They saw an infuriated Suleyman raise the curved blade, sharpened to a keen edge, and bring it down on the back of Phoebe's neck. Sally's scream drowned out everything else. Suleyman raised the bloody blade and struck again. Phoebe's head hung by a strand of skin—her eyes staring unseeing into an unknown distance, her soul gone from this nightmare chamber—and then dropped off. The head rolled onto the floor in front of Sally, who screamed again.

Suleyman roared even louder, "Now you see that I am not to be trifled with." He turned to his disciples and said, "You see that I am out of practice: One slash should be enough. Remember, cutting from the back severs the spinal cord, but if you cut from the front, blood spurts everywhere."

He left the room, leaving the body for his comrades to clean up. Trafik brought in a bedsheet and lay it on the floor.

That's some master you serve," Hal said.

"We must be seen as brutal," Trafik said. "We want your young men to see this woman's head and think, *This is what will happen to my mother if I don't give in.*"

Sally had curled herself into a ball, pulling away from the head that lay a foot away. Hal pulled impotently against his shackles, knowing he was powerless to do anything but sit and await Suleyman's next step.

Trafik moved slowly. He called to Mustafa to help, and together they removed Phoebe's body. But by Suleyman's orders the head remained to unnerve the prisoners. Fatima came in with a pail to clean up the blood.

"How can you stand to be married to him?" Sally asked.

"He is a brave man," Fatima said, but her hands were shaking. "Many women would be proud to be his wife."

"Are you proud?"

"He is my husband."

Hal forced the words out: "And what about Sally?"

"I will be proud that my master can afford more than one wife," Fatima said, keeping her eyes low.

"Very good," Suleyman said, coming in and overhearing her last remark. "But now, Mr. Bogikian. I will play you a game of chess."

"Go to hell. I'm not in the mood."

"Your mood does not matter. I am challenging you, and you must fight me. It's amazing how we freedom fighters challenge America and some of your people pretend they do not have to fight. You are not one of them."

After a moment Hal assented, "No, I'm not."

"Good!" Suleyman said. He promised that if Hal won, a ransom note would go out the next day: "Maybe your Pulitzer Prize committee will send some money so you can go home and then come back and fight me for the American beauty. Ha, you would like that, wouldn't you? But if you lose, sad to say, I may not be completely consistent with my ancestor's plan."

"Have it your way," Hal said sullenly. Trafik carried in a table and Mustafa followed with two chairs. Sulhaddin brought a chessboard and ornate pieces, with the kings turbaned as sultans and the bishops robed as imams.

Hal held up his shackled arm, raising his eyebrows in question but saying nothing.

"Of course we will unbind you," Suleyman said gallantly. "The game of sultans should not be played by slaves. And I will take white because you Americans taught me that the good guys wear white hats."

Suleyman opened with the most common first move: He pushed forward his sultan's pawn two squares. Hal moved his sultan's pawn forward the same two.

He asked Suleyman, "Could you please move Phoebe's corpse? It's hard to concentrate when her eyes stare at me."

The terrorist laughed. "I remember the song when I attended the university: 'The eyes of Texas are upon you.' Same here: You cannot escape these eyes." He moved out the knight on his sultan's side.

Hal brought out the knight on his queen's side and was content to see Suleyman moving his sultan's bishop five spaces on the diagonal. The terrorist was playing the Ruy Lopez, the one opening Hal had learned exceptionally well as a child.

"Yes, I see you have discerned my plan," Suleyman grinned. "I will show these students how the Ruy Lopez that they have studied can in a high-stakes game squeeze the life out of an opponent."

Hal moved out his other knight, waiting to see which variation Suleyman would adopt. When the terrorist made a defensive move, pushing out his queen's pawn one space, Hal went on the attack, aggressively moving his sultan's imam three squares along the diagonal.

Suleyman mocked him, asking, "Are the eyes helping you to concentrate now?" Then the terrorist again acted defensively, moving out his queen's imam's pawn.

When Hal castled, protecting his sultan, Suleyman drew first blood by using his imam to capture Hal's knight. Hal used his knight's pawn to knock off that imam, so each player still had the same number of pieces, but Hal felt increasingly confident in his position. He looked over at Phoebe's head, clenched his teeth, and was thankful that at last in this small way he could fight back.

Kemal's phone rang. He listened and then groaned once again. "Put him in handcuffs. I'm coming right now!" he yelled, and told Malcolm, "Come along." They jumped into a squad car.

On the way Kemal explained, "The shopkeeper now says he has no record of the big purchase. My inspector, Abdul, says he can't figure out the records—the shopkeeper used some kind of code—but he thinks the man saw something on the record that frightened him, so now he's lying. I'll get the information from him."

He called the special assault force. "Meet me at the tobacco shop by the museum. We'll go straight from there."

Suleyman captured a sultan's pawn, but Hal aggressively moved his queen's pawn forward two spaces. When Suleyman castled, Hal picked off his opponent's sultan's pawn and gained good lines of attack.

"You Americans always want to attack," Suleyman said. "You leave yourself exposed." He used his ninth move to forward his queen's pawn one space, threatening Hal's imam, but it was easy to pull him back one space.

Suleyman then used his advanced knight to grab Hal's unprotected pawn and threaten his queen. But Hal moved his queen over one space so it threatened that knight. "We always counterattack," he snapped. "We won't let you get away with murder."

Suleyman scowled and pulled his knight back to the margins of the board. That allowed Hal, now controlling the center, to move his queen four spaces to the knight's column. Suleyman, with his errant knight threatened once more, had to retreat again. He began to sweat.

Hal attacked by moving his previously waiting queen's imam five spaces, threatening the white queen, which stepped one space forward to stay alive.

Then came Hal's first sledgehammer blow. He moved his sultan's imam four spaces along the diagonal, grabbing a pawn and, more importantly, putting the other sultan in check.

Suleyman's options were rapidly decreasing. Looking anxious, he had no choice but to take Hal's imam with his sultan, which allowed Hal to advance four spaces with his queen and demolish Suleyman's castle. He moved his queen next to Hal's imam, which Hal then moved one space to where Suleyman's pawn could take it off.

"I can gain only a temporary advantage," Suleyman announced, "but I must take what I can." He took the bait. Hal's queen nabbed the pawn directly in front of it, placing the sultan in check once again.

Suleyman dodged by placing the sultan in the square where his castle originally was, but Hal kept on the pressure by capturing the sultan's one remaining, protective pawn. When Suleyman tried to protect the sultan by moving his queen directly above it, Hal moved his queen to the spot in the first row from which the sultan had begun his wanderings.

Kemal, followed by Malcolm, stormed into the tobacco shop and shouted, "Where's that lying shopkeeper?"

The shopkeeper, shaking, said he wasn't hiding anything. Kemal, pulling out a heavy service revolver, asked him how he would be able to run his shop with every finger crushed.

When the shopkeeper said he feared great trouble with violent people, Kemal brought down the butt of his gun on the man's left pinkie. As he howled, Kemal said, "I didn't hit your finger that hard. Next time I will crush it and all the others."

Malcolm remonstrated: "Surely you won't do that! It's barbaric." Kemal punched Malcolm in the stomach, doubling him over, and told the shopkeeper, "I've done that to an American. Just think what I'll do to you."

The shopkeeper rushed to his file and gave Kemal the address. He ran out of the station and called to Abdul, "Put the American in protective custody. We may have to do something else barbaric."

Now you are dead," Hal insisted to Suleyman. "Check—and soon, checkmate."

Suleyman examined the board in desperation. Anywhere the sultan moved would still leave him in check. If he moved the queen to shield the sultan, Hal could move his pawn forward one space and put the queen in danger, but the queen could not move without leaving the sultan in check once again.

Time to choose. Suleyman could lose his queen and fight on against enormous odds, or he could gracefully resign.

He did neither: In a fury, he knocked over the board, sending the pieces flying in all directions. The queen landed near Phoebe's severed, staring head.

Sally, still weeping, applauded, and that made Suleyman even angrier. Through clenched teeth he said to Hal, "Tomorrow I will send the ransom note."

"I don't believe that," Hal said. "After what you did to Phoebe, I believe you intend to kill both of us."

"There you have misjudged me. I will keep my word. And if you want to hatch another feeble escape attempt, go ahead. I always have backup plans, and those plans have backup plans. No man can fool me."

He told Trafik and Sulhaddin, "Put the Armenian back in his shackles and guard him." To Fatima, Mustafa, and Fadil he said, "Come with me, and bring Miss American Beauty." He told Zubeyir, "Ride your motorcycle to the south cliff above the gorge and wait there, armed and ready, just in case."

CHAPTER FIFTEEN

Suleyman, Mustafa, and Fadil sat on the passenger seats of the Ford van while Fatima guarded Sally in the cargo area, looking at her with both jealousy and pity before concluding, "You could never become a Muslim. My husband is deluded."

Sally tried to pull herself together. "W . . . Why did he murder Phoebe?"

Fatima shrugged: "I asked him not to kill her. Islam should not mean killing old women."

"But in your husband's view, it means exactly that."

"Yes."

"It also means casting you aside and marrying a younger woman." Sally stretched out her legs and massaged her ankles. She had to be ready to move.

"No, that's not true. He could marry three others and still honor me. In your country every man throws out his first wife through divorce and marries a young woman."

"Some do, but most do not. My father did not do that to my mother. They have been married for thirty years. They still go to bed together every night and can't stand being apart from each other."

"Is that true? That must be wonderful."

They were silent for a moment. Then Sally asked, "Did you feel pain when your husband killed Phoebe?"

"It's not my job to like or dislike."

"You are not a slave."

"We are all slaves to Allah."

A few minutes later Sally stepped out of the van under a cloudless sky. Mustafa prodded her to the mouth of a tunnel that, as Suleyman explained, the Emperor Vespasian had built through solid rock to celebrate his destruction of the Jerusalem temple in AD 70. She peered in: it looked to be much longer than a football field and three or four times her height. A tall, narrow wall divided the tunnel so that on the left stood ragged boulders and on the right a channel filled with water.

"Climb up," Suleyman ordered, pointing at the wall. The top was accessible by sloping earth that led to it.

"It's only three inches wide," Sally protested.

"Do it, or you die."

When Sally hesitated, Mustapha nudged her with the barrel of his gun. She scrambled up the slope and reached the top of the wall. Carefully she placed one foot on it, then the other. It was covered with slime formed from the constant dripping of the water from the walls of the cave.

Suleyman's voice came from below. "Mustafa and I will follow behind you. Fatima and Fadil will stay here to make sure no one interrupts us. If you stop moving forward, we will shoot you. If your balance is good and you try to run, we will shoot you. If you deliberately or accidentally fall to the boulders, you will probably be hurt, but you will not feel the pain for long, because . . ."

"You will shoot me."

"Ah, the beauty has a brain. Now move!"

Carefully she put one foot before the other, holding out her arms for balance. Sometimes when the tunnel narrowed, she felt her fingers brush against its slimy walls. Most times the walls were beyond her reach. Below her on the right she could hear the sound of water.

Two-thirds of the way through, Sally slipped toward the left, leaned too far to the right to compensate, and almost went over, but her early gymnastics training helped. *Stay on the balance beam*, she told herself, although this time killers were behind her.

Behind her she heard someone bulky falling onto the boulders and yelling angrily, but she didn't turn back. Soon Sally saw the bright blue sky becoming larger. She jumped down onto dirt. The view took her breath away. Two-hundred-foot-high cliffs rose on each side of her. In front, some fifty yards away, was a boulder-strewn passage that probably led to the sea.

Suleyman and Mustafa jumped off behind her. "Congratulations," Suleyman said, "you've won the first part of one of your American game shows. Mustafa is bruised, but he will heal. Mustafa, please rest behind the boulders down there."

"I am OK," Mustafa said. "I can stay here."

"Yes, but it is time for me to give Miss American Beauty the greatest prize I can bestow upon a woman. I want you to stand guard and shoot her if she does something devious. Do not be close by. That would be what the Americans do. 'Kinky,' they call it. But we are Muslims, living by the Quran."

"I understand. I will look the other way."

Suleyman grabbed Sally and forced her to a sandy area. Her legs buckled and her body went limp as the strain of the past hours caught up to her, but Suleyman was indifferent to her suffering. Toying with her seemed to excite him. He leaned over and whispered, "What do they say in your movies? 'At last we are alone.'"

"They also say, 'You're a pig.'"

"Those are bold words, but in truth you are my slave. Do not think you can escape me: I have planned for everything."

Sally saw that he was right. Behind her sat the tunnel with its guards at the other end. Ahead were huge boulders and Mustafa. The cliffs loomed above.

"No escape," he again insisted. "Every exit is guarded. Even if you were to fly up to the sky, one of my men would shoot you down."

"I'll never give in to you," Sally said. Even as she spoke, Sally realized how futile were her words and how foolish they must sound to her captor. She had to play for time in the hope that help somehow would come.

"Could you recite a poem for me?"

"So, a romantic spot like this excites you? Malcolm told me that." Sally fought against grimacing and put on an expression of rapt attention.

"I know that you are merely humoring me, but here is one of my favorites, 'The Elegy of the Old Women of Uzbek' by Necati Cumali:

> This morning at Ozbek
> We ran out at gunfire
> This morning at Ozbek
> Windows were opened to gunfire
> A tearful daylight flooded our homes.

"Do you like that?"

"I guess I'm like most American girls. I can get . . . excited by guns."

"You can?" Suleyman crooned.

"Yes, but"—Sally was desperate—"I'd like our ecstasy to come in your home, not in the open air."

"Ah, but this to me is a sacred spot. See the plaque on the wall? 'Vespasian-Titus,' it says: the father named the tunnel after himself and his son, with whom he was well pleased. I am sad that my father has chosen a traitor's path, but perhaps I will be the new sultan and have a son. I heard your story that you did not kill your unborn child. I respect that."

"Then respect me."

"I will. If you honor me, I will someday make you my second wife, and we will have a son. But that is in the future. Now, take off your clothes and worship me joyfully—or do I have to rip them off? I am much stronger than you. My patience is great, but it has come to an end."

———————

Trafik resented being left behind to guard Hal while Suleyman had his fun. He wished he had a cigarette, but that morning he had smoked his last. How could it hurt to leave for a few minutes?

He told Sulhaddin, "The Armenian is shackled and locked in the room. I'm going to get more cigarettes. The store is only a kilometer away. Could I get you something?"

Sulhaddin said, "I like those Doritos."

"I'll bring you a pack. Do not let the American get away."

"I'll guard him with my life."

Sulhaddin paced the floor. He could already taste the corn chips. He heard a sound at the front door and moved toward it. Suddenly he heard a blast at the back and was engulfed by an explosion of light and the sound of a firecracker going off next to his ear. A police assault! He yelled *"Allu Akbar,"* Allah is great, and jerked off a shot that grazed Kemal's shoulder. A second later Kemal shot him through the heart.

"What a pity," he said, kicking the body.

As the officers searched the farmhouse, Kemal heard thumping from behind a door that was locked. "Search that body for keys," he yelled. An officer found them, unlocked the door, and freed Hal.

Kemal entered the room and stared at Phoebe's head until Hal's anguished cry jolted him: "We need to find Sally. Suleyman took her."

"Any idea where?"

Hal shook his head. "Suleyman said something about a place of Caesars, a tunnel of love."

"The Vespasian-Titus tunnel," Kemal said. "Let's go."

"You're wounded!" Hal exclaimed, and Kemal for the first time noticed blood on his shoulder.

He looked back at Hal, who was fighting off leg cramps as they hurried out the door. "You and I have been wounded for a long time. This is just a scratch."

In the police car a torrent of words poured out of Hal. He described the beheading, and Kemal called to make sure that Trafik's video camera would be secured.

———————

Just on the other side of the tunnel of love, Sally stared at her captor with fear and loathing. Then a movement caught her eye: *Why was Fatima here, and carrying a stone?* Sally forced herself to concentrate on Suleyman as he preened before her.

"One more poem, please."

Suleyman stroked her arms, and Sally fought back the revulsion. "The poet Nazim Hikmet wrote:

> I am a walnut tree . . .
> My leaves are sheer, sheer like a silk handkerchief.
> My leaves are my hands, I have one hundred
> thousand
> I touch you with one hundred thousand hands.

Fatima crept closer. Sally slowly unbuttoned her blouse. "You know what we American girls say: 'I'll do anything for an A.'" Suleyman's grin became a leer. She pulled off her shirt, revealing her blue sports bra underneath, and flung the end in Suleyman's face, striptease style.

"Ah, you are finally becoming playful," Suleyman started, but he didn't complete the sentence. As his limp body fell before her, Fatima stood by with the big rock she had used to knock him out.

"I decided," Fatima said. "Murdering old women is wrong. You must escape. Climb the south cliff, here. Head west to the sea and the jandarma station. Tell the officer *IMDAT*—help—and have him contact your Director Kuris. The house where you've been kept is at the end of Scimitar Street."

"Come with me," Sally implored.

"I cannot. I am married to Suleyman. I must face him."

"He'll kill you."

"Perhaps. I will talk with him and pray that Allah will change his thinking. Perhaps not, yet I am still his wife. You must go." Mustafa heard their voices and emerged from behind the boulders. "You must climb," Fatima said. "The bushes will hide you. Go. Now."

Sally looked up. She saw at that spot not a ninety-degree wall but something that gave her hope: a seventy-degree climb to the first row of bushes located about a sixth of the way up the cliff. No time to think beyond that. Mustafa was huffing his way toward her.

Sally found a foothold, pulled herself up by a root, then found another and pulled up on a branch. She ignored Fatima's cries as Mustafa slapped the woman and sent her sprawling to the ground. Upward she climbed, one difficult step after the next, afraid to stop to take a breath until she reached a narrow ledge.

She peered down and saw Suleyman stagger to his feet. Behind her she could hear Mustafa's ragged breaths and the sound of dislodged rocks falling to the canyon floor. Again she climbed, grabbing recklessly onto anything she found. She had no time to test roots or branches for strength, and no energy to worry. She heard gunshots, but they struck off to the side.

When she reached the second ledge, Sally let herself rest, gulping in mouthfuls of air. She scrambled some more and finally hit the third ledge. Two more shots, but they were farther off, and it seemed that Mustafa was falling behind. Yet before she could relax, a bullet whizzed by her head. She moved furiously upwards, thorns tearing her skin. Each time she grabbed a branch the blisters on her hands opened a little wider. Her thigh muscles trembled with the effort, and her calves cramped painfully. Still she continued.

As she neared the top, she remembered Suleyman's insinuation that he had an armed guard stationed above. She scurried crablike to the left and then climbed again, as quietly as she could.

She peeked over the top. In front of her, far off, she saw the sea and the green flag of a jandarma station profiled against the blue of the Mediterranean. To her right, twenty yards away was Zubeyir, sleeping under a tree, his pistol in his lap.

Sally heard thrashing behind her and then a wail from Mustafa, followed by a thump on the canyon floor. She crept out onto the flat ground and over to a clump of bushes. Zubeyir stirred. She moved slowly, weighing caution against the need to get help to Hal.

She prayed for the first time in a long time, and as she did, she heard Phoebe's voice saying with quiet confidence, "If God is for us, who can be against us?" Then she stood up and began to run, not realizing how weak her legs had become. She stumbled and fell, just as Zubeyir opened his eyes. He jumped to his feet and saw Sally disappear behind a rocky embankment.

He charged after her, sliding down the same hill, waving a revolver in his hand. Sally disappeared into a field of chest-high corn. She could hear Zubeyir panting behind her, but she managed to stay ahead—until in front of her loomed a stone wall that bordered the field. She put one foot on the wall but felt the cold steel of the gun at her back. "Get down, miss."

She turned and faced Zubeyir, who regarded her mournfully. The gun trembled slightly in his hand.

"In captivity I remembered where I saw you before," she whispered. "It was after Phoebe's lecture. You were so sweet. You said you would do anything for me."

Zubeyir hesitated.

"You know you don't want to murder me. Please let me go."

Below in the gorge, Suleyman berated Fatima: "I told the Americans that no man can fool me. But a woman did. A woman! You betrayed me. You betrayed Allah."

"No," Fatima said. "You have betrayed Allah by murdering an old woman. What's happened to you, Suleyman?"

"You'd better think about what will happen to you," Suleyman screamed. Just then he saw Mustafa falling from above, his hand still holding onto a root that had been unable to bear his weight. Mustafa fell with a thud and did not move.

From the other side of the tunnel, Suleyman heard the sound of squealing tires and shots. "More treason," he growled. "I know a path past the boulders to the sea. Come with me." He pulled Fatima, and she ran with him, still hoping for change.

———+———

Zubeyir's jaw clenched and unclenched as he regarded the woman in front of him. Sally said, "In my country we have a story of a woman of her own free will kissing a beast and turning him back to a handsome prince." She stepped forward and kissed Zubeyir on the forehead.

He said, "You are right. I do not want to shoot you."

"Then let me go."

He nodded. "Run that way," he pointed.

Sally sprinted past a farm family having a midday picnic under an awning. Once she heard footsteps behind her and turned to see if she was followed, but saw no one. She hit a dirt road and saw a car coming toward her. Whether friend or foe, she had no time to know and nowhere to hide.

She stopped and waited as the car came right toward her. Because of the light's reflection she couldn't see who was inside. It stopped a few feet from her, and Hal, Beretta in hand, jumped out. Sally fell against him. Suddenly she heard gunfire and the words, *"Allu akbar.* I am a jihadist," coming from behind her. Hal pushed her aside and fired. Sally turned and saw Zubeyir fall to the ground. His body jerked once and then was still.

Hal, his eyes dark pools that spoke of suffering, stared at Sally's face, which showed relief but a tinge of regret. "I had to shoot," he said.

"I know." She began to tremble. "He could have killed me, but he let me go."

Hal took off his shirt and put it on Sally. "I'm afraid it smells," he said. She leaned against him. "I didn't think I'd see you again," he murmured into her hair.

After a minute Hal said, "We need to find Kemal." The road went downhill and led them to the start of the tunnel, where the police director stood. "Sally!" he exclaimed, shaking her hand stiffly but enthusiastically. "I am so happy to see you. How did you escape?"

"Suleyman's wife, Fatima. She's my height, thin, hair dyed blonde. A very angry Suleyman might be with her."

Kemal reported that he had shot Fadil and that his squad was now bringing out a corpse, perhaps Suleyman's. They walked to the tunnel entrance, where a sergeant told them dramatically, "I give you the murderer of Mrs. du Pont." But when he lifted the sheet both Hal and Kemal groaned. It was Mustafa.

Kemal called for more police to join the search. "They've sealed off all the roads and they have Fatima's description," he told Hal and Sally. "Now I'll drive you to the hotel where you can have some rest."

They were all silent as the road took them to the Mediterranean. Sally started crying. "I can't stop thinking about Phoebe," she said. "I remember her telling us about the anniversary dinner by the sea that she and Andrew had. I hope they're together now."

She added, "Kemal, could we stop here? I'd love to put my toes in the water."

"This is just a fisherman's beach. Not very pleasant."

"Oh, just for a moment. Please."

"Certainly." Hal sat on a bench and looked at the water. But Sally, shoes off, walked to the waterline.

Life went on, she knew. Twenty yards down the beach seagulls were pecking at a huge clump of seaweed. Sally meandered that way, and the seagulls reluctantly flew off, leaving the clump more visible. The sun's declining rays struck something shining in the middle of the clump. Sally drew closer.

Suddenly she screamed. The clump was the body of Fatima Hasan. The glow was a reflection off the edge of a knife, stuck between her breasts.

CHAPTER SIXTEEN

Hal and Sally had never enjoyed a plane flight more than the one they took together to Frankfurt. Just sitting next to each other in comfort was heavenly. As they walked through the German airport, a few people stared at them, remembering vaguely seeing faces like theirs on recent television news reports.

After a tearful good-bye they parted ways, Sally heading to Philadelphia and Hal to Dulles. Hal had never felt stranger than when he walked on the high-gloss floors between the gleaming walls of Concourse B. The farmhouse dirt floor of Antakya seemed more real to him than the trinity of McDonald's, Starbucks, and All-Religions Chapel. He walked fast even on the moving sidewalk, occasionally stepping on the heels of those who stood placidly in the middle of it. He forced them to move aside as he brushed by without a word.

He stopped at a newsstand in the main concourse and scanned the headlines before picking up a *New York Times* and heading to the taxi line: He rarely took cabs, but now he didn't care. He wanted to get home fast.

In the back seat Hal read the *Times* story, "Wife of former US ambassador to Turkey brutally murdered." One of the paragraphs irritated him: "The hero who managed to escape, Columbia professor Malcolm Edwards, made his way to police headquarters. The police then raided the Hezbollah house, too late to save Mrs. du Pont but in time to rescue another hostage, journalist Halop Bogikian."

He pushed himself to read on: "Mr. Edwards turned aside questions about his own courage and emphasized his sadness at the death of his aunt and his appreciation for the valor of the other surviving hostages." Maybe he had misjudged Malcolm.

Then he read the *Times* editorial page: "We should not exaggerate the impact of one attack. If we react in anger, we are playing into the terrorists' hands." He threw the paper onto the floor and stared gloomily out the window at the Virginia countryside.

For the first time in years, Hal felt a twinge of excitement as the Capitol dome came into view. It was good to be in America. The cab took him to his apartment house and he jumped out, only to realize he had no key any more. It turned out not to matter: a banner over the front entrance proclaimed, "Welcome back, Mr. B," and the building supervisor opened his door and gave him a cake a neighbor had baked for him. Hal was touched, particularly because he hadn't exchanged many words with the other tenants.

His apartment had the stale odor of a place closed up for too long. He flipped the switch on the small window air conditioner that waged ineffective battle against Washington's summer heat. Opening the fridge he found one of the odor culprits, a half-empty carton of milk, and dumped it down the sink. Then he grabbed a can of Coke, carried it over to the table, and turned on CNN.

There was Malcolm being interviewed. "The terrorists have different kinds of tortures. They kept my aunt and my two friends in captivity, but they left me out in the desert without water. I struggled on and brought my information to the police.

It was horrible to learn that they had killed my aunt, but at least Hal and Sally survived."

Hal listened to the CNN correspondent noting conservative criticism of Malcolm's videotaped message. Then came a clip of Columbia's provost saying, "Professor Edwards's life is consistent with his bold philosophy. He has his critics, but perhaps now, in appreciation of his courage, they will relent."

Hal flipped through channels and saw MSNBC soothing those with Turkish travel reservations: "The areas normally visited by tourists along the Aegean are untouched. Turkish authorities are easing fears by increasing police patrols. The Turks worked hard during the 1990s to get a grip on their terrorist problem. You can bet they're not taking it lightly now."

Fuming, Hal picked up his phone and punched in the number of his office. His editor promised, "You write something, we'll run it." He spent the rest of the day mainlining coffee as he struggled to capture the reality of his experience and draw meaning from it. He was determined to avoid platitudes. He would not couch the story to protect tender sensibilities.

Sally took a cab for the twenty-five miles from the Philadelphia airport to Greenville, the old-money terrain northwest of Wilmington, Delaware, where Phoebe had lived. Her task for the next month was to work on details concerning Phoebe's estate. The housekeeper greeted her with tears, hugs, and a stack of phone messages from television producers who had seen a photo of her and were looking for a telegenic face with a tale of terror.

Propelled by her looks and a sense of innocence lost, she made the rounds of interview programs in New York and was astounded at how much of what posed as news was show business. She sat in various green rooms amid soft furniture and soft drinks as she waited to go on stage. Associate producers with clipboards listing segment times and cue lines suggested that she leave out this detail or add that one. Makeup artists added some powder here and there to help her look bouncier. Other guests went over their best movie-pumping or book-selling lines.

At first she felt true to herself. "Those two weeks in Turkey changed my life," she told Matt Lauer on NBC's *Today Show*. "I had never seen a vicious murder in real life."

"Mugged by reality?" he asked.

"More like raped," Sally said. "Before, I didn't truly care about those plastic shredders into which Saddam Hussein's men placed captives, usually feet first, sometimes head first if the murderers felt like being kind that day. I didn't pay attention to the torture, the mass graves. My slogan was, 'Climb Sunshine Mountain.' Now I look in the ravines."

But after telling the story a few times and getting sympathetic reactions from hosts and audiences, she didn't want to say the words any more. What she had yearned for upon arrival in New York four years earlier she now had: a part in a riveting Broadway drama. And she didn't want it.

Hal e-mailed his column to the *Post* editor. It concluded with the beheading of Phoebe and a warning: "Muslim extremists care nothing about our lives. Sometimes they kill us one by one, but if they can get a nuke and kill millions of us, they will."

The next day, wearing a new blue blazer and a red tie, he hit the Washington talk-show circuit. A producer sashayed over to where he was sitting in the green room for *Hardball* and said, "When you get on, don't hold your tongue." Hal grinned and said, "No chance of that." He found it hard to get in more than a few words in response to Chris Matthews, but what he did say was blunt: "Evildoers like Suleyman are plotting to kill us and our country any way they can."

The Republican majority on the Senate Foreign Relations Committee asked Hal to testify, so he called Kemal and talked over what might be helpful. "To many Turks the beheading of an old woman represents the killing of mothers. If the US pushes for it, Turkish public opinion right now would welcome a joint Turkey-US force against terrorism."

At ten a.m. three days later, Hal sat at a front table in a two-story-high Senate hearing room, looking up at the dais where senators slouched in their high-back chairs as aides whispered in their ears. He looked behind them to the Senate seal affixed to a white and gray marble wall. He tried to think not of the often-disappointing legislators but the scroll inscribed with *E Pluribus Unum* that dominated the seal and connected olive and oak branches, signifying peace and strength.

Hal, feeling himself amid such august surroundings very much the grandson of an Armenian immigrant, waited until his cynicism could knock down his choked-up emotions. Then he plowed ahead: "I can still see Mrs. du Pont's beheading and hear her scream. Mr. Chairman, you and your colleagues don't have those sights and sounds imbedded in your heads. You need foresight to take vigorous action against things that you have only heard about, but have not experienced for yourselves."

After Chairman Richard Lugar uttered soothing words, Joe Biden of Delaware said, "Your friend was a great citizen of our state, yet we cannot have a policy of first strikes against groups that have as yet done us no harm."

"Pragmatically, you may not want to," Hal replied. "Think what would have happened had Great Britain and its allies listened to Winston Churchill and acted against Hitler before his power became so great. Millions of lives would have been saved, but many pundits would have proclaimed that Churchill was overreacting and unnecessarily fearful, and that Hitler never did anything so bad."

Lincoln Chafee of Rhode Island declared, "We have to proceed deliberately, so I am glad we will be able to apply to this problem the pragmatic thinking of your friend, Malcolm Edwards, who was fortunate enough to escape."

Hal tried to stay cool. "That's fine, as long as we don't confuse pragmatism with cowardice. Sometimes it is most practical to damn the political consequences and take action when a threat appears, not when it becomes overwhelming. Liberals and conservatives in the past united to stop fascism. Today we must unite against an Islamo-fascist jihad dedicated to the destruction of the US and Western liberal democracy."

Barbara Boxer of California said, "I know that you are sorrowing, Mr. Bogikian, but if we act aggressively, more people will die. What exactly would you have us do?"

"We need to show that when terrorists murder innocent Americans who are traveling abroad, the United States will not shrug its broad shoulders. We should offer Turkey a specially trained US force to work alongside the Turkish military in rooting out terrorists. We should do the same with the governments of other countries. We should make clear that we will not carry on business as usual with them until we take care of *this* business."

Other Democrats and moderate Republicans asked perfunctory and condescending questions, praising Hal for coming through "the ordeal" and treating him like an emotional basket case. That's when he became angry: "This should not be a conservative versus liberal issue. Liberals who prize individual rights should not be useful idiots for a movement that kills those who think for themselves. You sit back now, but when you're in the terrorists' sights, you will wish that you had not just hemmed and hawed."

He wrote his next column for the *Post* on senatorial fools, throwing in heated rhetoric: "Not understanding the nature of the Islamic threat we face, they are eager to sink back into slumber. We're vermin in the eyes of many Muslims. Some of us are progressive vermin, but we'll be decapitated just the same."

His editor called to say, "Hal, I know you're overwrought . . ."

"I'm not overwrought!" Hal shouted. The discussion declined from there, the editor insisting that one column on Muslim terrorists was enough, and it was time to move on to other topics: "We need variety in your columns. You can come back to terrorism next month, but why not write now about, say, the failure of compassionate conservatism"?

"This is my column, right? Can't I write it the way I want to?"

"No, it's the *Post's* column, and you can't make it your soapbox."

"Then I'm out of here. Use the space to sell your soap."

Hal hung up and immediately asked himself why he had resigned once again. He had to admit that he was over-the-top sometimes, but the press attention span's brevity was so frustrating: The front of rage was quickly passing, and a few quickly forgotten thunderstorms would leave behind an unchanged landscape. The sense of powerlessness he had suffered through while a captive in Antakya was back.

On July 4 Sally kept her promise and met Hal on the Washington Mall. They spread out a blanket as close as they could get to the fireworks firing line and lay down on it, looking heavenward. The smells of hot dogs, popcorn, and apple pie mingled delightfully. *Back in America*, Hal thought, but he couldn't leave behind the odor of their cell room in Antakya.

"I e-mailed Kemal yesterday and asked for a Suleyman update," Hal said. "Kemal said some think he's left Turkey, but that seems unlikely. Destabilizing Turkey is his purpose in life. Why would he go to Iraq or Saudi Arabia when he has the Turkey franchise?"

The first rockets ascended and burst overhead, sparkling downward like tree limbs of red, yellow, green, and silver. "Those are palm shells," Hal said. Not wanting Sally to think he was showing off, he added, "I spent one summer selling firecrackers."

"I love fireworks," she replied, trying to put a bounce in her voice, but the corners of her mouth turned down.

Hal turned toward her. "You look depressed."

"I am. You'd be impressed: I'm not searching for sunshine everywhere. Sometimes I yearn for shade, even darkness."

"Welcome to my world. But I want to remember what you told me at first about taking delight in small things now, like that roundel." He pointed at a series of circles in maroon and gold.

"Hal, we've flipped. You used to see things that reminded you of massacred Armenians. Now I see a circle and think of Phoebe's head. Remember on the dock when I talked about you changing me? You have, but Suleyman has changed me more."

She wept. Hal hugged her and thought he had to find something to delight her. "Hey, that's a willow shell!" Red, green, and silver stars fell in the shape of branches that stayed visible until they approached the ground.

"That's pretty," she said, looking mournful. Hal felt that his own heart was breaking. He kissed her and she responded, then looked up as beautiful bursts of green bouquets and blue stars appeared above her. "I saw that," she grinned. "You must be a very good kisser."

They were about to retest that hypothesis, but a spectator yelled, "Get a room!" Hal rolled away but they stayed face-to-face, he on his left elbow, she on her right. "OK, it's time to think this through logically," he said.

"Yes, logic."

"Postulate one: We can't live this way. We have to do something."

"Right."

"Postulate two: Suleyman thought he was 'patient' with you. He won't be so patient next time with anyone he abducts."

"Right." Red and green serpentines burst overhead, sending small tubes of incendiaries skittering outward to oohs and aahs from the crowd.

"So here's a question: How patient should we be? Shouldn't we, for our sanity and for the sake of others, try to stop him?"

"We should, but how? If the Turkish and American governments can't do anything, how can we?"

Ring shells burst toward them, exploding spectacularly in multiple colors.

Hal answered, "Most of the Turks who commanded the mass murder of Armenians in 1915 escaped punishment. That wasn't acceptable to Soghomon Tehlirian, a twenty-four-year-old Armenian who had witnessed the murder of his parents, the beheading of his brother, and the rape of his sister on one of the forced death marches in 1915. Soghomon, left for dead in a pile of corpses, had awakened and escaped."

Blue and gold round shells burst almost directly overhead, showering them with stars.

"In 1921, Soghomon walked up behind one of the leaders who had ordered genocide. He shouted, 'This is to avenge the death of my family,' and pulled the trigger. When the jury heard the story of his experience, it found Soghomon not guilty because of what today would be called temporary insanity."

"I'd like to avenge the death of Phoebe," Sally said, "but that story doesn't bring us any closer to what we can do now."

"I've been thinking," Hal responded. "Maybe I should go back to Turkey with some guns and go hunting for Suleyman."

Sally sat up. "Sure. I can picture you going through airport security. You'd tell the luggage inspector, 'Oh yes, I'm bringing weapons into Turkey.' Maybe they'd let you through if you talked like Elmer Fudd: 'I'll be weally quiet. I'm hunting wabbits.'"

Hal faced her. "I could hit the Istanbul black market."

Sally pounded her fist on the blanket. "Logic. You don't speak Turkish. You don't know the country." Her voice quivered and tears began to run down her cheeks. "Don't you get it? This is so over our heads. There's nothing we can do. If the Turkish government and the US government can't find Suleyman, we certainly can't."

"You're right." Hal stared off into the night. "We're stuck in abnormal normality, but I won't give up." For several minutes they lay back and watched colored pearls chasing comet tails, and tails then chasing the pearls.

"See the chased becoming the chaser?" Hal asked. "I have an idea. How about . . .?" But Sally couldn't hear the rest of Hal's question over the booms of the finale. They watched flying fish, falling leaves, silver spiders, and other phantasms, all to the sound of titanium bangs.

Hal thought more about his idea and decided not to broach it further. He walked with Sally to Union Station and to the door of the last car of the last Metroliner of the night.

She turned to him, grabbed his hand, and said, with the saddest of looks, "I want to forget about Turkey. I know you won't give up, but I need to. Thank you for tonight, and thank you for everything you did in Turkey, but let's not see each other for a while, please."

"Sally, we can't forget about . . ."

"Shh." She kissed him and ran onto the train. "Good-bye." She sat on the side away from Hal so he couldn't look in the window and see her crying. When the train left Washington, she looked out into the darkness. Arriving in Wilmington, she took a cab to Phoebe's mansion in Greenville and tumbled into bed, wrapping herself in a sheet.

Hal walked back to his apartment, frustrated and angry. Unable to sleep, he turned on the television and watched as Rocky Balboa began to train, getting stronger. He looked out of the apartment's single window at the new gym across the street. Its neon sign proclaimed, "Grand opening. One month trial membership."

The next morning he stopped by the gym. The manager, Phil, showed him the Life Fitness machines and said, "Let's see how you measure up."

Hal did chest and shoulder presses, lat pullovers, bicep curls, and leg extensions, with Phil adjusting the weight. He asked, "When was the last time you regularly worked out?"

"Never have."

"That's OK. You'll be surprised at how quickly you can advance if you work at it. But let me ask: 'What do you want to accomplish?'"

"I want to kill a terrorist."

PART THREE

CHASER AND CHASED

CHAPTER SEVENTEEN

In Greenville, Sally received news about Phoebe's will: $10,000 each for Malcolm and three other nephews, $50,000 for her, and many millions for Christian antipoverty work around the world, with as much of it in Turkey as the government would allow. The nephews announced that they would contest the will, but the lawyers said they didn't have much of a case and asked Sally to stay on for another two months to go through Phoebe's papers, remaining in the mansion until it was sold.

After that she went a week without answering the phone or talking to anyone except Phoebe's housekeeper. She took over Phoebe's bedroom and surrounded herself with records of Phoebe's life. Hal left messages, but she didn't call back. And yet, instead of forgetting about Turkey, she leafed through albums of photos taken when Phoebe lived there, as if she could exorcize her memories and replace them with new ones.

She sank into depression, often not bothering to shower or dress. One morning she looked at herself in the mirror and burst into tears. She looked like a street person. How could she come out of it? She knew Phoebe would not be acting like this; her faith was too strong. Sally wanted to be like her.

She called David Carrillo's church, but the secretary told her the pastor had needed a second operation and wouldn't be out of the hospital until the next day. She thought about going to the church Phoebe had joined, but it was a small one full of old people who reminded her too much of her parents and their friends.

She decided to comb her hair and stop by the big, cathedral-like church that Phoebe had left after her husband's death. She was soon introducing herself to a blue-haired receptionist whose eyes widened: "Weren't you with Phoebe du Pont in Turkey?"

"I suppose that was me."

"My, Pastor Jim will certainly want to talk with you."

Sally flinched. She could picture the gossip hotline firing up to carry tales of her visit. She was so cold: *Was the church air conditioner pumping out refrigeration?*

Soon a tall, fleshy man held out a manicured hand in greeting and invited her into his study. She looked around the well-appointed room with its oak bookcase filled with brand-new books about contemporary Christian living. Jim asked her to sit in a deep, leather chair and pulled another close to her.

Sally wondered where to start. "I'm having a particularly hard time getting over Phoebe's death."

"That must be difficult." Jim's face wore a sober expression, and his fingers were steepled.

Sally didn't know what to ask, so she blurted out what was on her mind: "Isn't it cold in here?"

"We do keep the temperature low." Jim leaned forward conspiratorially: "I'll tell you why: lots of people perspire when talking with a pastor about personal things, and that embarrasses them more. We want everyone to be comfortable here."

"Do you know how I can get comfortable? I'm a mess."

"I'd say that you shouldn't let tragedy sour you on life. Did you ever hear that old song, 'Climb Sunshine Mountain'?"

"I remember it vaguely."

"If you live out your life with the same joy that Phoebe had, then you are fulfilling her spiritual destiny."

Sally nodded, although that made no sense to her. She bit her lip and threw out one more question: "Where does Jesus come in?" She was surprised to see sweat form on the minister's brow.

"Thinking about Jesus can comfort you. Some people your age are hard pressed to believe the Christ story. It's a stumbling block, and I don't want people to stumble." Sally could now see sweat on Jim's neck, just above the Windsor knot of his tie. "It's also good to pray, if you'd like."

"I don't want something I'd like. I want something that's solid, that's true."

Jim said that was a good notion and handed her a pamphlet about choosing a life of meaning. As he promised that it wouldn't make her uncomfortable, Sally saw that his underarm was soaked.

"But I'm already uncomfortable." Sally stood up and asked the question she didn't know was in her until that moment. "If God exists, how could he let Phoebe die that way?"

Jim stood as well. Big splotches of moisture bedecked the front of his shirt. "You want me to answer in a black-and-white way. I say, embrace the paradox. It's good that you're asking questions."

Tears came to Sally's eyes. "That's all you can say? Why can't you say, 'Here I stand'?"

Jim smiled. "Isn't sitting more comfortable? Miss Northaway, here is my counsel: Forget about the tragedy that occurred. You're back in America. We're safe here."

Sally looked out the window at the parking lot outside. "Do you just bury and forget your family members?" she asked, and then thought, *That's what Hal said about remembering the Armenian holocaust.*

The next afternoon Sally combed her hair again. She planned to visit Phoebe's doctor and didn't want him to think she was hopelessly depressed. As she sat in the waiting room, she listened to patients chattering about a new television reality show. Then she told Dr. Chandler, "I'm sleeping poorly."

He listened to her breathing, peered into her ears, and said, "You went through an ordeal." He was about sixty and had a regular stream of mostly elderly patients whom he had known for years. "I don't want to intrude, but sometimes it helps to talk with a minister."

"Sometimes." Sally slumped in the chair, fighting to hold back the tears. "I've had enough of pastors."

"Well, then, how about talking with a psychiatrist?"

"I'm just tired, really." Sally eked out a smile. "Maybe this will all go away if I get some sleep."

"Worth a try," Dr. Chandler said. He looked at his watch and gave her a prescription for Dalmane, a fast-working sleeping pill: "We'll get you back to a normal sleep pattern."

"Yes, sir," Sally said with a wry smile. "Back to normal."

Sally filled the prescription, returned to Phoebe's office, and bored through more folders of papers for the next three hours. The office had big windows with views of the oak trees that sprawled behind the mansion, but Sally kept the drapes closed. She checked her e-mail: She could buy Viagra or send money to Nigeria and get millions back from the widow of General Abacha. Spam, bam, thank you, ma'am.

One e-mail with the title "News from Turkey," caught her eye. She hoped that Suleyman was captured.

She opened it and read the message: "Miss American Beauty, do not think you can escape me. I have comrades everywhere, some not far from you. How was church yesterday? How was your doctor's visit today? You see, anytime I choose, I can have you seized."

Sally jumped up and locked the office door. Then she peeked out the curtain. Was someone lurking outside, waiting for her?

She felt faint but forced herself back to the computer screen: "I offer you a choice: You can return to Turkey and become my slave and perhaps some day, if you are worthy, my wife. Or I will have you captured and raped repeatedly in Delaware because that's what you deserve. The eyes of Suleyman are upon you. You cannot get away."

She ran to Phoebe's bedroom and locked that door. Call the police? They wouldn't assign her a bodyguard. Call Hal? She had given him the brush-off. As she threw herself on the bed, memories of Suleyman washed over her. She gritted her teeth. *I can't bear it. I won't let him touch me. Not him. Not anyone. But I can't escape him.*

She shuddered and reached for the bottle of sleeping pills. A thought occurred to her: *I can escape him.* She instantly dismissed thoughts of suicide: *That's not me. I'm no tragic heroine in a novel. I'm Sally, climbing Sunshine Mountain.* But she stared at the bottle some more.

Hal, at that moment, was finishing a day of research for the *Harper's* article on MS-13 gangs that, free from newspaper pressure, he was now able to write. His Jetta was in the shop—that was happening often in its old age—so he had taken the train that day to Baltimore for several interviews, and it was time to head home.

He thought of returning to his apartment alone, and then thought of Sally. *Might as well try calling her again.* Thankful for cell phones, he punched and waited. Her phone rang once, twice, six times. He was ready to hang up when Sally's soft voice came on.

"Sally, thank you for picking up, but what's wrong? You sound awful."

Her voice trembled. "He's here."

"Who's here?"

"Suleyman or his friends. They're following me."

"Wait. Calm down. Tell me from the beginning."

"I received an e-mail from Suleyman. Executive summary: Come back and be my slave, or I'll have you kidnapped and raped."

"Just big talk. He's thousands of miles away."

"He knew where I had been yesterday and today." Her voice rose hysterically. "I won't let him get me. What am I going to do?"

"Sally, I'm coming to see you, right now."

"Promise?"

"I'm coming. Will you be OK 'til I get there?" He could hear her sobbing.

"I'll wait. I'm glad you called, Hal. I had these sleeping pills in my hand."

"Sally, I'll hurry. Don't go anywhere or do anything. Promise."

For a minute she didn't answer. Hal began to panic. "Sally . . ."

"I'll be here."

Hal raced onto the street and hailed a cab. "Greenville, Delaware, northwest of Wilmington," he yelled at the driver.

"That's at least sixty-five miles. It will cost you plenty."

"I'm not cheap," Hal screamed. "Step on it."

The housekeeper buzzed Hal in at the gate and guided him through the mansion's many rooms. Sally had kept her word and was waiting for him. Hal was shocked not only by the bags under Sally's eyes but also by her general lack of luster. He tried not to appear dismayed, but Sally saw that he noticed.

Hal said, "I'm sorry. I should have realized . . ."

"I thought I could handle it." Her eyes teared up. She reached for a tissue and said, "I'm doing this a lot these days."

He walked over to the nightstand and, with his back turned to Sally, picked up a picture of Phoebe and Andrew. He slipped the sleeping pill vial into his pocket.

Sally didn't like feeling helpless. "Thank you for coming, but there's no need for you to stay."

"Yes there is. Starting right now I'll take care of you. Think your housekeeper has some chicken soup?"

Sally let out a tiny smile. "That's sweet, but I'm a mess."

"Do you think I care what you look like?"

"Yes."

Now Hal smiled. "You're right. Take a shower. When did you last eat?"

"Yesterday."

"I'll find some chicken soup."

By the time Sally came back into Phoebe's bedroom in a white bathrobe, she was looking much better. Hal presented her with a tray—soup, sandwich, and one sleeping pill—and said, "Your housekeeper has made up a guest bedroom for me, if you don't mind."

"I don't mind. You took my pill bottle, didn't you?"

"Yes."

"I don't mind."

Hal kissed her on the forehead and closed the bedroom door behind him.

The next morning Sally made Hal a cheese omelet. "I slept so well," she exulted. "Will you stay with me today?"

"Yes, but I don't want to be a slob. I'll need to pick up some clothes."

Sally said shyly, "I thought of that. Here's something strange: I think you're the same size Andrew was, and Phoebe couldn't bear to get rid of his clothes. There might be something you could wear."

"Hey, I'll look like a rich guy," Hal grinned. "But I still have basic tastes: The Orioles are playing a game against the Red Sox this evening. After the game we could drive down to Washington, and you could stay with me."

Sally's eyes opened wider and Hal quickly added, "I'll be on my couch. Want to come? There's a friend I'd like you to meet tomorrow."

"Yes."

At Hal's insistence, Sally phoned the police before they left. The local chief sent a squad car to the mansion as a courtesy but said he wasn't equipped to deal with terrorist threats: "Tell the FBI." As they drove south to Camden Yards, the beautiful Baltimore ballpark, Hal said he would talk to federal officials but didn't expect much action. With rumors of potential biochemical or nuclear terrorism in the air, no one had much time for an e-mail threat against one person.

So Sally, with a new Red Sox cap, and Hal, in one of Andrew's lime green polo shirts, stood in line at the ticket window, determined to avoid Turkey talk. They were startled to see Malcolm walk up.

Sally was angry. "What are you doing here? Does a Benedict Arnold care about batting averages?"

"I have a board meeting in Washington tomorrow. I remembered that, in Antakya, Hal suggested we go to this game. Didn't expect to see you here, but I'm ready to buy three tickets."

Sally still smoldered, so Malcolm pleaded, "Please hear me out. In Antakya I thought I could go for help, and I did get to Kemal. I said on the videotape pretty much what I believe: You don't agree with me, but that doesn't make me a traitor. And about Phoebe's will: I don't need the money, but my cousins do, so I joined them to be a team player, something I've never been."

Hal said, "Sally, let's give him a chance."

Malcolm jumped ahead as they reached the ticket window. He said, "Three. Best seats you have left." The best turned out to be close to the field but down the line at the right field foul pole. This time Hal deliberately sat between Sally and Malcolm, hoping to keep the peace.

Both men loudly sang the national anthem, hitting with particular vigor the lines, "And the rockets' red glare, the bombs bursting in air, gave proof through the night, that our flag was still there." It was Youth Day at the ballpark, and behind them groups of teens, bused in from numerous summer city park programs, gave proof through the singing that they were there by hauling out random obscenities.

"They don't know what they have," Hal fumed. "I've never felt more patriotic than I do now."

Malcolm turned to Sally: "Please believe me: I never thought Suleyman would kill Phoebe. Now my eyes are open. I no longer want to be pragmatic all the time, and I know I can't be neutral."

Sally stared at the field, where centerfielder Coco Crisp led off for the Red Sox in the top of the first and received a walk. He took a big lead and stole second.

Malcolm went on, "And I haven't given any speeches or interviews since the day I got back, when all the interviewers were pestering me and I hadn't had time to think things through. I could have testified before Congress, but I didn't because I'm reconsidering everything."

He looked so sad that Sally felt sorry for him. She wondered if Malcolm was putting on an act for some reason, but she dismissed that as post-traumatic suspicion.

"And there's one other thing," Malcolm was saying. "Suleyman sent me an e-mail yesterday, complaining that he had freed me to be a propagandist for Islam. He said that if I kept quiet, his comrades in New York would kill me. To show that his eyes were upon me, he told me what I had done the day before."

"Sounds familiar," Sally said.

"He e-mailed you too?" Malcolm asked.

"Scared me. But I'm glad Hal hasn't received any threatening notes." Hal looked away, and Sally caught that. "Have you?"

Hal watched Mark Loretta hit a ground ball to the right side of the infield, making an out but allowing Crisp to take third base. He pointed out the importance of moving up runners and then told Sally, "I've been getting notes every week since we got back. He doesn't like Armenians."

"Why didn't you tell me?"

"Didn't want to depress you further."

The smell of hot dogs wafted their way. "Ballparks always make me hungry," Malcolm said. "Want one?"

"You are one," Hal laughed, and Malcolm laughed as well. "And yes, a hot dog would be great. But before you go, watch Manny Ramirez hit. He has the sweetest swing in baseball."

They watched Ramirez hit a long fly ball to centerfield. It was caught, but Crisp scored easily. Hal said, "Sacrifice fly. Not embellishing your batting average but helping the team. That's my plan to catch Suleyman."

"So you want to sacrifice yourself?" Sally asked with a catch in her voice. "How?"

"You were right in Washington to see that I can't do this alone. But what if I work with Kemal and travel through Turkey with lots of police protection? Think about those e-mails. Suleyman for some reason is fixated on all of us. We're the ground ball that bounced off his glove, and he can't stop thinking about it."

Malcolm was incredulous: "After almost being killed, you want to put yourself under Suleyman's control again?"

"I'd be the bait. He'd see I'm taunting him and consider it an insult. He'll snap at the bait, then the police will grab him."

"Bait gets eaten," Sally said. "Bait can't fight off the fish. Remember Mustafa? You couldn't trust the jandarma to swoop in, save you, and nab Suleyman."

Malcolm said, "I need to think about this. I'll get the dogs."

While he was gone, Hal reassured Sally that he'd seek Kemal's advice: "I care about you. I'm not about to sit still when you're in danger."

She looked at him miserably. "And I care about you. I couldn't bear it if something happened to you. I wish this would all go away."

He grabbed her hand. "Sally, it won't just go away. I have to do something."

Designated hitter David Ortiz came up to bat. "And if Suleyman kills you?"

"He won't."

Ortiz hit the ball high and deep to right field, just inside the foul pole, right toward them. All the fans reached up, but Hal lifted Sally. She took off her cap and extended it high: the ball plopped into it. The cameras caught and lingered on her face, momentarily shining.

It was 2–1 in the second when a group of teens behind them started a chant. It took Hal and Sally a minute to understand what they were saying: "La mara salvatrucha. La mara salvatrucha." That turned into another chant: "MS-13. MS-13."

"Trouble in Turkey and trouble here," Hal moaned. "That gang is spreading all over."

Malcolm returned with hot dogs and sodas, which he handed out as if making an offering to Hal and Sally. He told them again that he was sorry and that he had made a resolution: "No more chasing after students or women in museums."

When Red Sox closer Keith Foulke came on in the ninth inning to protect a one-run lead and struck out the first batter, Sally turned to Malcolm and said, "You have two strikes, but Hal's right: You're still up at bat." When Foulke ended the game by striking out Miguel Tejeda with the tying and winning runs on base, Hal kissed Sally, and Malcolm turned away.

They drove down to Washington and dropped Malcolm at the Capitol Hilton. He went to bed feeling lonely and lay for a while staring at the dark ceiling. Hal and Sally headed east to Hal's apartment.

Sally took a look around. She saw the pile of unfolded laundry in one corner and the dirty cereal bowl on the counter. Her eyes rolled over the battered IKEA furnishings. But with great self-control she turned to Hal and merely said, "Tell me about some of the Armenian leaders on the wall."

CHAPTER EIGHTEEN

Malcolm screamed at two a.m. as a scimitar blade cut into his neck. He awoke and realized it was only a nightmare but could not wipe from his mind the image of Phoebe's severed head. He finally fell into a fitful sleep, only to be awakened by hard rapping on his door.

"Room service breakfast, sir," the young woman called through the door.

Malcolm no longer opened doors unconcernedly. "I didn't order one. Go away."

"Dr. Edwards, it's Barbara. I no longer work here, but I brought you some Krispy Kreme doughnuts."

He flung open the door and saw the Georgetown student, this time wearing a T-shirt and shorts. "It's a great pleasure to see you, but how did you know I was here?"

"I'm starting my dissertation now, and I want you to be on my committee, so I called your office to find out when you were coming again." She put her arm around his waist and smiled. "You're in your boxers again."

"Barbara, I've been thinking about my life."

"I saw on the news a story about the terrible experience you had in Turkey. I wouldn't mind helping you to forget it for a while."

Malcolm hesitated and then explained that the terrorist leader used against him the American way of consensual sex, and he was thinking . . .

"What's wrong with giving each other what we like?"

"Well, I decided not to sleep with students."

"I'm not a Columbia student." She pressed up against him, and Malcolm's resolution weakened. "You'd just be the outside dissertation committee member, not the chairman."

"I have a foundation board meeting at noon."

"We have all morning."

———

Hal and Sally slept late that morning. When Sally woke up on top of the thin mattress on the floor, she imagined for a moment that she was back in Antakya. Then she looked out the bedroom door at the wall of Armenian portraits and smiled. *He's strange,* she thought as she turned on the shower, *and he has a wounded heart; yet when the spine is strong, everything else can be aligned.*

Hal woke up in his boxers on the couch and stared at the ceiling. The sound of the shower came through the thin walls. It was just kissing last night, but he could remember every touch of her lips and even more than that, her warm presence. Could this be love—and if not yet, was it getting close? He paced the floor and then stopped to watch Sally as she came out of the bathroom with a blue towel wrapped around her.

"Hi," she said shyly.

"Good morning," he responded, moving towards her. "Wouldn't it be easy to drop that towel?"

"It would be."

"Everybody else is doing it."

"Almost everybody."

"We're plenty old enough."

"Uh-huh."

"But not too old."

Sally smiled. "Not yet."

"So, why not . . .?"

"You know."

Hal stopped, his hands on her bare shoulders. "You're right, I do know. But why?"

"I'm not sure, but I know that too. I'll get dressed."

———

Just before noon Hal and Sally walked up to the door of the Mongolian Barbecue in Chinatown, smelling the pungent food as they entered under a big neon sign to meet Hal's mysterious friend. "You'll be surprised," was all Hal said, and Sally was when she saw Kemal.

He shook hands with Sally and hugged Hal. "I've been reassigned from the directorship to a position in personnel. I know little about that, so my new superiors sent me here to a training conference in American methods. But I never miss a chance to eat at a Mongolian Barbecue wherever I am. Meats, seafood, vegetables, sauces—and all you can eat."

Hal appreciated Kemal's desire to look on the bright side. He asked, "How bad was it for you in Ankara?"

Kemal's face fell. "It will take years for me to regain what I've lost unless I can do something spectacular."

"Any news on tracking down Suleyman?"

"That's out of my hands. Our army has taken over." Kemal collected lamb, pork, and chicken, and brought it to a chef for stir-frying on an enormous metal plate. "Did you know that Marco Polo wrote about Mongolian soldiers cooking on upturned shields?"

"Will the army find him?"

Kemal stared at his food. "In the police force we tell a story about soldiers who guarded a bench for years. When a new commander came on, he wanted to know what was so important about the bench that it needed round-the-clock guarding. He discovered that many years earlier a commander had posted a guard to keep people from sitting on wet paint. It became part of the routine."

Hal explained his plan. "Since the army is not agile enough for that type of operation, it will only work if you and your policemen are there to catch Suleyman."

Kemal listened intently and then outlined two major problems. First, he no longer had authority over vast numbers of police, so he could provide for security only four policemen who were personally loyal to him. Second, the plan—even under optimum conditions—was too dangerous: "Operations like this can easily go wrong. You could fall into the hands of terrorists again. It is foolhardy."

"I'm a fool. Do you have another idea?"

"Turkey does not tolerate fools," Kemal said. "Ours is a hard country where, for centuries, mistakes have meant death. Even prudent decisions have often meant death. And as terrible as your experience was, it could have been worse. Suleyman dripped burning nylon on the naked body of at least one of his victims. I believe another was buried alive. How's your food, Sally?"

"Excellent. And the luncheon conversation is wonderful also. I hope you'll say no to this crazy plan."

Before Kemal could answer, Hal asked, "Wouldn't you like your own shot at Suleyman?"

Kemal went back for seconds. He returned and sat down heavily. Silence. Hal counted . . . 1, 2, 3, 4, 5.

Kemal spoke: "I could redeem my career, but there's something much bigger. You are not the only one who has a personal reason to bring Suleyman to justice."

They walked a few blocks to the National Portrait Gallery, Hal's favorite Washington museum. In front of Andrew Jackson's portrait, Kemal asked about Malcolm and mused about Hal's plan. "The bait has to be ample enough to attract the fish. Hal, you might not be a big enough mouthful. You say that Malcolm despises Suleyman for killing his aunt, and Suleyman thinks

Malcolm isn't coming through. Do you think Malcolm would be willing to come? And is he trustworthy?"

Hal pondered the questions. "Yes, I suspect he'd come, but it's hard for me to judge his reliability. All I know is that I want to trust him, and he is good bait."

Sally broke in. "I don't want to seem vain, but I'm the best bait of all. Maybe I should go."

"Absolutely not," Hal and Kemal said simultaneously.

"Good. I don't want to go anyway."

Kemal returned to his conference, and Sally drove Hal north to Baltimore and dropped him off there so he could continue his research for the magazine article. "Hal, these last two days have been a lifesaver. Thank you."

He gave the sleeping pills back to Sally. "I need to work tomorrow, but I'll come by the next day."

"I'm OK now," she said. "You're giving me a lot to think about, but I'm OK.

Malcolm took the Metroliner back to New York after the Edwards Foundation meeting. One minor problem: He had turned off his cell phone when the meeting began and must have left it in Washington. But even that was good because he could go through the evening undisturbed and then sleep the sleep of the just in his Morningside Heights home, amid his new Turkish carpets.

Lying in bed, he made firm resolutions. He would become a disciplined, radical fighter for justice worldwide. He would refrain from any more sex with Columbia students. And things were already looking up: the students who threatened him hadn't gone public, so he could retain his position and reputation.

He walked to his office at the Center for New Values at Columbia. Carol, the secretary and former sexual partner who had turned against him, gave him the first smile she had offered in months. "A lot of calls already this morning," she said. "You'll want to look at page 11 of the *New York Times*, which I've put on your desk."

Malcolm dropped his briefcase next to the well-used leather couch in his office and glanced at the newspaper. Then he fixed his eyes on the page 11 headline: "NOTED COLUMBIA PROFESSOR CHARGED WITH SEXUAL HARASSMENT."

He groaned and read: "Ten current and recent students have testified that he offered them 'A' grades in return for sexual favors. Detailed logs and tapes of telephone calls kept by the professor's secretary supplement the students' testimony. Mr. Edwards, who recently returned from a harrowing experience in Turkey, did not return calls requesting his comment."

He was about to yell at Carol, but his phone buzzed. "Provost Brewster is here to see you," she crooned. *Good*, Malcolm thought, *a friend: Maybe he has a way to save me.*

Dispensing with small talk and shaking his jowls, Brewster said, "This looks bad. Both feminists and conservatives are calling for your head. These details in the *Times* are devastating. Ten, Malcolm, ten: we could have handled one or even four, but ten! Do you have any way to save yourself?"

"How about, 'I don't sleep with Columbia students any more'?"

"Really? If this was the past but you've been clean for awhile we could make a case that you've, uh, finally grown up. When did this behavior stop?"

Malcolm arose and stared at the portrait of John F. Kennedy over his desk. "When I went to Turkey."

"And you've just come back. Almost no time spent on campus without indulging yourself? That won't cut it."

Both men were silent. Then Brewster shook his jowls again and suggested that the best chance to keep the matter one for internal disciplinary hearings and not the courts was for

Malcolm to take a leave of absence without pay for this next academic year: "Maybe it will die down. I hope you've banked the money from that best seller of yours."

"Does it help if I say, 'I'm sorry?'"

"Times have changed. Perhaps a generation ago you could have gotten away with it. But you've hurt Columbia. You should have been more discrete."

"Do I have a choice? What if I stay and fight?"

"The administration will have no choice but to get rid of you permanently. Ten, man, ten! You won't have much support."

Malcolm decided to answer only one of his phone messages, the one from Hal: "Kemal has approved my plan to lure out Suleyman but wants me to double-bait the hook." He explained further.

Malcolm leaned back in his ergonomic chair. "You wouldn't expect me to make a hasty decision, would you?"

"Doesn't matter what I expect. What will you do? Time to choose."

Malcolm paused, then said, "I'm not worried. The police can protect me. Or if not, I have money. I can afford to hire a security person here. I can hire one for Sally, too."

"You think that if Suleyman wants to get you or Sally, a guard in New York or Delaware will stop him? Do you want to shudder every time you walk down Broadway? Do you want to wonder every time you turn on the ignition, whether your car will explode? If you're on defense, you have to be on your guard 100 percent of the time. Suleyman's agent only has to be there the one time you let it down."

Malcolm swiveled in the chair. "He can't persist month after month. He'll get tired and move on to other opportunities."

"You think so? Remember what he told us about Algeria and how month after month the terrorists waited? You can either fight him or appease him; nothing in between will work for you."

Malcolm swiveled some more. "Those are my only choices?"

"Yes. E-mail Suleyman that he'll be your daddy, or stand up and fight him."

"I'll call you in a couple of hours."

As Malcolm left his office, saying he'd pick up files later, he congratulated Carol on having her revenge: "You were devious, but I can admire that." He walked and walked, up Broadway to Washington Heights and beyond, finally ending up at The Cloisters, the reconstruction of medieval monasticism at the northern tip of Manhattan. He stood before paintings of the crucifixion and shuddered.

"Fight him or appease him." Those words rang in his head. He looked out over the Hudson River and started walking back. Near the end of his hike, he called Hal: "I'm going with you." Then he returned home and went through his e-mail.

———•———

As Hal was finishing his Baltimore interviewing, he called Sally. "The plan's developing," he blurted out, without even asking how she was doing. "Malcolm's coming with me. It looks like Phoebe's dream of the two of us working together will be realized. I'll talk with Kemal and see how quickly we can set it up. Then I'll come to see you tomorrow."

Sally was silent on the other end. Then she said, "I'm thinking," and was silent some more.

Hal waited.

"I've decided you're right," she said slowly. "Shooting does have a function. You're right to go after Suleyman. But I've also realized that I need you. I won't sit home and have nightmares. I don't want my heart in my throat each time this phone rings, thinking it might be bad news about you. I know now what I have to do. It's the best way under the circumstances. Bye."

"Sally?" She had ended the call. He called again. No answer. He called the regular number for Phoebe's estate. No answer. *She seemed so happy yesterday,* he thought. *But what if I misjudged her?*

Hal suddenly felt both stupid and afraid. He ran out to the street and hailed a taxi again. "Greenville, Delaware, northwest of Wilmington."

"OK, bud, but that's sixty-five miles or so. It will cost you a wad."

"I know, I know. Money's no object. Just step on it."

He called four times on the way: no answer. At the estate gate he yelled on the intercom. No answer. He climbed the fence and banged on the front door. Still no answer. He opened it and almost ran into the startled housekeeper. "Do you know where Sally went?"

"What's the rush?" the elderly woman asked. "I was dozing, but so much ringing, so many loud noises. Let me think: oh yes, Mrs. du Pont kept a pistol in her bedroom in case of intruders. I saw Sally heading out back with it. Don't be alarmed: Mr. du Pont built a shooting range out there, and . . ."

But Hal didn't listen to any more. He ran through the hall and dining room and then yanked open the French doors leading out to the oak trees on the immense acreage in back. At that moment, he heard a shot.

"Sally!" he yelled. No answer.

"Sally!"

She walked out of the trees in a yellow sundress, gun by her side.

Hal ran to her, put his arms around her, and kissed her.

She laughed the Sally laugh he knew well from Turkey. "I'm so glad to see you," she said, eyes sparkling. "But why did you rush over here?"

Hal hesitated. "When you dropped the call, I thought that you might . . ."

"Might . . ." Sally prompted.

"And then when the housekeeper said you had a gun . . ."

"You thought I might shoot myself?" Sally laughed again. "Oh Hal, I shouldn't have been so sudden on the phone. I'm so sorry. That's the second time you've hurried here. That's so romantic. Hey, I better put this gun down." She did. Then she hugged him.

He looked at her. "You said you had decided something. And why were you in such a hurry to get off the phone?"

"I had to see whether I could shoot," Sally said. "A boyfriend took me to a shooting range years ago, and I didn't do well, but I've been practicing just now. I'm going back to Turkey with you and Malcolm. Together we can beat Suleyman."

"Whoa! There's no 'we' here. You're not bait. You can't go. I won't let you."

"Whoa you! Remember Suleyman's line about Americans always saying, 'I won't' or 'You can't'? Why not?"

"Because I love you and . . ."

"What did you say?" Sally stood with her hands on her hips, staring at Hal. The wind tugged at her hair, blowing a strand across her face. Hal reached out a tentative hand and brushed it back.

"I said, 'I love you,' and I want to protect you."

Sally's lip began to tremble, and tears flowed freely down her cheeks.

"Did I say something wrong?" Hal asked.

"Shh!" Sally reached out a finger and touched his lips. Then she kissed him.

Later they walked around Phoebe's rose garden, enjoying the old-fashioned roses she had gathered from her travels.

"I *am* going with you," Sally said. When Hal protested, Sally shook her head. "You don't understand how bad it was before you came the other day. I was scared to be alone. I kept seeing Phoebe's head."

Sally stopped and brushed the air as though sweeping away the memories. "But when you came, I felt better. You cared for me when I was ugly. And now you're giving me a chance to do something instead of just waiting like a lamb for slaughter." She paused. "Do you understand?"

He was silent.

"If you want to protect me, you have to say OK. If I'm here, Suleyman's men could get me. If they don't, maybe I'll get myself. I know what I'm getting into, but I also know what I'm getting out of. Besides," she smiled, "it felt good trying to hit those trees, pretending they were Suleyman."

Hal nodded, but his penetrating eyes were full of pain. "If anything happens to you because of my harebrained scheme."

She stopped him with another kiss.

"OK," Hal said finally. "I'll call Kemal." He got him immediately and said that Malcolm had decided to go. "Problem is, Sally wants to come too." He went to the speakerphone so Sally could hear.

Kemal thought for a moment. "What I'll say might surprise you or an imam."

"Go for it."

"I'm not an orthodox Muslim. If Sally wants to do it, she should, in the interests of the mission. She is the best bait we could dangle in front of Suleyman. He will not only be attracted to her but distracted about our objectives."

Sally picked up the gun and began pointing it at imagined assailants. Hal, watching her, momentarily dropped out of the conversation.

"Hal?"

"Yes, . . . how will Suleyman be distracted? He'll figure out what we're trying to do."

"Yes and no. In one sense, of course: He could not think that you are coming to Turkey just as tourists. But keep in mind our stereotype of Americans: that you are people with no memories."

"Capable of forgetting a beheading?"

"Able to put it out of your mind to pursue your own selfish pleasure. Suleyman and his followers will scout you as they did before. If you seem playful, like children, they may think you are childish enough to feel secure because I am with you. If they see you as weak, they may not see the need to bring out all their own strength."

Kemal said he would need some time to set up police protection: "This will not be an official governmental activity, but my superiors will look the other way if I do this, and then claim credit if we succeed. Be in Ankara on August 1."

"Thanks, Kemal," Sally said. "I'll use that time to practice shooting."

"Sally, you're not coming here to shoot. My policemen will do the shooting."

"I'll be backup, Kemal. Does anything go as planned?"

Kemal muttered, "American women. Maybe I should become an orthodox Muslim. Hal, she is yours to teach. Good-bye."

Hal looked hard at Sally. "You're mine to teach? I don't think I can teach you anything."

Sally smiled at Hal: "I've seen you shoot."

"I worked on a small newspaper in Texas for a year right out of college. The publisher taught me how, but I'm out of practice."

"Then teach me, please. We'll both feel better if I'm not helpless. Teach me now."

"OK. I can't believe I still remember anything that guy taught me. He knew nothing about journalism, but he did know how to shoot."

Sally teased, "Do you regularly have problems with father figures?"

"Do you want to learn to shoot, or do you want to change my psychology?"

"Both." She looked him in the eyes.

Hal felt wobbly. He concentrated on action. "Let's look at the gun. You have here a .45 automatic. Good. Let's check: empty clip. Good: You need to learn a lot before you start firing."

"Show me."

Hal showed Sally as he talked: "Controlled shooting starts with balance. Feet shoulder-width apart. Legs straight. Head erect and turned toward the shooting arm. Arm needs to be still:

get it that way by having the arm straight, elbow locked, wrist straight, firm grip. Now you try."

Sally's stance was good, but her arm wavered. Hal moved his right arm next to hers, his right shoulder behind hers, and showed her: "If you lower your head toward the arm, your front sight will drop."

"I get it." They were cheek to cheek.

Hal gently turned Sally's cheek and kissed her. And again.

"My," she finally said. "You're good for someone who's out of practice."

He stroked her soft neck. "You bring out the best in me."

"We'd better get back to shooting. How firm a grip should I have?"

"Wrap your fingers firmly around the grip. See what feels comfortable to you. Equal pressure by all the fingers. Squeeze the trigger with a smooth, even pressure. Don't jerk it." Suddenly Hal laughed.

"What? Am I doing something wrong?"

"No. It's just . . . gun imagery and all that."

"Hey," Sally laughed. "Dirty mind."

CHAPTER NINETEEN

Malcolm, Sally, and Hal used July to prepare in different ways.

Malcolm refused all press inquiries and turned down Hal's invitation to another baseball game. He imagined, wherever he went, looks of scorn and pity. He read student affidavits about his conduct: It all appeared so tawdry. He hid and read about Turkey and Islam, and read e-mails from Suleyman that became increasingly insistent.

Sally continued going through Phoebe's papers. In her spare time she took up knitting, using Phoebe's fine number two metal needles to make baby hats that she lined up on the kitchen counter. She wore on her belt Phoebe's small yarn bag and tried to find an emotional midpoint, carrying grief but not staggering under it.

Hal helped. One morning he drove north in his reinvigorated Jetta and bought Sally an old China doll and two pork, cheese, and pickle sandwiches from the Cuban restaurant next to the gym.

"The doll is beautiful," Sally said, "and I want to give you something, although it's not from me: It's from Phoebe. Here's the pocket Bible she read from every night."

Hal drove north every other afternoon and practiced shooting with Sally. He often sat in the drawing room next to a grandfather clock and fiddled with an ornate Turkish chess set as Sally knit. He enjoyed seeing her fingers ply the needles. He gave her a Patty Griffin CD, and she liked to play what she said was the theme song for their return to Turkey:

It's a mad mission, but I got the ambition,
Mad, mad mission, sign me up.

One afternoon when Hal arrived, a surprise visitor awaited him: Pastor David Carrillo. "I came here to thank Sally for saving my life. And Sally told me—don't worry; I'm tight-lipped—that you probably saved the lives of some of my congregation members."

Hal glared at Sally for the first time in a long time, but she smilingly stuck out her tongue till he laughed. "No harm done, I guess. Pastor-parishioner confidentiality, right?"

"Right."

"Pastor," Sally said, "Here's something for you: a book of Christina Rossetti's poems from Phoebe's library. I read it last night and can't get this verse out of my head: 'And all the winds go sighing, for sweet things dying.'"

"That line is lovely. There should be sighs; Jesus wept when his friend died." Carrillo looked over at Hal, who thought, *Oh no, here comes some theology.* "Sally and I have been talking about whether she's spiritually prepared to head back to Turkey. Are you?"

"Sure. I wrote a column at the beginning of the year about Charles Frohman, the American producer who staged *Peter Pan* in 1905. He said, 'Why fear death? It is the most beautiful adventure in life.' He died ten years later when Germans sank the *Lusitania*. I suspect he didn't consider drowning in the Atlantic much of an adventure. I'm prepared like Frohman was prepared."

"That's nice and cynical."

"Me?" Hal wasn't about to talk straight with a clergyman. "No, I like James Earl Jones in *Field of Dreams*. Remember how he smiles broadly when reaching into the cornfield that is the realm of the baseball spirits? Then he walks right in, joyfully entering the afterlife."

"Can you believe that?"

"No. Can you? Would you like to step into the cornfield?"

"I'd rather be a skydiver with a parachute. Back in seminary I heard a sermon about two skydivers, both freefalling at the same speed but with a crucial difference: one had a parachute, one did not. Only the person who knew he could land successfully could dodge panic as the ground approached. I don't fear death because I know it's not a smash-up but a new beginning."

"A beginning of what? Endless hours of playing a harp in the clouds?"

"How did you get that idea? A silly Sunday school class? A cartoon? Please forgive my sharpness, Hal, but the Bible has those who believe in God living on a new earth, enjoying work and adventure, free from frustration and failure."

They talked through the afternoon and dinner.

On other days Hal and Sally swam in Phoebe's pool. Twice more he told her, "I love you," and she smiled but didn't say anything in return. Still, Hal's soul sang each time he drove back to Washington.

He kept finding out more about youth gangs and decided that if—when—he made it back from Turkey he'd write a book about them. He kept hitting the gym every morning, an experience that was the opposite of his relaxation with Sally. A Darryl Worley country song on his I-pod, "Have You Forgotten?" often accompanied him:

I hear people saying we don't need this war.
I say there's some things worth fighting for.
What about our freedom and this piece of ground?
We didn't get to keep 'em by backing down.

On July 25 he was so caught up in his Rockyist zeal that he started bellowing out the chorus. Runners on adjacent treadmills turned around and stared:

Have you forgotten when those towers fell?
We had neighbors still inside
Going through a living hell
And you say we shouldn't worry 'bout Bin Laden
Have you forgotten?

On July 30, grunting and grimacing, he hit double his starting strength on all the machines: chest and shoulder presses, lat pullovers and bicep curls, leg extensions and curls.

"This has been terrific, Phil," he told the manager.

"Great. So you'll sign up for a year?"

"No, I'm heading to Turkey tomorrow evening, and I'm not sure when I can come again. But if—no, when—I make it back, I'll be by."

———— • ————

Although Malcolm was flying to Ankara from New York, Sally and Hal decided to leave together from Dulles. He had a surprise for their last afternoon in the United States: tickets to a weekend matinee performance of *Macbeth* at the intimate Folger Theatre, one block north of the Capitol.

"This is wonderful," Sally whispered during the fourth act as they sat close to the stage, "but don't we need to get to the airport?"

"Soon," Hal said, and watched as Macbeth attacked rival Macduff by having his henchmen murder Macduff's wife and children onstage. Sally worked to keep back her tears, but Hal had to keep from cheering as Macduff, almost undone, listened to the counsel of his ally Malcolm: "Let us make medicines of our great revenge, to cure this deadly grief."

As they left, Malcolm's words reverberated in Hal's ears:

> Be this the whetstone of your sword: let grief
> Convert to anger; blunt not the heart, enrage it.

On the overnight flight to Ankara, Sally slept fitfully with her head on Hal's shoulder. When they arrived in Turkey's capital, government officials feted them. Turkish Prime Minister Tayyip Erdogan said, "These three Americans had a terrible experience, but they still trust the people of Turkey. They still want to learn about the country and see new sites. They are not giving in to terrorism, and neither will we."

Sally, blonde and smiling, was a popular interviewee on Turkish television. "It was horrible," she told Espen Askalad, a journalist with a highly rated interview show on the government station TRT1. "But in America we have an expression: 'When you fall off a horse, get right back on.' If we stayed away, that would be letting the terrorists win. We're not giving in."

Askalad persisted: "You are very brave. But isn't the terrorist leader who held you hostage, Suleyman Hasan, still at large?"

"Yes, he is," Sally said, "and if he is watching this program, I have one message for him: Suleyman, you're not a man at all. You're a weakling who brags about killing an old woman. You'd probably kill your own mother, you poor excuse for a human being. I hope you rot in hell."

Askalad lost his professionalism. "Turkish wow," he said, in awe and laughter. "Now I know the meaning of that song line, 'American woman, stay away from me.' Miss Northaway, I admire your courage. Mr. Hasan, if you are watching this, if I were you, I'd give up now."

Suleyman was watching via satellite dish in the south-central city of Diyarbakir. He fumed as he sat on a plastic chair in a two-room house by the ancient city wall.

He muttered to Trafik, who was smoking an ordinary Camel next to him, "Bad enough I was dumb and never entered her. Now she has to mock me before the whole nation."

"Let it rest, Suleyman," Trafik said. "It's obvious that they are laying a trap for you. We've never gone after hardened targets. We've taken the soft opportunities. If that police director emphasizes protection of those Americans, some other target will be softer."

"Easy for you to move on," Suleyman retorted. "She hasn't dishonored you in every home throughout Turkey. She somehow corrupted Fatima. Maybe she's one of those evil goddesses referred to in the Satanic verses."

When Hal wrote a guest column for *Hurriyet*, a big Turkish daily newspaper, he tried more psychological warfare: "Suleyman thought that by beheading an old woman he would create fear and keep Americans from coming to Turkey. We are here to show him his folly. We relish the stronger ties between Turkey and America that his evil action has unintentionally created."

The next morning Trafik bought with his cigarettes a copy of *Hurriyet* and, as always, turned to the soccer scores first. Suleyman looked quickly through the editorial matter as usual and then stopped as if transfixed: A photo of a grim Hal stared out at him, next to the headline, "The brave American versus the cowardly terrorist."

Suleyman screamed, "Look at this!"

They both read the copy, Trafik with his lips moving. He howled as he read aloud, "'One of our captors, Trafik, dangled a cigarette like a minor character in an American gangster film.' How can he say that?"

Suleyman laughed. "So now you understand that we must destroy these people?"

"Yes. Look, here he calls you 'a weak, pitiful, cornered rat.'"

"I will be sure to kill him. Look, the American is so arrogant: He says they will travel from Ankara to Cappadocia and then to Urfa, Diyarbakir, and Van."

"Amazing," Trafik said. "He lists each place they will visit. Unless he is a fool, he is trying to lure us."

"Lure, certainly, but think of the poetry. While the hunted are hunting the hunter, we plan ahead and hunt the hunted-hunter."

"That's one move ahead too many for me."

"Then I'll put it in a way you can understand," Suleyman said. "We have a way to neutralize whatever security they have. Then we will kill them, all except the woman. She is mine."

As Suleyman and Trafik plotted, Kemal picked up Malcolm, Hal, and Sally in another government-issued Opel and told them a quick way to understand much about Turkish government. "Note that Ankara's three main boulevards—Mustafa Kemal Pasha, Gazi Mustafa Kemal, and Ataturk—are all named for the same person, Mustafa Kemal."

He turned to his passengers and said, "I'm named for him, too, and proud of it. Mustafa Kemal stopped the British and the Australians at Gallipoli in 1915 and founded the Turkish Republic in 1923. He took the name *Ataturk*, which means 'father of the Turks'. Pasha and Gazi are titles."

Kemal parked at the base of a hill west of Ankara. He led them down a broad path to the Ataturk Mausoleum, past towers highlighting Ataturk's goals: independence, freedom, reform, peace, victory. "He's like your George Washington, Thomas Jefferson, and Abraham Lincoln rolled into one."

Helmeted soldiers like those at Buckingham Palace stood without moving a muscle. Kemal pointed to the nearest one and told Sally, "You must go and stand close to him. Each soldier is tested in this way before being given the position, which is a great honor. Let's see if this soldier can still pass the test."

Sally at first declined but then girlishly vamped next to him. The soldier didn't even twitch. But Malcolm did. He thought about how he could have been close to Sally, and he wished for another chance.

Kemal chortled and led them up the steps to a first level, then a second, third, and fourth. They walked toward bronze doors that opened into a vast marble-lined hall.

"Should I wear a head scarf here?" Sally asked.

"To the contrary. This is a shrine to secularism, which Ataturk strongly promoted. A scarf would be blasphemy."

As they waited in line to move slowly past the tomb, Sally said to Kemal, "We know about something hard in your past. I asked Phoebe once, and she said you should be the one to tell us."

"Yes, I should be the one," Kemal replied. He was silent for a time.

Finally, he said, "Late in 2001, I reviewed videotapes our police had seized while raiding a Hezbollah safe house. I couldn't take my eyes off one of the videotapes. It claimed that a thirty-eight-year-old woman named Zeliha was an advocate of secularism and an enemy of Islam. It showed her being tortured."

They shuffled forward. Hal examined the carpet-like ceiling design and the latticework behind the tomb that allowed birds to fly into and out of the mausoleum.

"I interrogated two terrorists we captured. They told us where we could find several corpses, in the frozen ground underneath a house in Konya. The men were buried below one corner of the basement. One woman was buried below a different corner."

They came to the austere tomb. Kemal passed a hand over his face and explained, "The woman's body was so disfigured that she had to be identified by dental records. But finally a positive ID came in, and my worst fears were realized. The dead woman's name was Zeliha Kuris."

Kemal bowed before Ataturk's tomb, turned to Sally, and said, "She was my sister."

They walked toward the exit and saw a tablet on the wall with an English translation of Ataturk's last message to the Turkish armies: "I address the Turkish army whose record of victory started at the down of the history of mankind."

Hal thought, *The record's not so great and the knowledge of how to spell English*—down *instead of* dawn—*isn't terrific either.* He would have blurted that before. Now he held his tongue and was glad he did when he listened to Kemal's expression of faith.

"We all have our duty," he was telling Sally. "When I was young, I memorized Ataturk's speech to the youth in 1927. Here is how the noble speech starts: 'You, the Turkish youth! Your primary duty is to forever protect and defend the Turkish independence and the Turkish republic. This is the mainstay of your existence and of your future.'"

Hal stifled his sardonic tendencies and merely asked, "Do others still say that as enthusiastically as you do?"

"Not all," Kemal said grimly. "But I take personally what Ataturk said: 'Your duty is to redeem Turkish independence and the republic.' I believe that. I want to be a redeemer. I watched the tape of my sister's torture. The chief terrorist stuffed a picture of Ataturk into her mouth."

"Did you ever find that terrorist?" Sally asked.

He gritted his teeth. "Came close but did not capture him."

"Sounds like you desperately want to get him."

"I do. His name is Suleyman Hasan."

Malcolm walked toward a museum that exhibited photographs from Ataturk's life. Hal watched an old man with a cane painfully making his way up the steps of the mausoleum. Twelve steps to the first level. Eleven to the second. "I'll help him," he said.

"No," Kemal replied sharply. "It is a question of honor for him." So they watched: Ten steps to the third level. Nine to the fourth. Then the old man proudly joined the line for the tomb.

As they caught up to Malcolm, Kemal scowled at a young woman in a "Latin Lover" T-shirt and a boy in a Mickey Mouse shirt. "That is not appropriate here," he said. "This also worries me: kids without faith in Ataturk and his vision, kids imitating Americans." He glanced at Hal: "No offense."

"None taken."

They stopped for lunch on the street, buying *gozleme*, griddle-cooked, fresh dough wrapped around cheeses, parsley, red pepper, and other spices. "Not fancy food," Kemal said, "but good."

Hal ran into a record store: "I have an idea for some travel music. I'll be quick."

Malcolm spotted a soft swirl ice cream machine. "Would you like a cone for dessert?" he asked Sally.

"I could never resist that offer." She licked it and asked Malcolm, "Would you like a taste?"

"I thought you would never ask." He kissed her upper lip.

Sally blushed. She wanted to be gentle. "That's not exactly what I had in mind. You know that Hal and I have been spending a lot of time together."

Malcolm's faced shadowed over. "I know, but can't we start out fresh the way we did in Istanbul? I'm sorry about the way I treated you before."

"I know."

"I've changed. This last month I've been living like a monk. I want to do what's right, and I want to do right by you."

"I know."

Malcolm spoke with urgency. "Will you give me another chance?"

Sally put down the flat-bottomed cone. She gestured at Hal, who was walking out of the store examining his purchase. "We've all gone through a lot together, but I love *him*."

Malcolm nodded. He looked so forlorn that Sally hugged him. When Hal saw that, all his old jealousies reared up. He hissed, "My back's turned for one moment . . ."

"Hal, you're an idiot. She loves you." Three Turkish women dressed in Western clothes turned and watched.

"She's never said that." Hal turned toward her. Sally put her hand gently on Hal's shoulder.

"What?" he asked. Two Turkish men also watched.

"It's true," she said. "I love you."

There, on the sidewalk, he kissed her. The Turks applauded.

"Americans," Kemal said with a shrug and a smile. But Malcolm turned away.

———·———

As Kemal drove east in the Opel on a straight, two-lane highway, he explained the security precautions: "A well-trained, well-armed team of four guards in plainclothes, led by my friend Abdul, will trail us by two kilometers, in a plain car. They will change vehicles every day and change clothes as well. My hope is that Suleyman and his accomplices will not notice."

Malcolm said he was certain that Suleyman already had noticed. When Kemal asked why he was sure, Malcolm said, "Suleyman scouted us thoroughly last time."

"True, but his network has been disrupted since you were here last. Let us hope so, anyway. I am trying to walk a fine line between unnecessary risk and showing such a hardened target that he will look elsewhere, despite his desires."

"He could have a suicide bomber blow us up."

"No, that would be inartistic. Besides, he desperately wants Sally."

"I've practiced my shooting," Sally said. "Hal says I'm good."

"He told me," Kemal said gruffly. "But I want to see for myself." He left the highway and drove down a dirt road. No other people or cars were in sight, so he stopped near a clump of bushes and opened a backpack.

"You asked me once what was in here," he told Sally. "Look, communication equipment." He showed them a device and explained that cell phones would not work in the distant places they were visiting. "And here are the weapons." He handed each American a .45 automatic.

"Just like the one I practiced with!" Sally exclaimed.

"Exactly, and now we'll see what you learned. Sally, load in the clip, take off the safety, and hit that tree over there."

Sally complied and knocked chips off the dry wood. Hal shot similarly well. Malcolm displayed poor form and poorer results. Kemal offered to show him how to improve, but Malcolm responded, "No, I don't expect to do any shooting. Your men are well trained."

Kemal was surprised, but he could understand Malcolm's embarrassment. "You're right: We will not need you. Each of my men is worth in a gunfight at least four of Suleyman's recruits. I have these weapons for you just in case, but remember: If you ever have to shoot for survival, it will not feel like a practice session. Your hands will feel clammy, your arms and legs will tremble, your mouths will be dry."

"My mouth is dry now," Malcolm complained. "Anywhere around here to get a beer?"

"Yes, a wonderful place not far away." Kemal drove them to the Mushroom House, where he excitedly said, "You can get anything made of mushrooms. Mushroom soup, mushrooms with cheese, mushroom casserole, mushroom beer. It's great."

Malcolm looked distraught, but Kemal stopped there and, after scouting the terrain and seeing no problems, asked Abdul, the leader of his team, to join them: "I'd like you to meet him."

Over mushroom pudding Abdul showed photos of his four children and his wife pregnant with their fifth. He said he would return to a desk job when this mission was over. He insisted, as an orthodox Muslim, that Suleyman was disgracing Islam by killing the innocent.

Kemal said, "I wanted you to see that you can trust the policemen who will protect you, but you may not want to trust others. One Hezbollah training camp was right next to a jandarma post. The president of Turkey himself conceded that some state security forces had formed links with Hezbollah. So be careful out there. I believe we're safe from everything except treachery."

CHAPTER TWENTY

They woke up early the next morning to visit Hattusa, the ancient Hittite capital that lost its influence three thousand years ago. Stones showed the outlines of the huge temples that once were the center of a mighty empire. Malcolm pointed out where colonnaded courtyards and an audience hall had stood, along with a library that housed thirty thousand cuneiform tablets.

Sally imagined a time when marching feet would have stirred up the dust on which she now stood. "Walker Percy asked, 'Where are the Hittites?' and wondered why such a powerful people disappeared from history while Jews survived. Maybe their gods weren't powerful enough." When she saw a reference to Shupiluliuma, last king of Hattusa, Sally made up a song: "King Shu-pi-lu-lu-ma, last king of Hattusa. Sh . . . sh . . . sh, shuffle off to Hattusa." She danced on the stones.

"Hey, anyone watching us would think we're having fun," Hal laughed.

"We are," Sally smiled. "The sun's rising, and this is a beautifully bittersweet place. Look at these wonderful rock outcroppings. Look at the play of light on those hills. And look at that man in the parking area over there watching us."

Kemal already had noticed and was walking that way. The man ran to his car and sped off.

—————

Kemal drove them into the strangest landscape they had yet seen: the vast plain of Cappadocia, filled with thousands of conical rocky outcrops, some over one hundred feet high. They looked like red, violet, pink, and beige stalagmites exposed to the sun.

"We call them *peri bacalan*, which translates as 'fairy chimneys,'" Kemal said. He explained that volcanoes had blanketed the region with ash that solidified into what's called *tuff*, an easily eroded material overlain in places by a layer of hard, volcanic rock.

"What a strange, beautiful land!" Sally exclaimed. "Lots of those pillars look like they have fezzes or turbans. They peer into the valley like lords of the land surveying their property." She pointed to a herd of sheep and insisted that she was no longer a romantic. "I'm trying to think like you, Hal. Some see sheep, but I see rugs and walking shish kabob."

"But I'm becoming like you, Sally," Hal laughed. "Look at the sheepdog: cute, huh?"

Kemal reported that the police team trailing them had seen nothing unusual, but they should be on guard at the next two stops: Each represented a response to terror centuries ago, and their symbolism might appeal to Suleyman the poet. First up was the underground city at Derinkuyu: Christians hiding from Muslim assaults in medieval times had created it by tunneling through the soft *tuff,* which hardened when exposed to air.

Kemal led them down and down through ten levels of the underground city, noting that there were thirty other cities like it. The two uppermost levels had served for stables and grain storage. Below were bedrooms, dining rooms, kitchen, classroom, wine cellars, wells, cruciform church meeting place, baptistery, and tomb. Ventilation shafts often went down seventy-five yards.

"It's all coming back to me," Hal said. "My granddad must have made his way out of Turkey through Cappadocia. Once he told me a bedtime story about a place where fairies built homes with chimneys and the angels lived among them—until one day creatures that looked like bats flew in front of the sun, and the blue sky turned dark.

"What happened?" Sally asked.

"The angels were ready to welcome the visitors, but they turned out to be bad demons yearning to kill every angel. The angels defended themselves, but granddad said the demons won."

"That's so sad."

"That was my granddad. He told me the demons almost always won. I can see him now: With his cap down almost over his eyes, he'd put a cube of sugar between his teeth and sip his tea through it, just like his father had. I protested: 'But granddad, that's not how it ended, did it?'"

"What did he say?"

"He said the demons rule. He said they can see you with 'the evil eye' and hurt you. I remember shuddering. And then he told me—I guess he wanted to offer some hope to a child—that the angels who survived dug themselves a fantastic underground city where they could hide from the demons."

Kemal showed them half-ton, two-foot-thick round stones that the Christians could roll across passageways to stop the invaders. But he suddenly stopped speaking as the sound of shouting and scuffling came from a passageway above. They raced up and saw a burly man handcuffing a thin young man wearing an Erciyes University shirt.

"He was trailing you, sir, in a very clumsy way," the police sergeant reported. "He could be with Suleyman." The young man cringed when he heard that, and Kemal said, "You see, we've already identified you. Suleyman's previous trainees are dead. Do you want to die?"

When the student did not respond, Kemal said, "Sergeant, he's yours." The sergeant promptly walloped his prisoner in the stomach and, as he bent over in pain, kneed him in the jaw.

"Don't!" Sally said. She rushed to the young man, cradled his head, and looked into his eyes. "What's your name?"

"Zubeyir."

The name spooked Sally. "Kemal, must you do this?"

"If you want to stay alive, yes."

"Could you see again if he'll tell you anything?"

Kemal agreed and told Zubeyir that his new master, Suleyman, had murdered an old American woman and was now out to rape and kill the young woman holding his head. The student looked confused, so Kemal told him that if he remained silent, he would not suffer a martyr's death but would go to prison "until you're such an old man that young women like this one will look at you with pity but never with a flicker of interest in their eyes."

The student spoke: "And if I do tell you?"

"If you provide information that helps us catch Suleyman, you will go free the day he is in jail or dead."

Zubeyir hesitated and then blurted out that he had never met Suleyman. He was dedicated to studying and reading the Quran and knew of Suleyman only as a freedom fighter who follows the Quran.

"Who told you to come here?" Kemal asked. The student was silent.

Kemal glanced at Sally and said, "Your compassion for this student is misplaced, but perhaps he will tell us the whole truth later."

"Now we know that Suleyman really is on our trail," Sally said grimly. She hugged herself. "Oh, I'm cold."

Kemal said, "That's not surprising. The temperature down here stays at 10 Celsius; that's 50 degrees Fahrenheit, not changing much from winter to summer. And you are wearing only a thin shirt."

Sally, noting Kemal's expression of disapproval, replied, "Not that kind of cold. Hal's granddad talked about demons. Now I'm reminded of human ones."

"You should walk out into the sunshine. I'll be up soon."

As soon as the Americans left, Kemal turned back to the prisoner. "Sergeant, hit him again, harder."

Soon the student, gasping on the floor, said, "My imam told me to follow three American spies who are free to move around because of a government conspiracy. He said that if I proved myself, Suleyman's friends from Saudi Arabia would pay my tuition."

"Good," Kemal said. "And who else listens to this imam?" When the student again was slow to answer, he grimly told the sergeant, "Do whatever it takes to extract the information." He then hurried back to the surface and joined the Americans in the sunlight.

Hal was saying, "I think my granddad didn't tell me the whole story. Sure, the demons think they're in charge. They think the angels are afraid of them. But see the gleam from the sun on the pavement here? What if that's the gleam of some angels flying out of the underground city to take a fresh breath while the demons aren't looking?"

Sally laughed. "Hal, you sound as filled with wonder as I used to be. What's gotten into you?"

Hal almost said he was thinking that talk of angels and demons wasn't as foolish as he once thought, but he wasn't ready to say that out loud. So he gave an answer that was also true: "You."

———

For lunch they ate *durum*, a mixture of grilled meat, cheese, and vegetables within thin layers of bread, and watched students walking home, the younger ones all in blue and the teenagers in blazers. "Like prep school," Malcolm commented, but Hal looked closer: "They have blue glass eyes pinned to them."

Kemal laughed. "That's to prevent someone from casting an evil eye on them. It's the original antiterrorism device. Remember that even if some things look the same, Turkey is not America." He herded them into the Opel and headed to nearby Goreme, past a woman driving a donkey cart and wearing a loose cardigan jackets and baggy trousers. She had completely covered her hair and face, leaving only a tiny space for her eyes to peer out.

They drove toward a striated butte ahead. Clouds played over the brown and red soil, making puddles and then oceans of darkness. Kemal looked ahead, wondering what awaited them in the darkness. Sally paid more attention to the purple and gold wildflowers decorating fields where donkeys grazed. "What a wonderful field of sunflowers."

"In Turkey we call them moonflowers," Kemal explained. "Like the moon they depend on the sun for their light. Some used to say that the Turks are moonflowers depending on the mercy of Ataturk."

"I wish you could have heard Phoebe during her last hour. She hoped in the mercy of Jesus."

"I believe in Ataturk. I will be frank with you: I see Christianity as a weak religion mainly suited to women. I cannot see turning the other cheek when evil men like Suleyman torture and kill women."

Malcolm said, "He's not all beast. He's merely motivated by his religious beliefs."

Kemal replied, "I think his religion gives him an excuse to show his malevolence. The whirling dervishes of Konya, where my sister died, tell a story about a Christian and a Muslim who were traveling and reached an inn where the innkeeper gave them some sweet halva. They agreed to go to bed and the next morning compare dreams: Whoever had the best dream should eat the halva."

"Better than killing each other."

"The next morning the Christian told of a magnificent dream in which he had seen Christ and gone with him to heaven. The Muslim said, 'I saw the prophet Muhammad and he said to me, 'The Christian is dreaming about heaven. Get up and eat the halva.' So I did. How could I disobey Muhammad's command?"

"Convenient dreams for both?" Hal asked.

"Yes, but look who ate the halva. You see, Islam gives us permission to take what we want. On the other hand, Christianity has nothing to say about life on earth."

Sally said, "It changed Phoebe's life on earth, and she changed mine."

Kemal was silent until he pulled into a parking area. "Here we are at the caves. I have never been here, but people say they show the second way Christians reacted to the Muslim invasion: There was hiding, and there was . . . well, we'll see."

They climbed a ladder into what looked like a cave in the *tuff* and found themselves in a barrel-vaulted room with every inch of the walls displaying paintings of Christian soldiers on horseback and on foot. They marched with swords held high.

"Hey, I like these green and orangey colors," Hal said.

Sally laughed. "I'd call it seafoam green, pale ochre, and several shades of salmon."

"I'd call it a fighting church," Kemal said. "I had no idea that Christians fought back against the invasion."

Malcolm was primed: "These paintings are from the tenth century. Nicephorus Phocas, who became the Byzantine emperor, took back Antioch and Tarsus from the Muslim armies. It's one of about three hundred churches Christians made by digging into the *tuff.*"

They visited other cave churches and saw paintings of warrior angels, muscular Christs with oversized shoulders and big biceps, and serpent-killing St. Georges.

"Look at the olive green and ochre," Sally marveled. "The paintings are still vivid."

"Look at those swords," Kemal exclaimed. "They were fighters. Warrior saints."

———•———

They drove further south, heading to their hotel for the night, as donkey carts and occasional tractors made the adjacent fields seem peaceful enough. Kemal wanted to talk about the cave paintings: "I read about Jesus in several parts of the Quran when I was young—he's called Isa in there—but he didn't seem to have any power. Those cave paintings make him seem more powerful than Ataturk. You're from a Christian country. Can you tell me more?"

Hal demurred: "I don't attend church." Sally was able to tell him some basics about Christ dying for others. Kemal's only comment was, "Very different from Islam."

They checked in at the Nicephorus, a hotel built right into *tuff* cliffs and featuring barrel-vaulted rooms with unadorned stone walls. Outside the hotel stood a newspaper rack with *Hurriyet* as well as pornography on open display. Far fewer Americans came here than to the coastal towns, so the Americans with a Turkish police director were an object of interest to children who yelled out, "Hallo, hallo!"

"Aren't these kids cute?" Sally asked. "They like so much trying out their English." She sang out, "Hello, hello."

Hal was last into the hotel dining room, so Sally did not hear when one of the children said: "Die, American." Hal wheeled, and they all ran away.

Awaiting their lamb shish kabob, they all dipped their bread in a peppery olive oil as Kemal explained how he had grown up looking to the United States as Turkey's ally against an aggressive Soviet Union. "*Little House on the Prairie* was a popular television show here, and Turks praised America as a place where families prayed before dinner. Now America is better known for pornography."

"But I saw the porn on the newspaper rack just outside," Hal said. "That's a Turkish production. No one is forcing Turks to make or buy it."

Kemal nodded. "Yes, we complain about cultural aggression by the US, but we blame you for what we ourselves do."

As they went to their rooms, Kemal told them that his policemen were nearby, but he didn't expect any difficulties that night. He told them to bolt their doors because the locks themselves could be opened with any skeleton key. Sally said she didn't want to be alone, so Hal went into her room. She went into the bathroom while he turned on the television and was surprised to see *High Noon* dubbed into Turkish.

It all came back to Hal as he watched Gary Cooper talking with Kemal gutturals: The Miller gang coming to town on Cooper's wedding day to shoot him and shoot up the town as well. The citizens saying it wasn't their job to fight. The pastor saying right and wrong were clear, but he didn't want people to get killed. The just-married hero, faced with bad choices but knowing he has to act.

Sally came out of the bathroom carrying a small piece of paper. "Did you ever see *High Noon*?" Hal asked. "It's great." She shook her head, sat on the bed, and picked up her knitting needles as he quickly turned back to the movie. But he soon heard a sound that stabbed him. Sally was quietly crying. He moved to her side.

Wordlessly, Sally handed him a note: "Suleyman says, take off your clothes. Your breasts—smooth, firm, and insolent—will fill my hands. Do not forget. I will take you at my house."

"I wish you would go back to the US," Hal said, hugging her and rubbing her back.

Sally bit her upper lip. "I can't. We're bait." They watched some more as Grace Kelley, playing the sheriff's wife, prepared to leave town, but then came back to help her husband defeat the gang.

"Odds were four to one against him, but he won with her help," Hal said. "That's Hollywood, but our odds are a lot better." He turned off the television.

"I feel better now, but"—she smiled and quoted *High Noon's* theme song—"do not forsake me, oh my darling."

Hal looked at her yearningly: "You know what else they say in Hollywood? Wait, let me say it with full melodramatic emphasis: 'One last kiss before we die.'"

"More than one," she murmured.

They kissed. After a while, Hal said, "I respect what you've decided about sex, but how about an exception before going into battle?"

"Nice try, but no." She stroked Hal's neck. "I love you so much. Am I weird?"

"Well, except for this urge to tell the story of Armenian suffering, I hardly feel Armenian at all. I'm the product of American culture, so I should say, 'Yes, you're weird, let's do what everyone else does.'"

"But you're not saying that."

"No. I guess I'm Armenian, which means that when you get married you should trust that the other person will be faithful to you, and the best way to build that trust is to show before marriage that you take marriage seriously."

Sally smiled. "And you take it seriously too."

"Enough to ask you this: Will you marry me?"

Her lip quivered, and her eyes teared up. She was silent for a time and then replied, "My heart says yes, but my head says no."

Hal was disappointed. "You mean we haven't known each other long enough?"

"I mean I remember what you said in Antakya: that you've always backed away when it was time to commit. Now we're heading into danger and might say things we wouldn't say under normal conditions. I want to make sure the commitment is real, and I want to do things Armenian style: you meet my parents, I meet your mom, and you ask me again, at the right time and in the right place."

Hal couldn't keep from smiling. "Sally, you sound as filled with logical analysis as I used to be. What's gotten into you?"

"You," she replied.

CHAPTER TWENTY-ONE

The next day began with a big Turkish breakfast: hard-boiled eggs, cucumbers, tomatoes, bread, cheese, and olives. Kemal examined the note from Suleyman. "'I will take you at my house.' I don't know which city he means. Urfa? Diyarbakir? Van? I'm in contact with my men and also with jandarma in all three cities. They'll all be on alert as we come close."

Kemal questioned the hotel staff, but none admitted placing the note or seeing a stranger hanging around. So on they traveled, southeast across a flat, desolate plain toward Urfa, with the sun shining brightly.

"Couldn't Suleyman attack us on the road?" Malcolm asked.

"No, that wasn't the Algerian method, and it's not his—not theatrical enough. But if he does come at us while we are in this vehicle . . ." He flipped a switch, and the Opel quickly jumped to over one hundred miles per hour. "It's not a James Bond car, but it will do."

Hal decided it was time to give Kemal the joke gift he had bought for him in Ankara. "I picked up for you the top musical work of American culture," he said.

"Gershwin?" Malcolm asked. "John Cage?"

"No, 'Eye of the Tiger' from *Rocky III*." He popped it into the CD player, and they cruised down the highway listening to the pounding rhythm and words:

> Face to face, out in the heat,
> Hangin' tough, stayin' hungry,
> They stack the odds 'til we take to the street,
> For we kill with the skill to survive.

Hal started to say apologetically, "The song has become a cliché." But Kemal interrupted enthusiastically: "That song is perfect. You Americans have it right. Even a professor like Malcolm is willing to risk his life. What a strange and awesome people you are."

Kemal became even more excited as he listened to more. "Let's open the windows and let all of Turkey hear." As they headed through the barren terrain, he bellowed, with Hal and Sally joining in:

> It's the eye of the tiger, it's the thrill of the fight,
> Risin' up to the challenge of our rival.
> And the last known survivor stalks his prey in the
> night
> And he's watchin' us all in the eye—of the tiger.

———

As they entered Urfa, more minarets were visible. When they left the car, men in robes and turbans, and women cloaked in black *charshafs,* looked suspiciously at the American interlopers. They passed Halilurrahman Mosque, constructed on the site of a Christian church. The sign proclaimed that the church had turned into a mosque.

"Not exactly," Hal said. "Muslims tore down the church. Thousands of Armenians used to live here—the city was called

Edessa—but right after Christmas one year, Turkish troops broke down the iron door of the cathedral, shot or bayoneted everyone on the main floor, blocked up the staircases leading to the gallery, and set the church on fire. A mob ripped up Bibles and hymnbooks. Then came beheadings with axes."

They walked to the Mevlid-I-halil Mosque that advertised itself as the site where Abraham was born four thousand years ago. Malcolm said, "Abraham probably came from Ur near the Persian Gulf, but you can't blame Urfa for wanting a tourist attraction." They walked to the city's tourist center and its two rectangular pools of water filled with carp, as Kemal watched warily.

"I don't like this," he said. "Too many hostile looks. Let's go quickly."

"Just one minute," Malcolm said. "I want to see these pools. The Muslim story is that Abraham was destroying pagan idols, and Nimrod, the Assyrian king, became angry, so he threw Abraham into a fire, but Allah turned fire to water and coals to carp. Look how many there are."

"Let's move," Kemal said again, but Malcolm was staring at the pool and Hal was buying from a small boy a saucer of corn, wheat, and dried fish to feed the carp. They were so used to being fed that when a person approached they went upright and opened their mouths.

Despite Kemal's concern, the threatening message of the evening before seemed distant, and Sally was once again cheerful. "Be careful," she told Hal as he reached into his pocket for a bill. "If you drop your wallet in there, all the fish will go for it and we'll have carp-to-carp walleting." Hal smiled and created a feeding frenzy.

Malcolm leaned over to listen to a small boy carrying a bathroom scale and asking the same question he had first heard in Istanbul: "Want to get weighed?"

"More than ever," he responded. "Here's . . ."

"Get down," Kemal yelled, pointing at a rifle extending from a third-floor window of the apartment building across the street. He pushed Sally behind a stone bench.

Malcolm and Hal also took cover, and a moment later a bullet slammed into the dirt a few feet away.

Kemal barked into his phone to the police team, "Get here NOW!" He yearned to run to the building but decided he had to stay with the Americans. By the time his men arrived, it was too late to go after the shooter.

Abdul asked, "One shot into the dirt—that's it? That's crazy."

"Could be," Kemal said. "But maybe it was a probe by Suleyman, trying to find out whether it's just me providing security for the Americans or others as well. Now he knows. I don't think we'll have more problems today, but stay with us in case I'm wrong."

They bought sesame-seed *simit* bread rings from a man balancing a tray on his head, then drove further southeast to four-thousand-year-old Harran, a once mighty city identified in the Bible as one of Abraham's homes. Armies fought over it repeatedly before the Mongols finally destroyed it in AD 1260.

Stepping outside the car into desert heat, they saw what is now a desolate patch of land. Looking over the old Roman wall, Malcolm described how Crassus, on that spot in 53 BC led an army of forty-four thousand to a disastrous battle against the Parthian army. The Parthians beheaded him and killed or captured most of his soldiers.

Malcolm led them up a hill that was actually a tell, with level after level of ancient Harran beneath, one new town built on the ruins of the last. He said, "Harran had a period of harmony in the sixth century when Byzantium and Persia signed a Treaty of Endless Peace. It lasted seven years."

"We're walking on history," Sally said softly.

"But also hysteria," Hal responded from the top of the tell, which allowed a 360-degree view of invasion. "You can imagine the utter panic each time a new group of raiders came. You could see them coming up the slope, and all you could do was wait."

"None of you will panic when Suleyman attacks one of these days," Kemal said, scanning the area below. He pointed: "See our team's vehicle? That's a reassuring sight."

At the only food shop in the now-tiny town, they bought grilled *misir*, corn on the cob, and ate outside a house made out of bricks from ancient ruins. Many of the houses were shaped like beehives. The inhabitants sat, swatted flies, and stared at the Americans.

They bedded down cautiously at the Otel Gunbay, which had waterless rooms for seven dollars a night. Abdul guarded their doors and even sang for them the Turkish lullaby that he sang every evening at home for his children.

The night passed without incident but not without discussion. Malcolm took Hal and Sally aside and asked, "Are you sure that Kemal is trustworthy? We know that Hezbollah has infiltrated the jandarma. Maybe Kemal generated that note from Suleyman and is working with him."

Sally and Hal were surprised by that thought. They both objected, arguing that Kemal had always been honest and had hunted the terrorists in Antakya.

"But don't you think it suspicious that Suleyman escaped so easily? And this afternoon, how come the terrorists didn't shoot Kemal? If he's not working with them, wouldn't they have wanted him out of the way?"

Hal objected, saying it was a chess match: "We haven't wanted to spook the terrorists, but now it's clear that they don't want to spook us either by killing Kemal before they have us trapped."

Malcolm concurred: "Makes sense, but let's watch him closely."

The next morning they spread honey and fresh cream on large pieces of flatbread. As Kemal drove on to Diyarbakir, he described the past of the city now known for its watermelons: "Fought over by Romans, Parthians, and Persians."

Sally asked, "Turkey has so much history. What do you emphasize in school?"

Kemal laughed. "I remember the grotesque. One Roman officer described a defeat the Persians inflicted on his force near here: He survived by not moving for hours, wedged against a soldier whose head was split open like a ripe melon."

"Ugh."

"The Persians were angry in AD 503 that the city surrendered to them only after a three-month siege, so they crowded the men into the amphitheatre and kept them there for weeks until they died of hunger. They fed the women so they would be available for repeated rape. In all, they probably killed eighty thousand residents."

As they drove on, Kemal speculated about how Suleyman's knowledge that a squad of police was always close to his intended victims would affect his action. "He might back off entirely, but I doubt it. He wants revenge. At least you know that he does not merely want to kill you. He could have gotten at least one of you yesterday."

"Is that supposed to be good news?" Sally asked.

"It means that we can bring my squad closer to us," Kemal said. "No need to pretend anymore. We can walk through the old city with protection right behind us."

They did that starting at the Diyarbakir wall, three miles of huge blocks of black basalt, thirty-nine feet high. They walked briskly through the bazaar, past jostling shoppers speaking Turkish, Arabic, and Kurdish, skirting donkeys and pushcarts weighed down by merchandise.

They walked past booths selling watermelons and others piled up with spices and nuts, taking in the smells of cinnamon and rosemary. Then they entered the realm of hemorrhoid ointments and erotic aids, followed by carts ominously filled with knives, but the seller shouted out only, "Yes, yes, good cheap here."

As they left the bazaar, Kemal's eyes scanned left and right, but he needed little peripheral vision because the streets had a width designed for pack animals, not cars and trucks. Three-story homes overhung the narrow streets so that rooftops on opposite sides almost touched each other. They were stopped by a disturbance in front of them. A fire truck was pumping water at heavy, acrid smoke coming from the second-floor window of a columned building.

Kemal wondered whether Suleyman was behind this, but after asking onlookers, he smiled and explained: "Some people converted from Islam to Christianity and opened an unmarked church here. One Muslim ran in with a butcher knife a couple of hours ago, but the Christians locked him in their storeroom. He won't give up, and he can't get away, so he's burning Bibles and cassette tapes."

The onlooker spoke again, and Kemal translated. "His name is Mehmet, and he is a former Muslim who now belongs to Diyarbakir Evangelical Church. He says he is excited to meet American Christians."

Hal hemmed and then hawed. "Yes, we're from America, but . . ." His voice trailed off.

Mehmet recovered to say, "I know a little English. God bless you." He turned to watch the fire hose shoot more water.

Kemal asked in Turkish, "I'm curious about one thing: Why would you become a Christian here, of all places?"

Mehmet at first seemed suspicious of a policeman's question, but he saw that the interest appeared sincere. He said in Turkish, "I was also curious about one thing—actually, one person, Isa. I heard that the Christians wrote a lot about Isa in the *Injil*, the Gospels, and they called him Jesus. So I asked the imam if I could get a copy to read for myself. He became angry."

The fire was going out. Mixed cheers and boos went up from the crowd as the man who had run in with the butcher knife was brought out by the police. Kemal asked, "Did you ever get the *Injil*?"

"I took a business trip to Istanbul and met an American Christian. He got one for me. Now that Turkey wants to join the European Union, it is much easier. I even give copies to visitors. Would you like one?"

"Would I? Why would I want one?"

"Oh, excuse me. It was good to meet you."

"All right, you may give me one." Kemal slipped it into his pocket.

After Kemal led the Americans back through old Diyarbakir without incident, he drove them out of the city past a statue with a watermelon on top. His squad car followed.

The road southeast to Mardin was bare macadam, and Mardin itself seemed like the end of the world: a high-up town with houses around an ancient fortress, looking south into the Mesopotamia plain and Syria.

They stopped at the medieval Deur-ul Zaferan Monastery because Phoebe had spoken highly of the priest in charge, Metropolitan Ozmen. Dressed in his long black robe, he greeted them and asked their names as they walked in past pomegranate bushes with bright red flowers, pistachio trees with dark green leaves, and stone walls that had stood for eight centuries.

Sitting next to a tomb in his office, Ozmen offered condolences regarding Phoebe, then said, "Now I know your names, but what are your callings?"

They answered: "Professor." "Journalist." "Police director." "Aide-de-camp."

Ozmen peered at Sally, amused by her self-description, but then turned to Kemal and asked why they needed police protection.

"They are Americans."

"I see." Ozmen stared at Malcolm and Hal: "You are coming back to Turkey soon after being kidnapped. I did not ask for your occupation. I asked for your calling. Do you not have some other purpose in being here?"

Hal said, "We have other interests."

"Yes, I suspect you do."

"Phoebe is on our minds. Those who killed her have not been caught."

"And you think you can do justice when the security forces have not?"

"Do you ever go fishing?"

"I have done that. You're saying that you are the bait."

"That's right."

"Mr. Bogikian, you have a good heart."

"I never thought so."

"You do, but are you prepared to be eaten?"

Sally broke in. "I don't feel it will come to that."

"Feelings, yes," Ozmen replied. "But I did not ask about feelings. I asked about preparation. Miss Northaway, do you go by feelings or by what you know in your brain is the right thing to do?"

"I don't know."

"Use your brain. It is a good one. Here, let me show you something."

He stood up by the tomb. "This monastery has had a metropolitan in charge of it for centuries. The bones of every metropolitan are in this tomb. When one metropolitan dies, the tomb is opened and his body is deposited on top of the remnants of the previous one. Each is literally sleeping with the fathers."

Malcolm asked, "Don't you have anxiety about dying here in the middle of nowhere?"

"This monastery has seen grander days," the metropolitan continued. "Now we have only two priests. For twenty years no metropolitan was here. I was comfortable serving at an Orthodox church in New York. My heart told me to stay."

"Then why are you here?"

"Because in my head I know what's right. I am an instrument of God's will, and in his mind everywhere is somewhere. I will die here. I am prepared to be eaten. Are you?"

Malcolm was silent but increasingly impatient through the discussion that followed. He finally said, "I don't want to be rude, but I once tacked up on my bulletin board a line from Woody Allen: 'It's not that I'm afraid to die. I just don't want to be there when it happens.'"

Ozmen, instead of snapping back, gave a big hearty laugh that made his eyes crinkle so that they almost disappeared. "I've lost touch—is he still making movies? I enjoyed his humor: 'I do not believe in an afterlife, although I am bringing a change of underwear.'"

Kemal said they should eat dinner at their hotel, which he believed to be secure. Hal knocked on Sally's door to walk with her to the rooftop restaurant. She came out with tears in her eyes. In her hand was a piece of paper that she handed to Hal. "It was slipped under my door."

The note had block letters: YOU'RE GETTING CLOSER TO ME, AMERICAN BEAUTY. TOMORROW I WILL TAKE YOU AT MY HOUSE. "He's toying with me, with us. He's obsessed."

Hal responded, "And so am I. If I have to die protecting you, I'll die knowing that's worthwhile." Then he grinned: "Sorry, I'm getting melodramatic. You won't die, and I won't die."

They showed the note to Kemal and Malcolm, who declared, "Have you been looking around the past couple of days? Evil looks, and women with only their eyes showing? Turkey is part Middle Eastern, part European, and we're in the Middle East. Suleyman has home-court advantage. Maybe we should go home."

Hal replied, "I'd like to go home, too, but there's no home until we've destroyed this evil."

"Other evils will come," Malcolm insisted.

"Not this one, though. Not Suleyman. He thinks slaughter is poetry. He won't kill any of us unless he can do it in a way he considers elegant."

Kemal still was chewing on Suleyman's phrase, "take you at my house."

Sally said, "It should be 'take you *to* my house.' Suleyman's English is good."

Hal added, "He wrote that on his first message as well. I thought it was a mistake. But the 'at' seems deliberate."

Kemal again questioned the hotel staff, but no one had seen anyone unfamiliar except for the guests. The message's delivery, like its grammar, remained a mystery.

Not to Malcolm, though. He took Hal aside and argued that Kemal must be a traitor. "I'm surprised that you of all people should trust a Turk."

"I trust you, Malcolm, but you've been foolish in the past. Why shouldn't I trust Kemal, who, in my experience has always been honest?"

CHAPTER TWENTY-TWO

This will be the day," Kemal said solemnly. "We'll see Lake Van and a church there, then Castle Hosap and Castle Van. We're almost at the end of the line."

Hal said, "Makes sense that Suleyman would want to get us in Van because Castle Van was the citadel of what used to be the most important Armenian city in Turkey, a Christian stronghold against Islam. My people in 1895 put up their strongest defense in Van. Maybe six hundred or seven hundred Armenian men defended their section of the city against a Turkish army."

"I thought the Armenians always lost," Sally said, putting her hand on Hal's arm.

"No exception here. After a week the sultan promised that if the fighters agreed to leave Turkey, he would guarantee the lives and safety of all Armenians. The Armenians said yes. They also agreed that Turkish troops could march them to the border. They gave up their weapons."

"Massacre, right?" Sally asked. Hal nodded. "Seems like too beautiful a place for killing," she said as they drove up a rise and could suddenly look out at the sparkling, deep blue Lake Van.

Sally took her knitting needles from the small yarn bag she had around her waist and finished a baby hat just before they stopped at a lake overlook. Kemal called the jandarma in Van. "Suleyman is playing into our hands," he exulted. "His desire for a dramatic, historical backdrop will kill him. The jandarma commander agrees with Hal that Castle Van is the place, and he's prepared."

Sally gazed at Hal: "The water is the color of your eyes."

"Yes, my ancestors called that color Lake Van blue. Lots of Armenians had it. Turks sometimes killed the blue-eyed first. After 1915 the sides of the road around the lake were strewn with corpses."

The day was windy, cloudy, and cooler than it had been since they had climbed out of the plain. They could still see the snow-capped mountains to the northeast, with Noah's Mount Ararat just beyond them. Kemal, believing this would be a day of combat, wore his police director's uniform. Sally wore a light-weight green jacket, and Hal wore one in red that had an inside pocket for his reporter's notebook.

When they stopped at a restaurant for Turkish coffee and *simit* rolls, Sally saw one turquoise and one amber eye watching her from the counter: "That cat is so cute. Are there a lot like her?"

"They're known as Van cats," Hal replied. "They look cute, sure, but the provincial governor here in 1915 used Van cats to claw and bite prisoners."

"Ugh." Sally looked away.

"That kindly governor also had his men pull off fingernails and toenails, tear off flesh with red-hot pincers, and then pour boiled butter into the wounds. Sometimes the jandarmas nailed hands and feet to pieces of wood, imitating the crucifixion. While the sufferer writhed in agony, the governor's men would cry, 'Now let your Christ come help you.'"

As they downed their coffee, they watched a woman feeding the Van cat. Wearing a kerchief, she washed wool by stomping on it in a basin. Kemal said that she had deliberately wrapped her kerchief to leave part of her hair visible: "That's how women in these parts act, observing Muslim rules but still maintaining some independence."

While Sally bought bread, cheese, and drinks for a picnic lunch, Hal was surprised to see Malcolm speaking with a young man who stepped into a white Mitsubishi and drove away. He asked Malcolm about that as they both headed to the restroom: "Do you know someone from around here?"

"No, he was asking for directions, but I couldn't help him."

"Strange that he would ask an American."

"Maybe he thinks we know everything."

Hal washed his hands quickly in the bathroom and then stood back to wait for Malcolm, who went through a more elaborate procedure: Lathering up his hands for a full minute, then washing, then lathering again and washing, until Hal told him, "Hey, we should be going."

As they walked to the car, Hal remembered the Shakespearian line he had planned to mention. "I don't know if you remember *Macbeth* from college, but Sally and I saw it just before we left Washington. In the fourth act Malcolm says, 'Let us make medicines of our great revenge.' I'm ready for this battle. How about you?"

"Of course I'm ready!" They entered the Opel and continued eastward toward Van on the bare, windswept highway. Kemal drove to a lakeside spot from which they could take a motorboat ferry for a mile-and-a-half voyage to a one thousand-year-old church built on an island.

He looked around carefully to see if they were being followed, but all seemed clear: "I don't expect them to do anything on an island where they also could be trapped."

The boat trip was a sweet relief. Hal watched Sally's hair blowing across her face. They disembarked and walked to a domed, pink jewel box, the sandstone Church of the Holy Cross. Reliefs that depicted nature and biblical scenes covered the outside walls of the church.

"Here's the one I like," said Hal, pointing to a grinning David holding his sling, ready to wipe out a lumpish Goliath.

"Here's the one that realistically depicts our situation," Malcolm said, pointing to a carving of Jonah about to be swallowed by a whale.

"It's all lovely," Sally said. Every time she spoke of beauty Hal had a lump in his throat and tightness in his chest, thinking of what might come later in the day.

Kemal put down his backpack on a picnic table set up in a grove of walnut trees. He took out his satellite phone and called his squad captain, who was watching the shoreline and reported that all was calm. Sally said, "Maybe this is all Suleyman's way of scaring us. Maybe we can just go home."

"I don't think so," Hal replied. "He'll attack at Castle Van: poetic justice from the poet wannabe. Back to the center of Armenian Turkey. Maybe we should go right there."

Malcolm objected. "Let's stick with the itinerary published in *Hurriyet*. Don't you think that any change might give Suleyman cold feet?"

Kemal said, "Malcolm has a point. I'll go to the boat and bring back our lunch. Then we'll leave and stay on schedule."

Hal and Sally wanted some privacy. They walked through the grove, leaving Malcolm sitting at the table. Hal felt his resolution weakening as he held Sally's hand. He had gained so much that he did not want to lose. Hal said, "Maybe Malcolm's right. We're up against the whale."

Sally stopped and faced him. "It's true that Kemal's the pro. It's his country, his job. So tell me: What do you really want to do?"

Hal looked out over lovely Lake Van, looked at Sally, and asked, "Is that the right question?"

"The metropolitan said I could use my brain. You're right. The question to ask is: What *should* we do?"

Tears came to Hal's eyes. "Do you know that this is the toughest moment of my life?"

"Yes." Sally looked at him. "Your eyes are as tender as those of the man on the ceiling at the old church in Istanbul."

"I have to go on. It's the right thing to do."

"I know. Then I'll go on too."

They embraced until Kemal returned. Then they sat at a table amid the trees, eating *vanotlu*, a sharp, juicy variety of cheese intermingled with grassy herb stalks, and sharing a bottle of Lake Van water.

On the return boat trip Kemal offered additional instructions: "We're prepared at Castle Van, but just in case anything goes wrong and you have to be in the fight, remember not to narrow your field of vision to what's immediately in front of you."

Hal said, "Funny, what comes to me now is a column I once wrote about Wyatt Earp. His maxim was, 'Coolness and steady nerves will always beat simple quickness.'"

"True, but you may have a different perception of time, with everything seeming to be in slow motion. You may think seconds have gone by when only a fraction of a second actually has. If you do have to be involved, don't jerk your shots. Aim smoothly and fire."

Their last stop before Castle Van was Castle Hosap. The remnants of the Ottoman fortress sat on a lonely, bare, brown ridge that ended in a cliff. One small car sat at the bottom of the ridge.

Hosap, Kemal told them, means "nice water" in Kurdish, but nothing in the area seemed nice. He told Abdul that they would stick with the itinerary but stay only a short time. Abdul said he would stand guard and let the other three policemen stay in the car so they could hear "A Long and Narrow Road," the new hit song by Tarkan, the Elvis Presley of Turkey.

Under a gray sky, Hal and Sally walked arm-in-arm through the castle, which sported towers, walls, reception room, small mosque, cistern, dungeon—all the comforts of home, with walls fifty feet high. When the swirling wind blew Sally's hair in front of her face, Hal gently brushed it aside and kissed her. They looked south toward Turkey's border, with Iraq and Iran both a short drive away.

The only other visitor was a woman wearing a large kerchief. She looked vaguely familiar, but she brushed by Malcolm and headed down. Hal borrowed Kemal's binoculars and followed an emaciated dog on the highway below as it approached a white Mitsubishi that had stopped. It looked like the same one he had seen at the Lake Van restaurant. The driver generously threw the mutt what looked like a whole steak.

Kemal pointed out the defense-minded layout: "One path past the lower level, one way up to the top. Attackers centuries ago had to come through here, under fire from the castle keep above. The attackers needed overwhelming force to win."

Malcolm stood off by himself, staring toward the west at the highway on which they had come. Hal and Sally walked on and stopped before a plaque telling the history of the castle, "Built by Suleyman Mahmudi in 1643." They looked at each other. "That note where he mentioned his house!" Hal exclaimed: "KEMAL. Here!"

He ran to them, read the plaque, and suddenly clapped his hands together: "That woman had her hair completely covered. She's not a local. She must be one of them."

He pulled out his phone to call Abdul, as Hal, looking through his binoculars, saw the white car with the generous driver heading east on the highway at high speed.

"THE ATTACK WILL BE HERE!" Kemal yelled into the phone, but at that moment they all watched with horror as the Mitsubishi headed straight toward the police car. Abdul emptied his clip, but the terrorist driver slammed into him and then into the vehicle. A fireball went up. No one came out of the inferno.

Kemal swore, "*Itouulu itt.* Suicide bomber! I never thought Suleyman would do that." He wiped his hand over his face. "Abdul, dead. How will I tell his wife? His poor children. My men, dead. What a fool I've been!" He slumped over a railing.

A few seconds later he resumed his ramrod posture and told Hal in clipped tones, "Time for the jandarma." He pushed buttons on the satellite phone, then pushed more, examined it front and back, and said, "I don't believe it. It worked at the lake." He pulled out a backup device: also not working. "I don't understand. This is sabotage, but how?"

He didn't have time to probe the problem because a brown van drove up to the base of the castle slope, and eight men jumped out. Through the binoculars Hal saw Suleyman pinching his mustache and carrying a revolver in one hand, a scimitar in the other. Trafik, cigarette hanging from his lips, carried an AK-47. Six young men held revolvers, and one had a backpack.

The woman in the kerchief, Kazasina, joined them. Kemal looked at his watch: "In half an hour the commander in Van and I are to be in contact. When he is unable to raise me, he'll send help."

Hal asked, "How do we hold them off until then?"

"We have the advantage of defense. Malcolm and I will stay behind this low wall. Hal, you and Sally go on top, there, overlooking us." He distributed the .45s and extra clips. "If they're foolish enough to come at me along this narrow path, they'll have to come right past you. You have the high ground. Remember, Suleyman's a self-styled poet, not a general."

When Hal and Sally hesitated, Kemal added sternly, "Obey orders. Remember, they have to come to us." Then he said softly, "Go now, and your God be with you."

Sally ran with Hal up to the top where they could stand on the stones of what had been the castle keep and look down from the wall. Through the binoculars Hal could see Kazasina showing the band some kind of drawing, maybe a sketch of the castle layout.

As he watched their adversaries, Hal was stunned to hear Malcolm screaming at Kemal, "You're working for Suleyman. You planted those notes, you had your men killed, you set us up."

Malcolm pointed his revolver at Kemal, who shouted, "You're a vicious liar, or you've gone mad. Our enemies will be here in a minute. Shoot at them."

"Hal, think it through," Malcolm screamed. "He's a traitor."

Hal looked down the ridge and saw the terrorists ascending. He made his decision. "Malcolm, I think you're wrong, but if you're right, we're dead either way, since without Kemal we can't hold them off. So you have to fight your fears and hope they're unfounded."

Malcolm still had the .45 extended toward Kemal, but gradually his right arm came down, and he leaned against the wall, his left arm covering his eyes.

Suleyman and the terrorists stood just out of range, and Suleyman's voice boomed toward them: "These hills are my witness: I will give this new group of four a new example of Allah's compassion. He who surrenders first will be freed, but the other three will die."

No one moved. Then Suleyman shouted, "Are you coming, Mr. Edwards?"

Malcolm suddenly darted toward the terrorist lines. Once there he kept running down the ridge, as the terrorists laughed behind him. He ran all the way to the small car parked at the bottom, started it immediately, and drove off toward Van.

Hal, Sally, and Kemal were stunned, but they didn't have time to ponder: the terrorists moved forward to a low wall and began shooting. One tried to sneak his way directly under the tall castle wall, where Hal and Sally would have to expose themselves to shoot him, but a shot from Kemal drove him back.

Suleyman called out, "Policeman, I know who you are. I know who your sister was. You're hiding behind that wall like a coward. Stand up so we can have a real gunfight, like in the movies."

Kemal did not move.

"Policeman, I will tell you what I did to your sister before I killed her." Suleyman proceeded to give specific detail, but Kemal did not move.

Then came the assault: One terrorist reached into his backpack, took out smoke bombs, and threw them as five others charged Kemal. But the swirling wind took away enough of the smoke cover for Kemal, his feet planted, to catch glimpses of the assailants and fire repeatedly from behind the wall as Hal and Sally shot from above.

The terrorists retreated. "We should be thankful for Suleyman's poetic impulses," Hal said. "No grenades." As the smoke cleared, they saw a terrorist sprawled below, dead.

Sally cheered.

"Wait!" Hal said. "Listen."

They were silent. Amid the whistling of the wind came another faint sound. Pebbles dislodged? Footsteps? Hal had thought their defensive position was excellent unless the killers grew wings. But then he wondered: Is there some other way up here?

He ran to the other side of the keep as a terrorist came around the corner, ready to fire. Sally watched as Hal's gun leaped and the first man toppled. But Hal, with tunnel vision, was slow to pick up a second man, Suleyman himself.

One of Suleyman's bullets struck Hal on the side of the head, and a second hit him full in the chest. He collapsed in the dirt, tried to get up, and fell again, his last shot merely plowing a furrow in the dust.

<hr />

Sally thought, *How can it end this way? This can't be happening.* But it was. Suddenly in her agony everything slowed down. "Get up, Hal," she implored him. "Get up, please, please."

But he did not move, and then everything speeded up. Sally jerked the trigger and saw her bullet slam into Suleyman's left hand as he ran toward her. She wanted to fire again, but he came fast, swatting the .45 from her hand and then slugging her with his own revolver, knocking her out.

Suleyman dropped the scimitar, ripped off Sally's skirt, and wrapped a piece around his bleeding hand. Then he called to Kemal again: "Bogikian is dead. The woman is mine. Why don't you stand up like a man?"

Kemal did not move, but he spoke: "My duty is to protect and defend the Turkish republic. If you dare, come and take me."

The commander at jandarma headquarters called Kemal's phone at the agreed-upon time, but there was no answer. "Something's wrong," he told his sergeant. "Let's get the chopper in the air and look around."

At Castle Hosap, Kemal looked at his watch and thought, *My friend will be heading this way soon.* But Suleyman signaled his squad to attack. And this time, with the terrorist ready to fire from above, the police director had to stay crouched behind the far corner of his wall until his adversaries were almost upon him, screaming *Allu Akbar.*

Kemal stood up and quickly fired, killing another man. But a bullet from Suleyman hit the left side of his chest.

He staggered and fell to his knees, and the remaining terrorists surrounded him, each taking a shot. He fell to the ground. His last sight was of the terrorists dancing above him and firing into him.

With his last breath he whispered two words: "Sorry, Isa."

CHAPTER TWENTY-THREE

The five terrorists left standing below—four men and Kazasina—raised their guns and shot off a victory round. Suleyman did the same above. Then he looked at Sally, lying in the dirt.

Suleyman called down to his band, "Give me five minutes for some unfinished business. Then we'll take the woman and leave." He slapped Sally awake. She opened her eyes and screamed.

"Listen to me," Suleyman roared. "Your Armenian is dead. Your Turkish policeman is dead. Now I will finish what I began." In a moment he was on top of her.

Sally furiously sifted the dirt with her right hand, hoping to find a stone, a stick, anything with which to beat Suleyman as he pressed against her.

She felt Phoebe's little yarn bag still around her waist, reached into the soft yarn, and found the short knitting needle. She yanked it out and with all her strength stuck it in her assailant's left ear.

Suleyman yowled in pain. He sat up, pulled out the needle, and yelled, "Now you will die." He reached out with his right hand to feel for the scimitar.

It wasn't there. He patted the ground again in surprise, then turned his head to look behind him.

The last thing he saw was a furious Hal swinging the scimitar with both hands.

The last thing he felt was its edge cutting into his neck.

But Hal's technique wasn't as good as Suleyman's. Blood exploded everywhere.

Sally scrambled up. "How . . . ?" Sally asked, looking at Hal's face, its left side caked with blood.

"Later," Hal said. "The others will be coming. We have to get out of here. Here, wrap my jacket around you."

"My god. It's a . . ."

"Ssh . . . Later. Let's get our guns." They put new clips in them.

Hal's plan was to climb down the secret path Suleyman had ascended, then circle around the remaining terrorists. But they had no time. Trafik, leading the other men up the main path, saw them, stopped behind a wall, and opened fire.

Hal and Sally scrambled behind a pile of rubble. "Suleyman is dead," Hal shouted. "Leave before you are too. The police will be here soon."

"Your policeman is dead, and you'll be dead in a minute," Trafik called back. "No more smoke bomb poetry. Now we'll kill you the old-fashioned way, with hand grenades."

Hal looked out over the countryside, facing east. Brown earth, grey sky, for as far as he could see: No hope on the horizon. He fired a shot at the terrorists' wall to keep them crouching down so their throws would be less accurate.

The first grenade came up short, so Hal and Sally were struck only by clumps of dirt.

"Good thing Turks don't play baseball," Hal said, "but the next one will be closer. We'll have to make a run for it."

He paused to kiss her. "I love you."

"I love you."

"And I love that sight." Hal pointed at the jandarma helicopter that suddenly emerged out of the eastern clouds. The terrorists heard the beating of the blades behind them, fired wild shots at it, and started running as its machine gun opened up on them.

Trafik also ran, cigarette still hanging from his lips. In his panic he headed toward the cliff and realized his mistake only when he was already in the air.

"I'm falling, falling," he screamed just before hitting the ground. His finger jerked on the trigger, and his gun fired one last dirt-disturbing shot, then was silent.

Kazasina, shot from the helicopter, also was dead, but the remaining terrorists dropped their weapons and raised their hands. The helicopter landed, and Sally helped Hal stagger to meet the commander.

"Kemal?" he asked.

"Dead," Hal replied. "Suleyman, too. Beheaded." Then he fell to the ground.

Two policemen carried him to the helicopter. "I'm going with Hal," Sally insisted. The commander agreed and added, "Please, take this for a dress." He handed Sally the helicopter's Turkish flag.

"Wouldn't that be dishonoring the flag?" Sally asked.

"Your bravery honors our nation."

Hal and Sally returned to Antakya for the emotional funerals of Kemal and Abdul. Kemal was buried next to his sister: one victim of terrorism, one avenger.

Turkish police arrested Malcolm as he tried to board an airplane in Van but released him the next day. They had no proof that he had conspired with Suleyman to plant notes to Sally, pass on information through a contact at the restaurant by Lake Van, sabotage the communications equipment left on the picnic bench in the island's walnut grove, and give Kazasina a green light when they brushed against each other as she passed him the keys to her car.

Turkish police did not press Malcolm hard: his American passport and a lack of imminent danger or witnesses against him worked in his favor. Suleyman and Trafik could no longer testify, Suleyman's computer had vanished, and the other terrorists said the strange American was only a coward.

New York police searched Malcolm's home, but his laptop was gone, and the desk computer had no record of e-mail traffic with Suleyman. Its hard drive did have a story, apparently written by Malcolm, in which he was the hero, the lone survivor of a terrorist attack that killed his best friends. A memo on the desktop read, "Hal says you can either fight him or appease him—nothing in between."

On the flight from Antakya to Istanbul, Hal talked with Sally about the clues he had missed: "Reporters are supposed to smell out deception. Why didn't I think that Malcolm was planting those notes? And that shooting in Urfa, could it have been a setup to make us trust him? When do you think he made the decision to betray us?"

Sally looked out the window as they approached the big city: It all looked so peaceful from above. "Maybe Malcolm decided in New York. He never practiced shooting because he never expected to do any. But maybe he was hoping all the way for some way out. Maybe that's why he wanted us to distrust Kemal."

They speculated about Malcolm's motives. Maybe he feared for his life unless he appeased Suleyman. Maybe the sexual harassment charges had diminished Malcolm's reputation so much that he was looking for a way to become known as a hero, but he didn't have the courage to attempt that in reality. Or maybe, as Hal was taking revenge on Suleyman, Malcolm was taking revenge on Hal for beating him out with Sally and on Sally for spurning him.

So many maybes, and then a Turkish detective met Hal and Sally in the international lounge at the Istanbul airport and immediately altered their theorizing. The Dutch woman involved with Malcolm at the Izmir Hilton, near the beginning of the first trip, had been powerfully affected by viewing the beheading of Phoebe and the TRT1 interview with Sally. She no longer wanted to help the terrorists: after agonizing for a week, she reported to the police her conversation with Malcolm.

The detective sipped Turkish coffee and continued: The woman said Malcolm had proven surprisingly sympathetic when she spoke about the one force ruthless enough to stop American imperialism, Islamic terrorism. When he said he'd like to learn more and even help out Hezbollah, she said she would put him in touch with a member who would make contact with him in one of the museums he would visit. The detective said that none of this was evidence enough to arrest Malcolm, but he wanted Hal and Sally to know that they were up against someone who may have plotted against them early and often.

Hal sputtered: "Could Malcolm have been in with Suleyman not just after Antakya but from almost the beginning? I don't think so." But as they boarded the plane back to America, he told Sally, "I'm thinking back to what I overhead in the museum when he met Kazasina. It was puzzling at the time. She said she and her friends would be glad to meet him. I wondered who her friends were, but then I forgot about it."

As they flew over Europe, Sally also pushed her memory: "That's strange. I remember what Malcolm said in the Antakya museum just before he left with Fatima. He was making a play for me, and when I turned him down, he said that I left him no choice. I guess that meant he was going through with the plan."

They both recalled Malcolm's calm, positive sense about Suleyman when they first were captured. No wonder: He knew he was getting out.

Over the Atlantic they speculated about reasons. Sally recalled, "Remember when we were approaching Izmir and drove by the shantytown, when Malcolm said he'd do anything so as not to be poor, and that without money life was hardly worth living."

Hal jumped on that: "Detectives say, 'Cherchez la femme,' but reporters follow the money trail. Malcolm must have known about the mess at Columbia before the public announcement, and maybe Phoebe had told him that he wouldn't get her money. His dad had lost the family money. He had grown up rich and was scared of being poor. Maybe he thought Suleyman would ransom Phoebe and they'd split the money."

As they approached JFK Airport, Sally shook her head: "I can't believe it was about money."

Hal stayed in one of the guest rooms at Phoebe's house. Sally brought him chicken soup, and he healed quickly. "You're ready for almost anything," Dr. Chandler told him after inspecting his head wound. "Don't let any water get in there." The doctor walked out to the waiting room with his recovered patient and saw a beaming Sally. "He's all yours."

"Is he?" Sally smiled.

"Yes," Hal stated.

Dr. Chandler added, "I reviewed my notes on your last visit, Sally. Are you sleeping well now?"

"Wonderfully. When I look back on how we survived the kidnapping and then the shootout, when the odds against us were so bad, I'm feeling so thankful."

"This goes beyond medicine, but I'm an old family doctor. Whom do you want to thank?"

"Hal. Kemal. And maybe God?"

Hal looked at her with surprise. In Phoebe's car, he asked, "God?"

At the first red light Sally turned to him. "Hal, I love and admire you, but are you sure we got out of this just by your guts?"

"My guts, your guts, Kemal's guts, and a lot of luck."

"Nothing else?"

"The jandarma commander."

"God?"

"If there is one, don't you think he has other things to do than to watch gunfights? Don't be stupid."

That comment set off Sally. "I'm not, and if you think of me that way . . ."

Hal tried to make amends. "I didn't mean . . ." But the light had changed, and Sally was fiercely staring ahead, her hands gripping the steering wheel. So Hal went further: "I'm sorry. Look, I jumped at you because I've been thinking the same thing, and it seems nutty to me. I'm worried about where this will lead."

***

Later that day Hal sat on a lounge by the pool at Phoebe's house, watching Sally float under the sun, eyes closed. The radio was on and playing the refrain of the Patty Griffin song that Hal had listened to while driving back to Washington in May:

> Just before the night falls,
> Just before the blood runs, into the valley, . . .
> Love throws a line to you and me.

He couldn't take his eyes off Sally in her gold swimsuit. He wanted to touch her, but he couldn't jump in the pool—doctor's orders. He thought hard, trying telepathy: *Sally, come out.*

She did and stood in front of him. Then she sat on his lap, facing him.

"Whoa," he said.

"Oh my," she responded, smiling. They sat there for a minute, just looking at each other. Sally said, "When I was floating, I started imagining that we were still at a Mediterranean resort hotel, with people putting chocolates next to the bed. But a lot has changed. Those days are over."

"Yes," Hal said, looking into a cloudless sky. "We have better days ahead."

Sally laughed: "'Better days ahead.' You sound like me, the way I used to be. Bright eyed, bushy tailed, climbing Sunshine Mountain."

"Hmmm, and do I see wisdom in optimism?"

His heart leaped as she looked affectionately at him: "You no longer rain all the time. I'm not as sunshiny as I used to be. Maybe we can share a climate."

Hal stroked her neck and shoulders. He leaned forward and kissed her soft lips.

"Do you plan to continue knitting?" he asked.

"Sure," Sally said. "Why do you ask?

"It was while you were knitting that I fell totally in love with you," Hal replied. "I watched you concentrating, trying to do it as well as Phoebe had. I watched the curve of your brows, the contours of your chin, the soft lines of your neck, the set of your shoulders. You were lovely but also poignant. You were sunflower but also moonflower, still independent but now conscious of dependence."

Sally looked at Hal with misty eyes, then kissed him. A minute later she was somber. "Phoebe. And now Kemal. I think of them. A lot."

"So do I."

"Phoebe's knitting needles," Sally laughed. "I didn't imagine I'd ever use one the way I did. And Phoebe's pocket Bible inside your jacket. That, smack up against your reporters' notebook, saved your life when Suleyman shot you."

"What a combination, journalism and the Bible."

They were silent for several minutes. Then Hal said, "I was reading last night the book you read on the airplane to Istanbul, *The Second Coming*."

"Like it?"

"I don't agree with Walker Percy that unbelievers are crazy and believers aren't. But when he says that he's surrounded by two classes of maniacs, those who think they understand life but act as if they don't and those who don't know diddly and don't care, maybe he's got something there."

"Which class do you want to be in?"

"I want horizontal love, you and me. Should I also be searching for vertical love, person and God?"

They agreed to see Pastor Carrillo again. He invited them to come over to his house in the evening: "My ten-year-old read some of the online news stories about the two of you. He wants your autographs."

"Makes me feel like a baseball player," Hal said when he obliged the boy, who then returned to the den to watch a DVD of *The Wizard of Oz*. The movie was at the point where the wizard makes clear that Dorothy's three friends had what they thought they lacked—a brain, a heart, courage—all the time, and just needed certification.

They had just entered the pastor's study and settled into bentwood rockers when Hal said, "Let's not mess around. Why did Sally and I survive?"

Carrillo said, "I don't know, but I know you should be thankful. Read Psalm 107, which explains how God delivered from distress 'those who wandered in desert wastes, those who sat in darkness and in the shadow of death, those who went down to the sea in ships and, amid storms, reeled and staggered like drunken men.'"

"Phoebe died. Kemal died." Hal responded.

"And you and Sally are alive. Why, do you think?"

"Luck. A thick book in my pocket—could have been any thick book. The helicopter arriving. But if you want to call it providence rather than luck, be my guest. Same deal."

"No, it's not. Luck is life proceeding by chance. Providence makes you part of the drama God is producing, and you don't even know yet what your role may be."

"I can't accept that. Because if I say God did something for us, then I have to ask why God didn't do something for Phoebe."

"Maybe he did. Maybe she's with her husband now."

"And what about Kemal, one of the most decent men I've ever met?"

"That's a mystery. But God knows hearts, and as Abraham asks, "Shall not the judge of the whole world do what is right?" Could it be that God has reasons of which you're unaware?"

"Could be, but if so, I sure wish he'd explain himself."

"Maybe he will, if you listen. You can start by reading that Bible that stopped the bullet."

"I read it when I was a kid."

"Good. Now you're an adult."

Hal was silent. Then he said, "What if you have some big sin in your past?" Sally perked up, thinking that maybe now she'd find out about that mystery.

Carrillo said, "If you grab hold of Christ, he'll pull you through it. He's already paid the penalty for you."

Hal said nothing more.

———•———

He stayed in a guest room at Phoebe's house one more evening and early the next morning received a phone call from Turkey. One of the captured terrorists had broken down and recounted for the police what Suleyman had told them about the Americans the night before the attack at Castle Hosap.

He said Suleyman had spoken of how the Americans hated one another, that the professor had wanted his aunt to be ransomed so he could be a millionaire, that he had wanted the journalist dead, but Suleyman had outwitted him by killing the aunt and planning to let the journalist go.

Since Hal couldn't swim until his wound healed, he and Sally went on a walk-and-talk in Phoebe's leafy neighborhood. Trying to fathom the latest news, they walked on under the oak trees, trying to recall facial expressions and words.

Hal asked, "Remember that weird look in Malcolm's eyes when I talked about going to the baseball game with him in

Baltimore. Did he think I'd be killed? Could he have wanted me dead? Was he that angry?"

Sally said, "That's hard to take, unless . . ." Her voice trailed off, and she shivered. "Hal, I'm scared. We're looking at real malice, real evil here." She put her palm against her forehead. "I thought his problem was drinking, which led to bad behavior. But what if his problem was far deeper, and the drinking masked it?"

They stopped beneath a willow and looked at each other. "Real evil," Hal murmured, taking Sally's hand. "You know what drove me in my research into the Armenian holocaust? It wasn't just to tell the history or keep alive the memory of my relatives. I wanted to understand why such evil happened. I wanted to find if evil really exists."

"And . . ."

"It does, Sally, it does. And this information about Malcolm points the same way. I don't know what got into him, and I can't figure out why, but it doesn't just stink. It's evil."

Sally tightened her grip on his hand and bit her lip nervously. "I didn't think that evil existed. I can understand money, drunkenness, fear, ego; but this goes much deeper. I can't stand it." She looked away, then leaned against Hal, desperate for support.

They were silent. The wind came up, and the willow branches swayed.

Hal suddenly smiled. Sally looked at him. "What?"

"It's nothing."

"What? You look like you've had a revelation."

"Not much of one, but I remember what the patriarch in Istanbul said, 'If there is a hell, there is also a heaven.'"

"He told me, 'If there is no heaven and no hell, nothing matters!' But what did he say to Malcolm?"

"I don't remember."

CHAPTER TWENTY-FOUR

That evening in Damascus, Ibrahim bin Musa paced in his Damascus villa, listening to the latest gossip before convening a crucial late night Al-Qaeda planning session. His second-in-command, Omar al-Hajji, gave him details about how Suleyman had died near Van.

"But what was he doing at an old castle?"

"He wanted to kill two Americans who escaped from him in June."

"Revenge? Suleyman always ran with his emotions. He should have studied the science of terror instead of wasting time on personal agendas. What a waste!"

"One of the Americans was a beautiful woman. Suleyman died as he was mounting her."

"Ah, that was my friend," Ibrahim said, raising his voice as he entered the main room so that the other three Al-Qaeda members sitting and leaning against cushions could hear the homily he was about to deliver. "Brothers, our fallen Turkish comrade and I watched some American movies together, but we sometimes took away different lessons."

Omar said mischievously, "You learned the line, 'You'll never take me alive'?" He popped a date into his mouth.

"No," Ibrahim said, fixing his lieutenant with a stare. "We saw the movie *City Slickers*, about Americans from a big city who had to live among cow herders for a time. Suleyman thought it showed that Americans were weak. I came away impressed that the toughest man in the movie emphasized the importance of working on one big thing rather than lots of small tasks and doing that big thing well."

The terrorists broke into an extended discussion on which big thing they should do well. They tore apart pieces of lamb on a tray as they kept coming back to the destruction of Israel. But Omar finally threw the question at Ibrahim: "So what is our big thing?"

He responded, "I, like our Jewish adversaries, will answer your question with a question for all of us: What was Suleyman's error?

"Lust?" the youngest member of the group offered, and others nodded. They looked hungrily at Ibrahim's buxom daughter, who brought in a watermelon for them to dissect.

"The Quran allows us to make use of the spoils of war but not the daughters of sheiks," Ibrahim said pointedly. "Think, my brothers, when we should concentrate on a big thing, why was Suleyman killing enemies one by one? Think: which of our Al-Qaeda actions in the past decade has made the imperialists sit up in shock and awe?"

"Our September 11 attacks."

"Exactly. It took great patience and planning, but was it worth it?"

The Al-Qaeda members thrust their fists in the air, and shouted, "*Allu akbar.*"

"Yes," Ibrahim exulted. "Allah is great. And if by acting bravely and wisely we can kill three thousand oppressors of Islam, why should we settle for killing one here and three there?"

"We should not."

"And if Allah gives us the opportunity to kill three hundred thousand in one blow, why must we settle for killing three thousand?"

"We must not."

Omar added, "That would be a magnificently big thing to do. But we would need a nuclear weapon to exert so much damage."

"Yes, we would," Ibrahim replied, smiling and nodding.

Now it was Omar's turn to look at him sharply. "Are you suggesting that we have one?"

Ibrahim's smile became even broader. "Yes, we do, one produced in the old Soviet Union. Purchased by several good friends from Saudi Arabia. And I've brought the four of you here to plan out how to make our dream come true."

Again the members stood and cheered: *"Allu akbar, allu akbar."*

"And we would detonate this in Washington or New York?" Omar said excitedly. "Are you saying that it's in our power to destroy the US Capitol? Or downtown Manhattan?"

"Not so fast," Ibrahim replied. He explained that Americans have Nuclear Emergency Search Teams—NESTS of vipers—stationed around Washington and New York with the task of detecting and dismantling bombs, so perhaps Houston, or St. Louis, or Philadelphia would be better.

Omar asked, "How would we get the bomb there?"

"We're in contact with an international gang, la Mara Salvatrucha, that has MS-13 groups in cities across the US. It started in El Salvador and expanded into Mexico. It now brings huge quantities of drugs into the United States and exports stolen cars and guns to Central America. For that gang, the Mexican border is nothing. Or perhaps the porous Canadian border . . ."

"And how will we interact with that gang?"

Ibrahim opened his arms wide: "Ah, this is the question I've brought you here to discuss."

As the meeting continued in Damascus, Hal and Sally were sitting by Phoebe's pool in the late afternoon sun. Hal said, "This shows my insecurity, but when we were prisoners, you mentioned a 'truth or dare' question that you said your friends used to ask. I'd like to ask you that now."

"Ask away."

"If you could kiss anyone in the world, who would it be?"

She kissed him.

Hal's cell phone rang. "This is Espen Askalad from TRT1. I've been trying to track you down. We're live on our evening show. All Turkey wants to know how you and Miss Northaway are doing."

"Ah, Mr. Askalad, can't I forget about Turkey?"

"Maybe, but Turkey can't forget about you. You and Miss Northaway are still a big story here: the Americans shooting it out with terrorists. And Kemal Kuris is a national hero."

"I'm glad to hear that. Kemal loved your country and gave his life for it."

"Our viewers want to know how you are recovering."

"Very well, thank you. Wounds are healed; new ones haven't opened yet."

Askalad seemed confused for a moment. "New ones . . . oh, that's your American humor."

"I guess so."

"Is Miss Northaway there? Our audience would like to hear from her."

Hal turned to Sally, but she smiled and jumped into the pool. "She's swimming now."

"That must be a beautiful sight."

Hal watched. "Yes."

"Here's my last question: Keeping both good and bad developments in mind, looking back, do you think it was worth it?"

Hal paused. "For the war on terror, yes. Still, I know that Kemal's parents and many others in Turkey mourn his death. So do we."

"But Director Kuris knew the risks he was taking. That was his calling. What about you two? You were amateurs, volunteers, going through a harrowing experience. Did it change your lives in some way?"

Hal responded slowly. "It has started me thinking about God and Satan. Why is there evil in the world? How should we then . . . ?"

Askalad was impatient. "But are you glad you did what you did?"

Hal smiled. "I'm glad Suleyman is gone. I guess relieving the world of him was our calling at that particular time. I hope life in Turkey is better." He looked over at Sally and smiled. "I know my life is better."

Hal put down the phone and picked up *The Second Coming*. He read the last sentence, where Will Barrett, having fallen in love and also come to understand a little about God, asks, "Am I crazy to want both, her and him? No, not want, must have. And will have."

Hal looked at the woman he loved, floating under the sun, eyes closed, a brilliant gold.